CATHARSIS

LANDSCAPES OF LOVE

Catharsis

Landscapes of Love

PHILIP TYLER

© Philip Tyler, 2021

philip@topspec.com

Published by Pickhill Publishing

A CIP catalogue record for this book is available from the British Library.

ISBN 978-1-7399815-0-1

Book layout and cover design by Clare Brayshaw

Prepared and printed by:

York Publishing Services Ltd
64 Hallfield Road
Layerthorpe
York YO31 7ZQ

Tel: 01904 431213

Website: www.yps-publishing.co.uk

Dedication

This book is dedicated to the Park Rangers who risk their lives every day to protect the mountain gorillas in Virunga National Park and the rhinos in the National Parks of Kenya.

In the year ending March 2021 alone, twenty young Park staff in Virunga were murdered in a 'ferociously violent and sustained attack' by armed poachers.

Mountain gorilla and baby in Virunga

"If we do not do something to prevent it, Africa's animals, and the places in which they live, will be lost to our world and her children forever."

Mandela

Contents

Artists and Photographers

Colsterdale – The Yorkshire Dales – England

They first met on Masham High Moor, that runs along the ridge between Wensleydale and Nidderdale in North Yorkshire. It was a beautiful spring morning, with dawn mists still hanging in the deep valley below. The curlews were flying high, filling the skies with optimistic concertos against a chorus of other less musically talented birds.

He was staying near Catterick with an old university friend, after a few months working abroad, and needed a day on his own in the peace of the English countryside to think. Apart from a JR called Suzi that is, which he had borrowed from his friend to keep him company. Dogs are such good companions when you need to be on your own.

The bitch put up a wayward red-legged partridge, and he was following its flight, along the gentle curve of the cloud-shadowed hillside, when he caught sight of a grey Arab stallion. It was following the narrow track down from Gollinglith Ridge, near the twin standing stones. The rider was wearing the kind of coat an Antipodean stockman would wear and one of those wide-brimmed bush hats. As

Red-legged partridge

they approached closer on the track, the wind caught the brim of the hat and revealed the aristocratic face of an English lady, slightly flushed by the cool morning air. She was carrying a Canon camera over her left shoulder; one of those with the rather glaring advert on the strap. He noticed the camera had a wide-angled lens, as used in landscape photography.

"Landscape photographer I presume?" he queried, in a pleasant manner.

"No, astrophysicist actually," she replied dismissively.

"Not with a Canon D5 camera you're not," he observed competitively.

With that brief encounter, she pushed the stallion on past him, forcing him to step aside off the pathway to avoid its extravagant movement. She half looked back at him quizzically and then pressed on down the hill towards Colsterdale.

Their paths did not cross again for two years.

CHAPTER ONE

Hydra – The Saronic Islands – Greece

He had been working on the Greek island of Hydra for three weeks and was having a quiet evening off at the Techne restaurant overlooking the cerulean waters of Avlaki Bay. The food was an inventive update of traditional recipes and he ordered the hylopites with apaki and mizithra cheese, exquisitely created by the talented young chef. The Savatiano wine, made from the old vines in Attica, was a particularly good complement to an excellent meal. He enjoyed eating on his own, planning the night's work ahead, and finished the bottle at a leisurely pace. At about ten, he thanked the owner for a pleasant evening and started back through the labyrinth of car-less, narrow streets and passageways up the hill to his friend's villa, where he was staying whilst on the island.

He passed sea-salted fishermen, lazily seated in tired wooden chairs, enjoying their evening smoke. Excited young lovers, mostly illicit in Greece, embraced in shadowy doorways. When he was about one third of the way up the hill, he turned a corner and ahead of him he saw three Albanian youths lurking in the shadows of one of the narrow passageways that make up the mosaic of thoroughfares on that side of the island. When he got nearer, he could see that they had cornered a young woman, holding her with her back against a flaking wall. They were tentative, yet aggressive in manner, as all cowards are. He could not see her face, to see if she was a local, or hear her voice at that point. He hung back not wanting to get involved, in case it was a family affair; however, the intensity of the conversation increased, and they were clearly intent on robbing her. She held her own for a while with deprecating remarks, interspersed with the occasional reference to their lack of a father. Suddenly the self-prescribed leader of the group, a particularly unpleasant character, pulled a long blade, changing the dynamics of the situation.

He walked slowly towards the youths and distracted them from their captive.

"Don't get involved mister," muttered the smaller youth with the grubby tee shirt.

"I think it's time to go and play somewhere else," he proposed calmly, in his best non-confrontational voice.

"You got money too?" asked the leader aggressively.

"I did have but I have just paid for my dinner at the restaurant, I'm afraid."

"You're a fucking liar – give me your wallet," the leader screamed, turning towards him with the knife in his right hand but relieving the intense pressure on the woman. She was now clearly very scared and staring down at the ground in apprehension.

The youth approached closer to him waving the knife, which unfortunately left him with no choice. He put hand behind his back and pulled his Heckler & Koch handgun from his belt and pointed directly at the leader's head. The youth's eyes widened with shock and he stopped in his tracks.

"You can't kill all three of us, before we get to you," blurted the youth bravely.

"But I will kill you first and I predict that when you are dead on the floor, with blood pouring out of your twitching body, your two friends will be running away at speed – it's your call."

The stunned youths looked at each other with indecision; but their bravado evaporated and they ran off down a side passage, into the shadows of the now setting sun.

He approached the woman, who was still looking at the ground. "Are you OK? Sorry about the graphic language but cowards always run away when faced with their own mortality."

"I had it all under control," she proposed unrealistically, in a broken voice.

"I know. I was just protecting them!" he joked, to break the tension.

She did that half-quizzical look again and he realised that they had met before in a more civilised landscape.

"A drink?" he offered kindly.

"I don't drink with strangers carrying guns," she replied.

"I'll let you carry it then. I am staying up there – at the top of the cobbled pathway."

He offered her the gun, grip first, but her hand was shaking uncontrollably.

"I think I will hold on to it for now," he smiled, and replaced it in his belt behind his back, under his loose denim shirt.

"Sorry about pushing you off the track up on the Moor," she added apologetically.

"It was my pleasure; I always give way to a lady!"

"Can I take your arm?" she asked.

"You can borrow it!"

She smiled for the first time and linked her arm in his.

They climbed the path to the white-painted villa and she sat on a Lloyd Loom chair on the terrace, looking out over the sea, now bathed in moonlight with fishing boats bobbing gently.

"What would you like to drink – sorry, we don't have Black Sheep," he said, referring to the famous Yorkshire brewery in Masham.

"Have you got a gin and Fever Tree?"

"Tanqueray OK?"

"Perfect – make it a double please."

"Are you OK now?"

"Just a bit cold. Do you have a rug?"

He fetched a warm, woollen blanket from the poolside and draped it around her shoulders. He passed her the gin and tonic in a crystal tumbler and sat opposite her. She looked vulnerable under the rug, but he realised for the first time how beautiful she was. She had long auburn hair held up with an artisan clip, classical cheek bones and a slender neckline. An English lady – confirming his first impression at their meeting on the moor in Colsterdale.

"What are you doing here in robbers' paradise?" he asked, trying to break the ice.

"Photographing the natural landscapes up in the hills for the Greek government. It's to do with a European funded, environmental project."

"I knew you weren't an astrophysicist," he laughed. "How did you get into landscape photography?"

"My father gave me his old Leica camera as a fifteenth birthday present and I used to take it with me up on the High Moor early in the mornings, when the light is so amazing. The skies change every minute and every day is different. I was lucky enough to get some atmospheric shots, which a local publisher picked up at my school photography club annual exhibition, and it just grew from there. Do you like photography?"

"Don't really have enough patience. My wife was into wildlife photography."

"Was?"

"Long story. I had better get you back. Where are you staying?" he asked, avoiding the painful question.

"At the Hotel Hydra down on the sea front. I'll be OK walking back," she proposed bravely.

"I am sure you will, but I was going that way anyway," he lied chivalrously.

With that, she took his arm again and they walked back down the cobbled streets to the hotel.

"How long are you staying for?" he asked.

"Probably another couple of days depending on the weather. Why?"

"Unfortunately, I have to leave on the early morning ferry, but I have a friend called Max who could pick you up from the hotel each day and take you wherever you want to go. He knows the island really well and could show you all the interesting views."

"It's not necessary, honestly I will be fine."

"You will be doing me a favour actually," he lied again, trying to protect her. "Max will enjoy a couple of days off. What time do you want to get going in the morning?"

"About six?"

"OK. Reception at six it is. It has been a pleasure meeting you again and I hope you get some good shots."

He arranged for Max to be there in the morning, as he walked back up to the villa to prepare for his night's work.

* * *

The following morning, when she came down at six, there was a very handsome and rather muscular young man sitting in reception, smartly dressed in a sand linen suit and with a Panama hat on his knee. Not what she was expecting.

"Morning ma'am. I'm Max." He greeted her in a broad American accent.

"Good morning, I'm Charlie. Thank you for offering to escort me around the island at such short notice. It's very kind of you."

"Absolutely delighted. Can I carry your equipment for you? That tripod looks rather heavy."

With that they set off, in the early morning sun, across the island to Limnioniza beach for the first location shoot. It required a long trek from the port, up past the old monastery of Agia Triada. When they reached the crest of the hills, that form the backbone of Hydra, they stopped to admire the spectacular view of the coastline below. Charlie decided to take some photographs and set up the tripod, whilst Max poured out some iced spring water which he had thoughtfully brought along. After taking a few shots, Charlie sat next to Max on a nearby rock and sipped her drink.

"Do you live on the Island, Max?"

"No, no I flew in this morning to meet you."

"Err, excuse me, Hydra does not have an airport!"

"Sorry, I flew over from Athens in a helicopter and landed on the beach along from the port, out of sight. Not really meant to do that but all the locals were asleep," Max smiled.

"Now I am really confused. I thought you were a friend of ....?" She suddenly realised she did not know the name of her previous evening's rescuer. "Don't get me wrong, I am very grateful, but who asked you to come and meet me this morning?"

"I have no idea. My boss just asked me if I would like a couple of days out of the office, helping a beautiful damsel in distress. Naturally, being a true American gentleman, I jumped at the chance. So here I am."

"Who exactly is your boss? Does he carry a gun?"

"Goodness gracious no ma'am, he is a diplomat at the British embassy."

"Firstly, will you stop calling me ma'am – its colonial – and secondly why would the embassy pay for you and a helicopter? .... don't bother to answer that."

"Great. That's sorted that out. How did the camera work?" replied Max, grateful that the interrogation was at an end.

"It's fine. It's only the photographer that's confused. Shall we move on before we lose the light. Just call me Charlie by the way."

Max collected up the bags, collapsed the Manfrotto tripod, and followed Charlie down the hill. A bit further on, they passed the smouldering wreck of a large mansion, with two police officers from the NCB Athens (Interpol) hovering near the gate. Evidently there had been a large gas explosion overnight, killing several people and burning the place to the ground. Max ascertained from the policeman that there were no suspicious circumstances and that they could move on safely down the hill.

On reaching Limnioniza beach Charlie did a quick reccy of the site and set up her camera at a strategic point and started collecting images. The light was still good and the cloudless blue sky helped with the tones she wanted. After an hour or so Charlie was happy, so Max broke open the packed lunch of crab salad, with a cool bottle of Prosecco Ca'Stella. They sat on the beach looking out over the blue waters between the Saronic and Argolis gulfs. The sun was intense and Max took off his jacket. He was wearing a tight sky-blue chambray shirt, as most young American men do when they want to impress a lady. Charlie pretended not to notice.

"What do you do at the Embassy?" asked Charlie.

"I am a commercial attaché."

"What does that involve?"

"Mainly arranging business meetings. Pretty boring stuff really. It's all about imports and exports, tourism – that sort of thing. I understand you live in Yorkshire in England?"

"I do… But how do you know that?"

"Did a bit of homework in the sky; you are quite famous on Google. I love your pictures of the moors. Do you only do landscapes?"

"Yes, mainly now. I used to do some pet photography to make ends meet but landscapes are my love. Shall we make our way back now. It's getting too hot."

Max packed the bags again and they hitched a ride on a sea taxi that circled around the island and back to the port. Charlie trailed her elegant hands in the cool sea and was glad they had decided not to hike over the hill again. When they had disembarked and walked back to the hotel, Max offered to take her out for a meal at Omilio's Bistro, that evening.

"That's very kind of you but I must pay," offered Charlie firmly.

"No need. Everything you want is already paid for."

"Everything?"

"That is what I was told. I don't know who your friend is, but he obviously knows all the movers and shakers. I will pick you up at six. Is casual OK?" asked Max.

* * *

When Max reappeared, Charlie was sitting outside the hotel drinking a G & T. She was wearing a white cotton blouse with a mandarin collar and a long pale blue skirt with buttons down the front. Her hair fell loosely over her shoulders. Max was clearly impressed.

"Can I say you look amazing this evening," he flattered her, in a less than subtle American way.

"Thank you, kind sir. You're looking handsome yourself," she smiled.

They wandered down to Omilio's and took a table overlooking the harbour, where the rigging was tapping on the high-tech masts in the warm evening breeze. Max ordered two more drinks and they looked through the menu.

"I am having the fresh squid – how about you, Charlie?"

"I will have the same I think."

Hydra harbour

"Where are you from Max?"

"Just outside Boston, New England. Went to Harvard Business School and then did a PhD at Oxford, on the evolution of European languages."

"Any family?"

"No. My parents were killed in 9/11. Wrong place. Wrong time. I have two beautiful godchildren in California, who Facebook me all the time and give me a lot of fun."

The waiter finally made it to the table.

"Good evening. Are you two having a nice stay on our lovely island?"

"Yes, very pleasant thank you," replied Charlie.

"Have you been around the island yet?"

"Yes, we walked over to Limnioniza beach this morning," reported Max.

"Ah. You will have gone past the big house that burnt out last night?"

"Yes – it looked awful and several people were killed evidently."

"No one on the island will mourn that Chinese lot going. They only came to the island very rarely and never spent any money here. There have been rumours for years that that were mixed up in all sorts of bad things."

"What sort of things?" asked Max.

"Mafia type stuff. Two of them were accused of being involved in illegally trafficking ivory from Somalia to Thailand last year. The case got to court in Athens but was thrown out on some sort of technicality to do with diplomatic immunity. Everybody knows they were guilty as sin, so good riddance I say. What would you like to eat?"

"I don't think we should have a Chinese dish then Max," Charlie smiled.

"We will both have the squid please," Max confirmed to the waiter, "and a bottle of Vinsanto Argyros 20."

"What do you make of all that then Max?" enquired Charlie, not understanding the intrigue of her future with her rescuer on the island.

"These islanders love a bit of local gossip. I expect it was just an accident of some kind," lied Max.

"I suppose you are right. Max could you ask your boss if he has a contact email address for ....; whoever is paying for you helping me? I would like to write to him to thank him for his kindness."

"I will ask when I get back, but I doubt he will know. As far as I understand it, we just got a large bank transfer and a note asking for someone to come over and carry your bags. Best job I have ever had. Cheers!"

With that, the first course arrived. They thanked the waiter and dived in, being really hungry after a long day. It was a romantic, Saronic sunset across the bay. The evening shadows from the masts reflecting in the still waters and the seabirds were dipping for their own suppers.

"Shall we have a dessert ma'am?" teased Max.

"I thought I said ……."

Max smiled. "Only joking. Did I tell you that you look amazing tonight?"

"You did actually, and it's been a lovely evening but I think we should be getting back. We have another early start tomorrow."

Max took the hint and they walked back to Charlie's hotel.

"Sorry. I didn't mean to make you feel uncomfortable. Forgive me?" begged Max.

"No need to apologise. You are a very attractive young man and great company. I am just not in a position to start a relationship at the moment."

"Of course. Sorry. Can we rewind?"

"Never happened. Is six OK for tomorrow?"

"See you then," said Max, leaving the hotel entrance and pondering another unsuccessful conquest.

* * *

Charlie and Max spent the next two days travelling the island on foot or by water taxi. They laughed a lot and she took some beautiful photographs for her portfolio, that she hoped would please her clients. On the final morning, Max carried her bags and equipment down to the ferry and loaded it on board.

"What time does your flight leave for Manchester?"

"Not till late afternoon, so I have plenty of time. Thank so much for all your help, Max. You have been great company and I have really enjoyed my few days on the island," said Charlie sincerely.

She gave Max a friendly hug and he smiled as she climbed aboard the ferry. He waved, as the ageing, white-painted ferry, tinged with rusty streaks, eased its way out of the historic harbour. Unknown to Charlie, their paths would cross again, when he could help her revenge her past.

CHAPTER TWO

Masham – North Yorkshire – England

Three months passed and Charlie had completed the post-production of the photographs for the Hydra portfolio. It was mid-November. The trees were losing their golden leaves and the shooting season was in full swing on the estate. Charlie was working in her studio in the loft above her modest flat, over the old heavy-horse stables. She was organising her next landscape shoot for a wealthy American conservation group in Africa.

Going through her routine emails she nearly deleted one from a Gmail address that she did not recognise and thought was junk. For some reason she opened it out of curiosity and read it.

"Dear Charlie, I was pleased to hear that the rest of your trip to Hydra was less eventful and a success for your photography. I hope Max was helpful and not too impetuous! I am travelling to the UK for a few days in late December and was wondering if you would be free for us to have a meal together at the Blue Lion in East Witton, or somewhere else if you prefer?"

With best wishes.

No name. She noted.

Charlie sat back in her chair and felt a tingle of excitement that she had not felt before. Her immediate reaction was to reply but she had learnt over the years to suppress such impulsive actions to avoid being hurt. She turned her computer off and put on her Schöffel coat against the chill November wind blowing up the Dale. She walked across the stable yard and set off through the wicket gate, up the track to the in-bye fields where the Swaledale ewes were running with the elegant Bluefaced Leicester rams. The rooks were calling in a parliament above the old oak trees and the last dying leaves swirled in the gusting wind. Charlie always went up there to think. Being near to nature was the greatest joy in her life and gave her a peaceful place to make important decisions about her solitary life. Did she want to risk her safe haven? She had never felt like this before. The more she thought about the email, the rescue and that safe arm to hold, the more the fire started to smoulder. She walked for an hour or so and then headed back to the Hall for tea with her mother. They were very close, more like sisters, and always consulted each other on all matters of a womanly kind.

"Come on then. Tell me what's happened?" her mother enquired.

"I don't know what you mean."

"Your eyes betray you my darling. Have you won a new landscape contract or bought a new camera?"

"Neither actually. This is a very good Victoria cake mother."

"Come on – let me in on the news," asked her mother, with a hint of frustration in her voice.

Charlie briefly explained what had happened on Hydra and how she had been rescued by this rather charismatic gentleman.

"I told you Greece was a dangerous place. You are never going there again."

"Yes mother. Anyway, out-of-the blue he has emailed me to say he is coming back to Yorkshire at Christmas and wants to take me out for a meal. What should I do? You know how I feel about men, but he does seem a bit different."

"I think you should be careful my darling. We know nothing about him. What's his name and where does he come from?"

"Can I have another cup please and that cake is delicious."

"Now I am really worried. And ???" questioned her mother, cutting another slice of the cake.

"Sorry! I don't know his name or where he lives. But he did save my life!"

"Mmm. It all sounds a bit odd to me. Let me talk to your father first and we can decide what to do tomorrow."

Charlie returned to her flat but did not sleep much that night. She kept replaying the events on Hydra in her head and indecision swirled around her normally objective brain.

* * *

Over coffee, in the farmhouse kitchen the following morning, her mother said that her father had given it some thought and suggested they invite him to stay over Christmas at the Hall, as a thank you for rescuing her. "We can then get to know him a bit, without you committing to a meal on your own. Your father will enjoy interrogating him!"

"The Blue Lion is not exactly a big risk; it's only down the road and I am thirty-five!" exclaimed Charlie, wishing she had made the decision herself.

"I didn't mean that. We love you, and after everything that's happened, we just want to protect you."

"I know. It's a lovely idea, thank you. Can he come for a few days?" asked Charlie grinning.

"I haven't seen that spark for a long time. For as long as you like darling. We can even teach him to shoot properly," proposed her mother, not understanding what that would lead to.

* * *

Charlie returned to her flat, trying to contain the excitement she felt at actually meeting her mysterious rescuer again. She sat down at her computer and drafted a reply.

Dear Whatever you are called,

We would love to see you over Christmas and Mummy and Daddy would like to invite you to stay at our house for a few days, if you are free, as a small thank you for your chivalrous rescue.

Please say yes. I will protect you from my family.

Kind regards C
(She thought a lot about the kind regards)

To her surprise she got an immediate response.

Dear C,

That is a very generous offer and please thank your parents. I would be delighted to spend a few days with you. I should be landing in Yorkshire on the day before Christmas Eve about midday. Would it be convenient to arrive at your home in the afternoon at about four o'clock?

Kind regards.

Whatever.

Dear Whatever,

That's great. I look forward to seeing you again and talking over old times together.

Charlie x
(She thought even more about the x but went for it.)

He turned into the long drive, through the stone pillars set back off the Leyburn Road. The gatehouse had seen better days. The Capability Brown landscape lay before him, with ancient oaks and a herd of roe deer lying peacefully under the drooping leafless branches. The Hall stood well on rising ground, with the moors as a stunning backdrop against the winter sky. A small lake lay off to the left in a hollow. He drove up the drive in an old Series II Land Rover station-wagon in army green, at two minutes to four. The punctuality and the car impressed Charlie's father.

He drove around the circular gravel drive, ensnaring a well-kept lawn in front of the Hall. He parked at a respectful distance to the left of the old stone entrance. As he swung his legs out of the car door, Charlie and her parents appeared to meet him. Charlie did not know what to do next. Her father saved the day by stepping forward, hand outstretched.

"Hello sir. We are so pleased you were able to come and meet us. My name is Edward and this is my darling wife, Elizabeth. And I think you know this young lady?"

"Daniel Knight. Thank you for having me." Charlie looked directly at him and they both smiled. At last, she knew his name.

With that, Charlie stepped forwards and risked an awkward kiss on his cheek. He took her in his arms and gave her a hug, breaking the ice perfectly.

"Shall we go inside to the warm fire? We can collect your things later. Like the Series II," observed Edward knowledgably. "Most of them are still going you know. Very good for the environment!"

An immaculate, old Robert Menzies grandfather clock sat in the hallway ticking away the generations. A variety of boots, country coats and thumb sticks made from antlers, cluttered the stone-flagged passage.

Elizabeth had prepared a spread of homemade cakes and scones. They were laid out on a coffee table in between the two Chesterfield sofas, positioned in front of the open log fire in the cavernous hall. Charlie sat down next to Daniel and her parents sat opposite.

"Earl Grey or Indian?" asked Elizabeth.

"Earl Grey thank you."

Mummy was impressed with the choice.

"Have you had a long journey?" enquired Edward.

"We had a good flight from Washington to Heathrow and then I hitched a ride in a friend's plane up to Leeming. He kindly lent me the Series II for a few days."

"I thought I recognised it. Do you know John well?" asked Edward.

"Old university friend. He was a mature student when I was at Oxford," replied Daniel.

Charlie had learnt more about Daniel in five minutes than the whole of the time on Hydra. Well done Daddy she thought.

"I thought we might go for a ride in the morning. I assume you can ride?" suggested Charlie. "The forecast is good; if we wrap up warm."

"A bit rusty, but used to point-to-point a bit, a long time ago."

"Mummy breeds Arabs, so we can take a couple of the geldings out on the moor."

"I wondered where that magnificent stallion came from when we first met."

Elizabeth looked quizzical. "You two have met before the trip to Hydra?"

"Not exactly. I was walking on the moor with John's JR and this beautiful young lady rode me off the track!" smiled Daniel, looking at Charlie.

"I'll ignore that! Would you like a tour of the stables to see the horses?" asked Charlie, rapidly deflecting her indiscretion.

"That sounds a good idea. I'll get my coat from the car and bring my bag in if that's OK?"

"Daddy will show you your room whilst I grab a coat too," said Charlie.

* * *

The stable yard was immaculate – not a straw out of place. The walls were white-washed in the traditional way and the mahogany stable doors gleamed with their natural oil coating. There were ten large boxes, bedded deeply with bright yellow oat straw, led in from the Yorkshire Wolds. The six brood mares stood quietly in their boxes munching on sweet-smelling summer hay from the high, flower meadows in the Dale.

Two geldings and the magnificent grey, Arab stallion were at the other end of the barn, in a separate section, away from the mares.

"This is your ride for tomorrow," said Charlie, leaning over one of the stable doors. He is very quiet and my favourite."

"What's he called?"

"Darley. And mine is called Byerley…. It's a family joke. Ask my mother at dinner tonight. She can talk for hours about Arab horse breeding."

Daniel stroked Darley's neck and was rewarded with a low whinny. A good start he thought privately.

They went into the old tack room with saddles, bridles, and girths, all kept in immaculate condition. Each piece of fine English leather carefully positioned in its rightful place. The walls were hung with row after row of championship rosettes won across Europe at all the main Arab horse shows. A shrine to the love of the horse.

"My little empire is above the stables. Would you like to see my finished Hydra photographs?" asked Charlie.

"Of course, as long as there aren't any of Max!"

Charlie liked the slight hint of jealousy.

They climbed the old wooden staircase that creaked with age and Charlie opened the door to her flat. No key.

The room inside took Daniel's breath away. The old loft was flooded with lights and magnificent old masters hung on the walls alongside more modern works by hugely talented artists like Kirby and Upton. A Turner hung over an ancient sofa and a Herring graced the opposite wall.

"I adore the work of really talented artists. Their paintings have a soul that photographs can never aspire to," perceived Charlie passionately.

"I hope you have some good security up here?" joked Daniel, referring to the valuable works of art.

"No. This is Yorkshire not Columbia!" Little did she know how ill-judged that remark would prove to be and the pain she was to face.

"Anyway, you are the only person that knows they are here. I have never brought anyone up here before. I hope you can keep a secret," she smiled. "I'll go and get the Hydra file."

Charlie disappeared up another rather rickety staircase into her studio. She reappeared carrying a large green leather portfolio. She opened it on the solid pine table she had acquired from her mother's kitchen.

The photographs were stunning and the colours so intense, they brought alive the magical early morning Saronic light.

"They are amazing Charlie. You have done a fantastic job. I am sure your clients must be pleased?"

"Yes, they seem happy and have bought the copyright to most of them. I don't like to Photoshop them too much – I prefer to try and get the light and composition right, through the camera. I only take out stray aeroplane trails and the odd delinquent seagull."

Charlie looked at her watch. "We had better be getting back to get ready for dinner."

They walked back to the Hall across the stable yard; the light had gone and the stars had risen brightly in the dark sky. Low on the horizon Venus outshone the stars to the northwest.

"Dinner is at seven – totally informal. Cords and jumper are fine. Father hates formality except at funerals." Charlie informed Daniel. "Is your room OK?"

"It's really warm and inviting. The bed is enormous. I will need GPS to find my way out."

"Mummy loves having guests. See you in a while. Thank you for coming," smiled Charlie.

"The pleasure is all mine."

* * *

Daniel came down promptly at seven, dressed as instructed. Green cords and a Finch Hatton shirt. No sign of Charlie.

"Good evening Daniel. Can I get you a drink?" asked Edward.

"Thank you, Sir, that would be very welcome."

"Gin and tonic? Ice?"

"That would be great thank you."

Edward made the drinks on the side table and passed one to Daniel.

"Good health. Nice to have you here. Would you like to choose a gun for the Boxing Day Flush?"

"I will have to take your advice Sir. I have not had any experience with shotguns."

"Call me Edward please – we don't stand on formality here."

They went into Edward's cluttered study. There were piles of paperwork on the leather topped, walnut desk and heaps of magazines on the floor, mostly shooting and CLA. The heavy curtains looked a thousand years old and there were a couple of old paintings of spaniels, long ago buried in the woods, with proper headstones. There were two gun-cupboards, properly secured, with rows of wonderful old guns. Edward unlocked the first cupboard and took out a beautifully engraved side by side.

"This is my favourite gun. Bought the pair years ago at Tennant's in Leyburn and never regretted it. Elizabeth coughed a bit at the price, but women don't understand how important a good gun is. It defines a man. You can't hit things without the right equipment."

"What make is it?"

"Made by Churchill in London. Twenty-five-inch barrels, twelve-bore, quarter and half choke. Nice light gun. Takes a two-inch cartridge. Less weight to carry around. You can borrow one for the shoot if you like. You'll enjoy handling it."

"That's very kind of you. I will look forward to it."

They returned to the big hall and sank into the deep sofas surrounding the crackling log fire. Elizabeth brought through trays of hot food and bowls of homemade chips, fried in duck fat. Charlie arrived in jeans and a thick Shetland jumper and sat next to Daniel. It was the first time he had noticed her wearing perfume. It had the desired effect.

"We usually just have a light supper the day before Christmas Eve, as we will probably eat too much over the next couple of days," Elizabeth laughed.

"The pie is delicious and the chips are amazing," said Daniel sincerely.

Edward brought out a bottle of Merlot. He liked wine and had an extensive cellar that was his exclusive territory – except when Elizabeth stole the odd bottle for her culinary masterpieces.

"You have some lovely broodmares in your stables. How long have you been breeding Arabs?"

"Probably about forty years? Edward bought me a mare as a present, going back to Crabbet bloodlines, and she has left me some lovely stock over the years. They are all home-bred and I enjoy showing them occasionally."

"Mummy you are being too modest. She has won championships all over Europe – you saw the rosettes in the stables. One mare even won at the World Arab Show in Paris a couple of years back."

"We are using a stallion from Al Shaqab this year for the first time. The stud is based in Qatar so it's a new line for us. He is beautifully bred, so we are very much looking forward to seeing the foals in the spring. Lemon mousse anyone?"

A unanimous 'yes please' set off another round of drinks and a second course.

"What time are you off riding in the morning Charlie?" asked Elizabeth.

"I thought we would leave it till about ten, to let the ice on the lanes melt away first. I will take a flask of coffee with us and some cakes. We will be having a big meal tomorrow night so that should keep us going till then."

"Where are you planning to take Daniel?"

"Not sure. Through the gate, turn left and see where we end up," replied Charlie, enigmatically.

"The forecast looks bright and sunny but it will be very cold on the tops so wrap up warm," advised Elizabeth.

"Yes Mummy. I have been up there before! Thank you for supper. I think I will have an early night."

With that, Daniel stood up and wished Charlie 'good night'.

"Thank you for making me so welcome," said Daniel to his hosts. "I think I will do the same. It's been a long day since starting off in Washington this morning."

"Have a fun ride in the morning. Darley is a spirited ride but he will keep you safe. See you for dinner in the evening."

* * *

Charlie did not sleep too well thinking about being with Daniel the next day. She felt like a schoolgirl with her first infatuation. Her history told her to be sensible, not to get involved; she would only get hurt. It did not work – her latent hormones were stirring and she could not control them. It scared her.

They both arrived at the stables at roughly the same time. Nine fifteen – Daniel did not sleep well either for reflected reasons.

"Good morning Charlie. You are around early. Did you sleep OK?"

"Like a log," she lied.

It was a bright, still, sunny December morning, typical of the Dales. The frost had burnt off by nine on the low ground, so they could make an early start. They went into the warmth of the stables and the smell of the meadow hay was evocative of long, warm July days and picnics under trees in full leaf.

"Darley's head collar is on the hook opposite his door and his grooming box is underneath on the shelf. He's not dirty but give him a quick flick over to get rid of the hay seeds in his mane and then pick his feet out. I assume you can manage that?" said Charlie in jest.

"The feet are at the bottom of his legs I presume?"

"OK sorry. I feel an idiot now."

"A very attractive one though," asserted Daniel, which made Charlie blush.

"I'll give Byerley a quick going over and then we can get the bridles and saddles."

They fetched the old Stübben saddles and simple snaffle bridles off their allotted spaces and tacked up. They led the horses out into the bright sunlight. Their coats shone with the sun's rays catching the newly groomed quarters. Charlie climbed on the mounting block, threw her slim leg over the saddle and leant over to tighten the girth. Daniel pretended to make mounting look difficult but Charlie was too experienced a horse woman to fall for that.

"Stop messing about you! I know you have been riding longer than me."

"How do you know that?"

"Because you're a lot older than me," joked Charlie.

"OK we're equal now. Where are we going, when we turn left?"

"We are turning right"

"But last night you told your mother we were going left?"

"I know, I changed my mind. Lady's prerogative!"

With that, they moved off at a brisk trot down the back drive, over the bridge spanning the leat and up the lane leading to Bramley Grange, passing one of her tenanted farms on the way. The farmer was holding his sixteen-hand grey hunter whilst the farrier was fitting the hot shoes ready for hunting on Boxing Day. The smell of burning hoof reminded Daniel of the last time he was at the dentists in York.

"Morning Tom. Should be a good scent on Boxing morning. Which cover are they drawing first?" asked Charlie.

"Up at Nutwith Common is the plan. I guess it will depend on the volume of the stirrup cup the huntsman quaffs!" he laughed.

"Have fun."

"We always do!"

Charlie and Daniel moved on up the lane and turned right onto Grewelthorpe Moor, through the gate next to the cattle grid. It was two coats colder up on the moor, but they had both wrapped up warm and the exercise was keeping the chill at bay. The cumulus clouds moved gracefully across the deep blue sky, a covey of grouse broke cover and the horses snorted. They reached some open grass, kept short by the Swaledale ewes, and free of stones.

"Shall we have a canter?" suggested Charlie.

"Why not. You take the lead and I will follow."

The Arabs had been here before and no encouragement was necessary. They took off at speed but in a safe way. Daniel had not ridden for a couple of years but the required balance and sensitivity came flooding back and he started to enjoy himself and rode up alongside Charlie."

"The views are amazing up here. Where are we headed?"

"We will go over the top to Jenny Twigg and stop at Fountains Earth to give the horses a rest. You can see Gouthwaite Reservoir from there – it's a great landscape."

Just as Charlie finished speaking, Byerley stumbled into a rabbit hole with his near side fore, dropped his shoulder and Charlie fell out the front door. She somersaulted onto her back on top of a heather thicket. Daniel dismounted rapidly and gathered up the reins of the two horses.

"Are you hurt?"

"Just a bit winded I think."

"Just lie there for a minute and catch your breath. Can you feel your legs OK?"

"Yes, I am fine. Can I have your hand please to get up?"

Daniel held out his hand, took Charlie's and pulled her to her feet. They ended up facing each other very closely. Daniel kissed Charlie on the lips. She looked shocked.

"Sorry if I misread ...." said Daniel hesitantly, but Charlie threw her arms around his neck and kissed him passionately. It seemed like an hour before their lips parted.

"Can you fall off again?!" asked Daniel and they both smiled. The smouldering fire was alight. "Are you sure you are OK to get back on?"

"Yes, honestly. I think the heather broke my fall. Is Byerley OK?"

"Seems fine fortunately. It's easy to lose a leg in a rabbit hole. We had better take it steady for the rest of the day just in case he develops a tendon."

"If we just walk down that hill, we will get to Spring Wood that overlooks Gouthwaite Reservoir. It's a dramatic view down to the water which is usually teeming with a whole variety of birds. A birder's paradise. We can have our coffee down there, in the lea of the oak trees."

They led the horses down the track to the wood, walked through the bare trees and out to the panoramic view of the reservoir. The low sun reflecting on the water, rippling in the light breeze coming up Nidderdale. They found a sheltered spot by an old log and loosened off the girths and let the horses graze. Charlie opened her saddlebag and retrieved the flask and a small oblong cake tin. She poured out the Taylors coffee, still steaming, and unwrapped the tea cake her mother had made specially the night before.

"That's an amazing view, Charlie. Have you photographed it before?"

"Yes. I did a series for the RSPB a couple of years ago, all around the reservoir. I got some really atmospheric shots early in the mornings, before the grockles arrived. Look, there's a group of snow buntings over there in that dead elm tree," indicated Charlie.

"They are winter migrants, I think. Do you know what they call a group of snow buntings?" asked Daniel, trying to impress.

"A snowflake"

"Mmm, I will have to think of a harder one next time," he smiled.

"There's a buzzard up there too," pointed Charlie. "It's catching the thermals from the lake. They are beautiful raptors but they devastate the ground nesting birds in the spring. It's difficult to get that balance right. Red kites have been artificially introduced round here and they are a nightmare, devastating curlew and lapwing chicks along the whole length of Nidderdale. Conservation is much more complicated than the urban naturalists on the television think. Don't mention badgers to our gamekeeper, Mac, by the way!"

"How long has your family owned the estate?"

Red Kite

"Over 200 years. My great-great-grandfather made his money out of the wool trade in Bradford and had a big sheep station in Australia. They used to import merino wool from New South Wales and make it into fine worsted for men's suits and so on, in the dark satanic mills!"

"In ancient times?"

"Do you still have the sheep station?"

"No, that's long gone, along with the mill. We concentrate on running the estate now, so agriculture, forestry and the shooting mainly, but we do run some special conservation projects like the one we have with red squirrels. The estate is over 17,000 acres so it keeps us busy. Most of it is let out to families that have farmed in the Dale for generations. You never really own land – just hope to pass it on in a better state than when you took it on. How about you. What do your family do?"

The question completely took Daniel by surprise, as he never talked to anyone about his past.

"Err, not as exciting as yours," he replied ambiguously.

"Please tell me a bit. I did let you kiss me." Charlie smiled at Daniel and he opened up a little.

"OK. Just for you. I was born in Kenya near Tsavo National Park. I was the only white child in an orphanage run by a very gentle and kind priest called Father Peter. The people who brought me to the orphanage at one week old did not leave a name but they did leave a trust fund for my education which enabled me to get to Oxford to get a degree. I owe everything to Father Peter. He is a wonderful man."

"That is an amazing story. You said 'is'. Do you ever go back and see him?"

"I try and go twice a year to Nairobi on business and always call in to see him. I help him a bit financially to keep the orphanage going. He deserves all the help and support he can get. Life is still pretty tough out there for the poorer families. This cake is fantastic," he said quickly changing the subject.

Daniel had always found it difficult to talk about his past, which Charlie would understand better when he overcame his painful memories and took her to Africa with him. Daniel put his arm around Charlie's shoulder and gently pulled her towards him. They sat for a few minutes in silence together.

"Are you sure you are OK to ride back to the Hall?" he asked tenderly.

"Yes, I am fine, honestly. I will probably be a bit stiff in the morning but I am sure a bottle of Daddy's favourite wine will help this evening. Talking of which we had better be getting back."

They checked the horses were sound, tightened the girths back up and Daniel gave Charlie a leg up. The sun was getting lower in the winter sky and the chill was returning. They followed the track that runs over Dallowgill Moor and dropped down into Swetton village; and then retraced their morning route back down to the Hall. The lights were already on in the stables when they rode into the yard. They dismounted and were glad to be in the warm building. They untacked the horses and put them back in the stables, which were full of deep clean straw with big banks around the edge. The haynets were full and James, the groom, would feed them later when they had settled.

"I think I am going for a nice hot soak in the bath," said Charlie.

"That's a good idea. I think I will do the same. See you in a while."

* * *

Daniel came down at seven, walked across the big hall, fire blazing in friendly welcome, and through a heavy oak door into the dining room. In the middle of the group, busily chatting away and laughing, was Charlie looking stunning with her hair down, a long black dress with a high neck, long gold earrings and a necklace left to her by her grandfather.

"Daniel let me introduce you. This is Tim and his wife Annabelle; they help me run the estate. This is Mac and his wife Sally; they look after all the shooting side of the business; I think you know John and Julia already. Julia works for the Inland Revenue so be careful." They all laughed.

"I better go and help Mummy. Sally, can you give me a hand to carry things through?"

"I thought we would celebrate with a good red from my humble cellar tonight," said Edward jokingly. "Mac brought us a nice haunch of venison a couple of days ago, which he's been keeping specially for tonight."

The enormous table was laid out with every type of plate and glass ever made and the sideboard laden with enough wine for the whole of Edinburgh at Hogmanay. It was going to be a good night.

Charlie, Sally and Elizabeth carried in steaming plates of vegetables, roast potatoes and a huge carving plate with the venison. There was also a multitude of different sauces and a rich gravy carefully created with love and skill in the kitchen. The venison was placed in front of Edward, for him to carry out the ceremonial carving.

Tim was delegated to look after the wine and they all served themselves the steaming garden vegetables, passing the tureens around the table with suitably insulating napkins. When they all had heaped plates and a full glass, Edward proposed the toast.

"Firstly, I would like to welcome Daniel to our annual pre-Christmas dinner and also thank him formally for rescuing our impetuous daughter from the hands of evil. Daniel!" They all took a sip of the Mouton Rothschild from Pauillac; a perfect partner for the venison.

"Secondly I would like to thank everyone for the fantastic job you all do to make the estate the success it is. We are already fully booked on the moors for next year and even have some Russians coming. Hopefully with Love and not Novichok! And finally, I would like to thank Elizabeth for creating such a wonderful meal and for putting up with me for another year. Cheers. Dive in!"

The meal passed in a flash. Interesting and surprising conversations, much laughter and debate, and enough food to fix the famine in the whole of central Africa. Charlie sat opposite Daniel and he could not keep his eyes off her smiling face. She was beautiful, elegant, sophisticated, funny and vulnerable. He was desperate to hold her in his arms, look after her, and be with her alone.

After the meal they retreated to the great hall and broke up into groups. Daniel got cornered by Tim's wife Annabelle, who smelt a romance and couldn't wait to find out more about him. He was polite and charming, making her giggle about something but gave nothing away. Charlie kept an eye on him and already had a tinge of jealousy.

Edward and John were standing in the window recess, carefully protecting the Bordeaux, and in deep conversation as old friends do.

"Tell me a bit more about Daniel then?" asked Edward.

"We were at Oxford together; he read chemical engineering and I read politics and international relations as a mature student. His wife was a doctor but she was sadly killed in Africa about ten years ago. They were deeply in love and he never talks about it. He has become a very private individual and normally finds it hard to interact socially, so he is doing very well tonight."

"He seems to have taken a shine to Charlie," remarked Edward. "I like the man but must admit I am a bit suspicious of him. What line of work is he in? He's not one of your lot, is he?"

"No definitely not. Works for himself. Something to do with business restructuring. He travels all over the world, so he must be good at what he does. He stays with us when he is in England and takes Suzi out for walks up on the moors. I think his job can be very stressful at times and he finds it peaceful to be on his own for a while."

"So, you think Charlie will be OK? – you are her godfather, and I worry she will get hurt again."

"I would trust him with my life Edward. He will look after her. Her problem was fifteen years ago now. You have got to let her find herself again."

"I suppose you are right. This red is exceptionally good. I think I'll get another bottle from the cellar!"

Julia was interrogating Elizabeth about the wild mushroom sauce she had made specially to go with the venison and Tim and Mac were planning how to make the last woodcock stand of the 100-bird flush as difficult as possible.

Daniel had managed to escape Annabelle's Spanish Inquisition and could not see Charlie anywhere. He was searching for her, when Tim called him over to discuss the Boxing Day Flush, shooting clay pigeons.

"Do you shoot much?" enquired Tim, hoping the answer was 'No'. Tim was very competitive and did not want any more experienced opposition.

"Only in self-defence," Daniel joked; well sort of. "Charlie has roped me in as her partner, I think it might not have been her best decision."

"It will be quite challenging. What make of gun will you be using?"

"Edward has very kindly offered to lend me one of his pair of Churchills. They look beautiful guns – the level of skill to do that intricate engraving is unbelievable."

Tim smiled and slightly raised one eyebrow to Mac. Daniel moved on in his hunt for Charlie, leaving Tim with his fiercely competitive concerns satisfied.

Daniel eventually found Charlie in the kitchen talking to Sally about their new litter of puppies born a couple of days before. They were out of Mac's best bitch and by a Field Trial Champion, Greenbriar Thunder at Drakeshead. They had got eight puppies, five bitches and three dogs and were obviously Sally's pride and joy. She loved looking after puppies and they were her domain until they were weaned. He did not want to interrupt the flowing conversation, thanked Charlie for a lovely day, and retired for the evening to his enormous enveloping bed. With a copy of the *Shooting Times* for some quick revision.

CHAPTER THREE

The First Flush of Love

It was a frosty Christmas morning and Daniel had agreed to meet Charlie at eight o'clock for a cup of Earl Grey and toast before going for a walk around the park. By coincidence they arrived in the great hall at the same time in front of the roaring fire. Daniel wondered who lit all these fires but never solved that mystery. He had bought Charlie a present and decided to give it to her whilst they were on their own. Charlie opened the immaculately wrapped small box. It was a gold bracelet with a small St Christopher charm attached.

"Oh, its lovely Daniel. Thank you so much. But I have not got you anything I didn't…" Daniel put his arms around her and kissed her gently.

"That's the best present I could ever have," he smiled.

They went through to the kitchen and Daniel brewed the tea, whilst Charlie made the toast on the Aga. As they were eating breakfast, Elizabeth came in with a bottle of red wine acquired from the cellar.

"Good morning you two. I have to steal the wine before your father appears or he moans that I have taken the wrong one!"

"Look Mummy. Daniel has bought me a lovely new bracelet."

Elizabeth took Charlie's hand and inspected the gift closely.

"A St Christopher; it's beautiful and very thoughtful of you Daniel. She really needs one of those! A great choice. Are you two off for a walk now?"

"Yes, we will look after ourselves today so don't bother with lunch. I will come back at about four and help you with Christmas dinner."

"That would be helpful darling. See you later, have fun and wrap up warm."

It was a beautiful December morning, the low sun lighting up the ice crystals clinging to the branches of the bare trees. The grass crunched under their boots as they made their way along an old pathway towards High Wood. When they were out of sight of the Hall, Daniel took Charlie's hand in his. She smiled happily and they silently enjoyed the winter landscape together. Occasionally a rabbit would appear on the track looking for breakfast, and a vixen could be heard at the other end of the wood – maybe looking for a rabbit. Such is the balance of nature.

"It's a bit late in the morning to hear a fox. She must have had an unsuccessful night," observed Charlie.

"Lucky rabbit!" jested Daniel

As they left the wood behind them, they met Mac walking two of his lovely black labs.

"Hi Mac. Happy Christmas." Charlie gave him a friendly hug.

"Happy Christmas, Daniel. Sorry we did not get much chance to talk last night."

"Happy Christmas. The evening did seem to fly by."

"I understand from Charlie you are joining us for the 100-bird flush tomorrow?"

"Yes, Charlie cajoled me into it I'm afraid. I believe we have to shoot in pairs? I've never shot a clay in my life. So, any tips would be most welcome – I don't want to let Charlie down."

"We can't have that can we. Why don't you come round in the morning and we will have some breakfast, then I will drive you up to the quarry and we can have a private practice run to get your eye in?"

"That would be great. Are you sure you have time?"

"Anything for Charlie," laughed Mac genuinely. "Will about eight be OK? Bacon and eggs. Don't bring Charlie, she knows how to shoot – she killed five more than me last year!"

Charlie laughed and put her arm around Mac.

"Fantastic. See you then," confirmed Daniel, pleased with the opportunity to get some practice in.

They continued their walk down towards the lake where the three black swans were serenely feeding, without a care in the world.

"Where did the black swans come from?"

"My grandfather was in Churchill's war cabinet and frequently stayed at Chartwell with him during the Second World War. They both had a love of wildlife and often walked around the estate in Kent, planning meetings and political strategy together. After the war Winston gave my grandfather a pair of black swans as a memory of their time together. They have been here ever since and occasionally breed, but I am afraid the foxes usually get the cygnets."

They stopped by the overgrown sluice gate, which controlled the height of water in the lake, to watch a kingfisher. It's azure and copper plumage was glistening in the sunlight. It was perched on a branch, staring into the water. Suddenly it dived and flew back up to the perch with a small fish in its beak.

"Do you ever photograph wildlife?" asked Daniel.

"I have enormous respect for wildlife photographers because they spend hours sitting in a hide waiting for the bird or animal to do its thing and get spectacular pictures. But mountains don't move, so I think I'll stick with them."

They completed the circumnavigation of the lake and walked slowly back up the drive, watching the deer grazing the short winter grass.

"We traditionally have Christmas dinner in the kitchen – just the three of us and obviously there will be four of us this year. It's nice to have an intimate family evening together, sandwiched between Christmas Eve and Boxing Day, which are lovely events but very busy, and a lot of work for Mummy. We always have a roast sirloin of beef, roast potatoes and Yorkshire pudding of course. I help mum do the cooking and washing up so I am afraid you will get roped in."

"Look, I am just so pleased they were good enough to invite me and I am able to be with you for a few days. It's a very long time since I felt so relaxed and happy."

"Shall we go back to the flat for a cup of tea; then I will have to go up to the Hall to help Mummy."

Charlie took Daniel's arm as she had done in Hydra. She looked at him and smiled. He gave her a quick kiss on the cheek and smiled back.

They climbed the old stairs into the warmth of the flat and took off their coats. Charlie put the kettle on and Daniel sank into the sofa opposite the painting by Herring.

"He was an incredibly talented artist. He just catches the characters of the individual horses; you feel you can touch them," observed Daniel knowledgeably.

"Sugar?"

"Two please."

"It's not good for you."

"I know but I like to live dangerously."

Charlie streamed some music quietly in the background. She chose Mozart's Flute and Harp Concerto, one of her favourites. It was to become theirs as their love affair blossomed.

Charlie deliberately sat closely to him on the sofa. He put his arm around her shoulders and she put her head on his, warming her hands on the hot tea cup.

"It was nice of Mac to invite me round in the morning for a practice. I will certainly need it."

"He is a brilliant coach. Just do exactly as he tells you and you will be fine. We have got to beat Tim and Annabella."

"I thought he shot for the England team?"

He does, but Annabella couldn't hit a partridge if it sat on the end of the gun. We'll get them. Not that I am competitive or anything!"

Daniel gave her a squeeze and kissed her head. Charlie looked up into his eyes and their lips met softy and sensuously. His heart missed a beat. She put her cup down and lay on his lap looking up at him.

"I haven't kissed anyone like that for a very, very, long time. Please don't ever hurt me?" pleaded Charlie.

"I have a feeling we both have painful histories, but that's not for now. You are very special to me. I will always look after you Charlie, if you let me. I do not believe in fate, but meeting you for the second time in Hydra was surreal for me and the moment I saw you, I knew I wanted to look after you and catch you whenever you fall."

"Promise?"

"For ever."

They kissed again. Slowly and very sensitively.

They spent the afternoon together on the sofa listening to Charlie's Mozart collection, looking at the books on her favourite artists, and enjoying the first flickering flames of love. The magic was interrupted by the ancient Charman clock hanging on wall, striking four times.

"Crickey, we had better get going or I will be in trouble with Mummy. Meet you in the kitchen at half six."

* * *

When Daniel entered the kitchen, Edward was opening a bottle champagne. "I thought we would celebrate your visit with a bottle of Larmandier-Bernier, one of the best vine-grower champagnes."

"That's very kind of you. I am having such a wonderfully relaxing time: I am so grateful you were kind enough to invite me, Edward. Can I help you do anything Elizabeth?"

"Can you stir the gravy on the Aga please, whilst Edward carves the beef?"

"Of course – it smells delicious."

"Mummy's secret recipe," said Charlie.

"It's no secret. It's just half a bottle of my best red!" muttered Edward, winking at Daniel.

They served up and all sat down around the old pine table and tucked into their traditional dinner. Daniel asked Elizabeth how Darley and Byerley got their names and Elizabeth explained that they both grew rather over-height for an Arab, so they were gelded to be ridden. The Darley Arabian and the Byerley Turk were two of the foundation stallions, along with the Godolphin Arabian, of the modern thoroughbred, which are bigger than traditional Arabs – thus the joke.

After two bottles of the excellent champagne, the conversation was freeing up and everyone was more relaxed.

"When did you take over the estate from your father?" Daniel asked Edward, not expecting the reply he got.

"Well actually, I don't own the estate, Charlie does. My elder brother, Roger, never got married and had no children to pass it on to, so he left it to Charlie. I am just the lacky that keeps the place going!"

"Daddy that's ridiculous and you know it is. You have transformed this estate since you took it over; when you took charge, it was run-down and had had no investment for years. It's now one of the top shooting estates in Yorkshire and that's all down to you and the team you have built up. They all respect you enormously and it was only left to me for tax purposes."

"OK I give in. You can have an extra glass of champagne for being such a wonderful daughter. I understand Daniel you are off for a bit of early morning shooting practice with Mac first thing?"

"Yes, he has kindly said he will let me see a few clays so I do not let your daughter down tomorrow. I hope he's good teacher."

"What Mac doesn't know about shooting is not worth knowing. He's an instinctive shot on the moors when it comes to grouse. Tim might be a genius at clay shooting but Mac will help you the most, if you know how to handle firearms. Don't aim the gun at the target as you would with a rifle – use your eyes to follow the clay not the gun. Anyway, cheers! Good health. And here's to family Christmases."

* * *

Daniel was up early on Boxing Day morning and made his way down to the kennels, where Mac and Sally lived in an ancient stone farmhouse complete with boot room, a bitch with puppies and an Aga kitchen filled with chaos; including two JRs arguing over last night's bone.

A pile of shooting magazines lay open on the kitchen table, along with Saturday's *Yorkshire Post*, slightly crumpled. An old spaniel lay on the rug by the Aga. A kettle steaming away with a broken whistle, sat on top, with a tea pot warming cosily in a knitted bonnet. Blue and yellow.

"Fried bread and two eggs? They're Marans," asked Mac.

"Yes please. It smells delicious."

"How long have you known Charlie?" Sally wanted to know.

"We met a couple of years ago up on Masham Moor. I was walking John's bitch Suzi and she was riding a grey stallion. We met on a path between the heather, passed the time of day, and she rode on."

"Very romantic! – sounds like Charlie, she can be a bit standoffish when she wants to be," said Sally in a blunt but not critical Yorkshire way.

"How does the clay shoot work then?" asked Daniel, rapidly changing the subject. "I have not used a shotgun before. More of a rifle man myself."

"Oh dear. Not a good start. What do you shoot? Deer?"

"No, vermin mainly," replied Daniel ambiguously.

"Don't worry, Tim always wins and gets the bottle of Malt. Edward always tries to beat him, but insists on using his old Churchill side by side which makes it harder."

They finished the excellent breakfast. Daniel thanked Sally and they drove up to the quarry, set in the hillside, in the new Range Rover. Grouse shooting pays.

"Ok, so it's a 100-bird flush. You shoot together in pairs on four stands each representing a different type of game bird. So, we are in this grouse butt first. There will be four pairs shooting today. Charlie and you. Edward and his old shooting friend, Nick, who farms on the estate in Coverdale. Super shot Tim and his wife Annabelle. And William and Paul who run the Auction Mart up at Hawes, where we sell the mule gimmer lambs in the Autumn sales. They have their own grouse moor above Cotterdale and know how to handle a gun.

So, you and Charlie will stand in the butt and there are three traps that loose the clays. When the whistle sounds, we will release twenty-five clays. Some singly, some in pairs and an odd four or five. You work as a team and kill as many as you can between you. It doesn't matter if you miss one, Charlie can kill it for you. If five clays are released together, one of you will have to reload. We draw straws to see which pair goes first etc. I have a clicker in my pocket and record the missed birds out of the twenty-five. So, if you miss five, you score twenty at stand one. Each pair then shoots here and we then all move on to the three other stands. As I said, each stand is meant to represent how a type of bird will fly. So, this is an easy grouse stand to start with. At the end we have a score out 100 for each pair and the highest scoring pair gets the Malt and it's a Balvenie DoubleWood 12 so it's worth going for. Ok so far?"

"Yes, thank you. Sounds like fun. Can I have a practice shot?"

"Ok. This is a Perazzi 12-bore over and under. A well-balanced gun and perfect for this job." Mac demonstrated how to break the gun, load and release the safety.

"I will release one clay and you try and hit it."

Daniel missed.

"OK relax. Don't aim like you do with rifle. It's a different technique. Keep your eyes on the clay. Say pull when you are ready for the next clay."

"Pull." Second clay. Missed.

"Pull." Third clay. Missed.

"OK what am I doing wrong? There is shot in these cartridges?" Daniel laughed.

"Plenty! The spread is about the size of a dustbin lid when it gets to the clay so there is a good margin for error. The shot travels at over 1450 feet per second, that's nearly 1000 mph, so there is no need to shoot in front of the clay. If you aim, you will always be behind the clay and miss it. That's what you are doing wrong. Follow the clay with your eyes. Ok try again"

"Pull." Missed.

"Charlie is not going to be impressed Mr Daniel! OK I am going to release a clay, start to follow it with your eyes, both open, and when I say 'now' I want you to shut your eyes and follow through. I will then say 'kill' and you pull the trigger, still with your eyes shut."

"Really?" said an astonished Daniel.

"Reload. Ready?"

"OK. Pull."

"Now…….Kill." In a puff of dust, the clay was completely destroyed.

"OK explain how that works? I am a better shot with my eyes shut!"

"Look, you are clearly a good shot with a rifle. You know how to handle a gun. Don't aim, just follow the clay with your eyes."

"OK. Pull." Dust.

"OK. Pull." Dust.

"OK. Pull." Dust.

Mac patted Daniel on the back. "You've got it now; you might just impress the lady."

"We better get back or I will be in trouble with Charlie for monopolising your time."

As they were leaving the quarry a badger silently appeared from the scrub at the side of the Range Rover.

"Look Daniel. That sow has been around for a few years now. She is heavy with cubs and the clan live in a sett at the far end of the quarry."

"Charlie sort of implied you didn't like badgers?" quizzed Daniel hesitantly.

"I love seeing badgers in the early morning, rooting about, but we don't need thousands of them. They are knee-deep in them further up the Dale. They decimate the food sources that other animals eat, so you will never see a hedgehog, for example, within a mile of a sett and if you have hundreds of setts, no wildlife diversity. The trouble with these plastic TV naturalists is that they have read a Beatrix Potter book and think they are world experts on conservation. That's apart from the fact that badgers carry TB and cause huge human catastrophe when herds of cows and calves have to be slaughtered. Just because nobody has the backbone to cull out the surplus badgers. They suffer an awful death with TB but it's underground where the so-called country lovers can't see them. There you are, rant over. Badgers are like cream cakes. Delicious in small numbers!"

Badgers

They drove back down to the kennels. "Thank you, Mac. I owe you."

"Pleasure. Just give Tim a run for his money. I can't beat the chap, but you just might, if you keep both eyes open! Oh, one last thing. Edward will offer you one of the Churchills. They are his pride and joy. Politely refuse and ask him if you can use his Browning over and under. It's heavier and gives you more shot in each cartridge. Might just give you the edge."

Daniel got back to the Hall about 10.30 and everyone was already there in the great hall having coffee and homemade scones. No alcohol before the guns. The conversations were all about Labradors, lambing and lunch. The latter being the halfway mark of the competition ahead. It was friendly, fun and fiercely competitive.

Edward called Daniel into his study and opened the gun cupboard.

"Now then. Is it to be the Churchill?"

"Would you mind if I went for your humble Browning over and under?"

"You've been talking to Mac, haven't you?"

"He thought the extra shot in each cartridge might help my lack of experience," said Daniel modestly.

"What he actually thought was that there was a chance, however small, of you beating Tim and everything he could do to make it happen was worth a try. If he thought you had no hope, he would have let you use the beautiful Churchill and feel important. Go for it. We all like Tim and he is a brilliant shot but this is meant to be fun!"

He broke the Browning and handed it to Daniel. "Good luck. Charlie always pulls to the left. Stand on her right and pick up her misses."

"Thank you very much, Edward. I will do my best." They returned to the great hall and everyone was getting their shooting gear on. All green and very country. Charlie came across to Daniel smiling.

"How did you get on with Mac?"

"His knowledge of shooting is encyclopaedic. He was really helpful, but said Tim has a whole row of malt bottles and he couldn't see that changing."

"No, he didn't. He said don't aim, and shoot with both eyes open."

"How did you know?"

"Because that what he tells me too."

"Let's go get 'em, Sundance," she laughed competitively. Tim overheard.

With that, they climbed into the Range Rovers and drove up to the quarry, for the first stand of the Flush.

Each team drew a straw from Mac's swarthy hand to decide the order.

"Edward and Nick to shoot first. The Hawes Team second. Tim and Annabelle third and Charlie and Daniel last. Six clays each to practise."

Edward and Nick Stepped into the butt and the whistle went. The clays flew. Single. Single. Double. Double. All down.

"OK, here we go for the real thing gentlemen," warned Mac.

The whistle went again and clays appeared from two directions at considerable speed. Much faster than at Daniel's practice session. Clay Armageddon followed.

"Two misses. Twenty-three scored. Good start gentlemen."

Next up we have William and Paul.

"Practice first. Six clays." One missed. The whistle sounded and the competitive clays flew erratically.

"Four misses. Twenty-one scored."

"Tim and Annabelle please. Practice."

All down, but Tim shot four and Annabelle two. He reloaded so quickly, if you blinked you would have missed it. Daniel was impressed. A lot.

"OK, real thing." The whistle went. Tim shot two, for every one of Annabelle's but they still only missed two.

"Twenty-three scored. Level with Edward and Nick."

"Charlie and Daniel next please. Practice first."

Three misses. Charlie one and Daniel two. Tim smiled at Annabelle.

"Just relax. You hit one." joked Charlie.

"I wasn't aiming at that one!"

The whistle went. The fun stopped. Time to impress.

No misses. Twenty-five scored. Daniel shot fifteen.

"Shit," whispered Tim to Annabelle.

"Thank you, ladies and gentlemen. The second stand Is the high pheasant and it's up by the stone tower, in Meg's pastures."

They all climbed aboard. Charlie smiling.

"Good start for us," she said quietly.

"Beginner's luck," lied Daniel.

The pheasant stand was more challenging and there was a side wind upsetting the flight of the clays.

"This is where a light gun comes into its own," said Edward confidently, walking up to the stand with his friend. A little conference took place slightly altering their strategy.

"All ready?" The whistle went. The pair worked brilliantly together even getting the three clays released together towards the end. A real test for any gun.

"One missed. Twenty-four scored. Well done gentlemen. Given the youngsters something to aim at. Your turn William and Paul."

The breeze was getting up and the clays were harder to follow, but they were used to shooting grouse up on the high moors, where the wind is horizontal half the time. They accounted for themselves well, under the circumstances and shot twenty out of twenty-five.

"Tim and Annabelle please." Luckily for them there was a lull in the gusts and this was Tim's strongest stand, having spent most of his life on big sporting estates with outstanding high pheasant shoots. He shot brilliantly, killing all of his, plus most of the ones Annabelle missed. A true professional. Everyone was impressed and he got a spontaneous round of applause.

"Only one missed. Twenty-four scored. Well done Tim – great shooting. OK Charlie and Daniel, let's see what you've got."

Half way through the stand the wind became very gusty again and the clays were everywhere. Disappointingly Charlie missed three and Daniel one.

"Bad luck – great job under the circumstances. Four missed. Twenty-one scored."

"Time for lunch ladies and gentlemen. Sally has put on a spread down at the kennels so we will head down there now. The scores at halfway are Edward and Nick are tying with Tim and Annabelle on forty-seven, great shooting you four. Charlie and Daniel, you are lying third just behind with forty-six. And William and Paul you have forty-one. All still to play for. Enjoy your lunch. Back in the cars for two o'clock for the third stand. The teal."

With that, they all piled into the Range Rovers and headed for the old cow byre. Tim had converted it into a warm haven for the guns to have lunch in, when they were shooting locally on the estate.

Sally had done herself proud, as usual, with an array of homemade pies, sausage rolls, baked potatoes, cakes and a whole variety of puddings. The enormous teapot, steam issuing from the spout, was at the end of the table. There was much talk about the gusting wind, Tim's brilliant shooting and endless praise for Sally's fruit cake which was her speciality. She took the praise humbly, but was grateful, as she always put in a special effort for this highlight of the year. Edward's comments were especially noted and repeated to Mac throughout the following weeks. "Edward said......" Mac was not very good at praising.

Towards the end of lunch Daniel had to take an urgent call on his mobile outside but said nothing to Charlie.

At the stroke of two, Mac rounded up all the replete guns and ushered them into the vehicles. They moved off down to the pond in the grazing field, next to the derelict stone barn.

"OK ladies and gentlemen, the pressure mounts and things are going to get a little more testing. Well a lot actually," he laughed.

"Twenty-five clays. At least one treble. Plus, an odd surprise!"

"Edward and Nick, are you ready?" They were again having a secret discussion.

"Ready." The whistle rang out.

Single, double, two singles in quick succession, a treble and then a very fast double which meant a fast reload. Edward dropped his cartridges, got confused and missed two. More followed in quick succession.

"Two misses, twenty-three scored. Good recovery," said Mac.

William and Paul next. More secret planning; just like a doubles match at Wimbledon.

"It will be dark soon! Are you two ready yet?" The whistle blasted.

William seemed to come alive after a lacklustre morning and Paul backed him up superbly.

"Two misses, Twenty-three scored. Great stand gentlemen."

"Now then Tim and Annabelle. Your turn." Tim was looking very serious and determined. "Ready?" The whistle rang out.

Tim was like a man possessed, clays shattering, empty cartridges flying everywhere and reloading in split seconds. The others were not sure if Annabelle hit anything but only two clays escaped the duo.

"Brilliant Tim. Great style. Only two missed. Twenty-three scored."

"Well, follow that!" said Mac to Charlie and Daniel. "I hope you've two have got a plan?"

Charlie and Daniel went into a huddle, pretended to be talking, but they had already devised a plan. Beat Tim!

The whistle went, and calmly, as if in slow motion, twenty-four clays bit the dust. They did a high-five – very out of character for both of them, but excitement was mounting. Tim smiled in respect. He knew the home of the Malt was in the balance.

"Amazing. That fruit cake is working a treat!" chuckled Mac.

"OK, now the woodcock. This should be fun. I've bought some special super-charged clays for the day," Mac joked. "Last stand. Up to Chapel Wood, on the far side."

The sky had clouded over and the light was dimming. Fast clays were going to be incredibly challenging. They pulled up next to the makeshift stand made out of old pallets.

"The scores before the final round are; Edward and Nick seventy, William and Paul sixty-four, Tim and Annabelle seventy, and Charlie and Daniel seventy. I can never remember it being this close. So, it's all down to this last stand. A bit like Custer!"

"Edward and Nick. Are you ready?" A small round of applause for support and sportsmanship. The whistle went.

They shot incredibly well considering the pressure. Edward had not been this close to winning in many a year.

"Four misses, twenty-one scored. Total for the day ninety-one. Brilliant day gentlemen."

"Now then William and Paul show us what you have."

"How many out of twenty-five do we need to win?" joked Paul.

"Thirty-six to be sure," laughed Mac.

"We will give our best. Ready!"

To be fair, they did very well but a treble clay proved too much of a challenge and they ended up five down.

"Total score for the day eighty-four. Well shot gentlemen and thank you for being such great company."

The scene was set for the final showdown. The final two pairs, both on seventy points, both youngish, both quietly competitive, and both with their own agendas.

"Tim and Annabelle. Good luck." The whistle went.

Their new strategy was basically that Tim tried to shoot everything and Annabelle tried to pick up the strays. It worked incredibly well and they missed only two which was unknown for a Boxing Day woodcock.

A genuine round of applause followed, built on respect for such a professional performance.

"Now then you two," said Mac, looking at Charlie and Daniel. "I think you have got your work cut out!"

They had a little conference. "We're ready to go Mac." Whistle.

Ten clean shots. Missed one. Nine more clean. It all rested on the final five – no more misses if they were to win. A treble woodcock, instantly followed by a double. Nobody knew how Daniel hit all five, but they lay in a heap of dust on the Yorkshire grass field just outside Masham.

Charlie threw her arms around Daniel and kissed him, Tim ceremoniously lay his gun on the ground and the others applauded for several minutes.

"Ninety-four scored. Just luck I think," grinned Mac.

Edward hugged his daughter and shook Daniel's hand vigorously.

"Well that has been a fantastic day ladies and gentlemen. Thank you for being so sporting. I haven't seen such amazing accuracy in many a year. We will run you all down to the kennels. Have a safe trip home."

Daniel was having a quiet word with Edward when they got out of the cars at the kennels.

"Is everything all right?" asked Charlie.

"I am afraid I will have to leave straight away. That call at lunchtime was to say my business trip to Lima in Peru has been brought forward and I fly out to Los Angeles tonight. I am so sorry. It has been a lovely few days and being with you again has been wonderful."

He took Charlie in his arms and kissed her slowly. "You mean the world to me. I will be back." He gave her a tender squeeze.

"Your mother has very kindly packed my things and there is a taxi waiting. John will collect his Land Rover next week."

Charlie was taken aback by the suddenness of his leaving but understood he had a business to run. They walked hand in hand out to the taxi. Daniel gave her another hug, kissed her softly and then he was gone.

She stood alone, looking down the long drive and wishing he was coming the other way.

* * *

The shooting party were putting their guns into their faded leather slips and into the boots of their cars. Tim came over to Mac.

"Did you see how he did that Mac?"

"No idea. It all happened so fast, but it was amazing however he did it."

Tim wandered off shaking his head.

A bit later Edward came over to Mac to thank him for such a marvellous day and Sally for the lunchtime spread.

"Go on then, how did he do it?"

"It was fantastic shooting but he was also very lucky. They had decided the only way they could possibly win was for Daniel to try and take all the last five clays. They were too fast for Charlie. So, Charlie did not shoot her gun. He had worked out where the clays were coming from and their trajectories. He reckoned that if he could hit the second and third clays together with one cartridge as they crossed over, he could then swop his gun for Charlie's loaded gun and hit the last two.

"I watched him and he did exactly what I told him not to. He aimed at the second clay, followed it with his eye on the crossover and fired as you would a rifle. Charlie then quickly exchanged guns and he killed the last two. You and I would never had achieved that with our technique, and it's why it has mystified Tim. I think we should keep it a secret from him. It will keep him baffled for weeks."

At that moment, Tim came over to Mac to thank him for the day. As he walked away, he looked back and said, "Who the hell is Sundance anyway?"

CHAPTER FOUR

The Dark Landscape

The next few days passed slowly for Charlie. Although she was not expecting any communication from Daniel, she was slightly disappointed that she hadn't heard anything, but then he hadn't promised anything either. The lead up to New Year was always busy with clients coming and going and there were always problems to sort. Collecting them from airports, getting clearance for helicopters to land and solving their endless problems like, "I only eat vegetarian food." "Err, you are here to shoot things sir."

New Year's Eve came and went. Charlie hated it.

Darley threw a shoe and the farrier had to fit a new one. The smell was evocative of their hack up to the moor when they saw the hunter being shod. She thought of Daniel and wondered what he was doing in Lima.

Two more days passed and she was walking Mac's dogs, Bess and Molly for company, when she saw the kingfisher on its branch. She remembered the kiss and his arms around her waist. She wanted that feeling again. She had lived fifteen years on her own, until Daniel had saved her life in Hydra. She could wait a bit longer.

A week passed and Charlie made herself busy with editing and filing photographs in her flat above the stables. It was bitterly cold and apart from walking the dogs she did not venture far.

Her mother invited her over for tea and a chat in the third week of January, as she often did when she wanted a woman-to-woman

Kingfisher

conversation. Edward was not good at conversation, if it did not involve running the estate or his wine cellar, but she loved him dearly. They had been married for forty years and had mellowed together.

"How is the planning going for your next trip darling?" she asked, pouring the Earl Grey.

"I've not really decided where to go next. I've got that commission in Africa but that's a long way off and I have to wait for grants to be approved and that could take years. I just feel like being at home for a while."

Hesitantly her mother asked, "Have you heard anything from Daniel?"

"No not yet. I am trying not to think about it. He has a very stressful business to run and I expect he is focused on that at the moment. He didn't promise to contact me, so I will have to be patient. This cake is very good."

"Yes dear. I am sure you are right."

They talked about other things but their hearts were not in it. Charlie drifted off to her flat. Edward came in for a cup of tea.

"Did I see Charlie going back to her flat?"

"Yes, she came over for a chat about things."

"Has he rung yet?"

"How did you know......?"

"I may be a man, but I am not totally insensitive to these things. It's a pretty poor show if he cannot pick up the phone after how well they got on over Christmas. I thought they were getting on like a house on fire."

"I know, so did I. I am a bit worried about her actually. It was the first time she had seemed really happy for years, with him. If he lets her down, I will be very cross with him. She doesn't deserve that."

"Do you want me to ring John to see if he has heard anything?"

"Would you mind dear. There may be a very good reason and we are being unfair or hasty."

"OK I will give him a bell in the morning. What's for supper I am starving?"

* * *

"Hello Julia. Is John about? .... Hi John. How's things with you? Really. When? Are you taking the Series II? Would love to come. It will be fun. Actually, I was ringing about Daniel. You haven't heard from him, have you? It's just that we haven't heard hide nor hair since Christmas and to be honest, Charlie is a bit sad about it. She really liked him and they seemed to get on so well. And you said he was a decent chap. A bit odd really don't you think? OK, that would be great thank you. I will wait to hear from you. Speak soon."

Later that afternoon John rang back.

"Can I come over this evening about seven. It's not good news I am afraid."

"Oh dear. That's not what I wanted to hear. OK see you later."

Edward went through to the kitchen. Elizabeth was making some fresh bread.

"I have just spoken with John and he is coming over later with some news on Daniel. He said it was not good, so you had better prepare Charlie for a difficult conversation."

Elizabeth rang Charlie and she rushed over to the Hall.

"What's happened Mummy; is he OK? Is he coming back?"

"We don't know Darling. John is coming over at seven to give us the news. But it does not sound good I'm afraid."

"Oh, Mummy no, please don't say he's been hurt or anything, I couldn't bear it. Please God he is all right."

John arrived at seven promptly. His face was solemn. He was experienced at delivering dire news to the families of his fallen troops, and how to handle the fallout that inevitably followed.

"I am afraid it is very sad news. Daniel was apparently caught up in some sort of violence as an innocent bystander. It appears it was a gang war of some sort and Columbia can be a very dangerous place if you are in the wrong place at the wrong time."

"But Daniel was in Peru. Why was he in Columbia? Maybe it's not him?" pleaded Charlie.

"I am really sorry Charlie but I am afraid he's gone. He was a great man and he thought the world of you."

"I can't believe this is happening. Why? Why? She burst into tears and ran out of the room."

"Will they bring the body back to England for burial?" asked Edward sadly.

"I am afraid there is no body. These bastards are worse than animals. It's best left that he is buried out there. We just don't have any information on the ground out there. I've contacts in the US agencies and they have no intelligence from that area either. I am afraid it's a closed book."

Elizabeth burst into tears. Edward put his arm around her and shed a few too.

* * *

It was a long hard February with bitterly cold snow blizzards, drifting even on low ground. Shooting was finished and spring seemed a millennium away.

The following Saturday, Edward was reading the *Yorkshire Post*, with his morning cup of coffee and cake and he came across a short article about a massive explosion near Caquetá in Columbia. Evidently, a huge warehouse of cocaine was destroyed, along with a large group of the traffickers who were having some sort of cartel meeting where they fixed the prices for cocaine going to the USA through Mexico. The reason for the explosion was not known and the CIA denied any involvement. The USA and the Columbian government were currently at a delicate stage in negotiations about controlling the supply of cocaine and its derivatives through Mexico and across the border into Texas. Edward wondered if they were involved in Daniel's death in any way, but decided he was only speculating and it would be best to keep the article to himself. He read the farming page instead.

Charlie threw herself into physical work on the estate to escape the grief. When she stopped, she cried desperately. She kept working till she dropped. It was the only way she could sleep.

One day in early March she was woken at five-thirty in the morning by a call on her mobile. It was George, the new young shepherd.

"Sorry to disturb you so early Charlie but there is a raging blizzard up here at Hagg's Gill and some ewes have got buried in a drift under the wall against the moor. I've tried digging them out with a shovel but the snow is beating me. I've tried ringing Tim but I can't get a reply."

"No. He is away for a couple of days with Annabelle. I'll go and get Mac and we will come up in the Gator. Tim got some tracks put on it, so we should make it. Give us half an hour."

Charlie rang Mac, pulled on some warm clothing and her waterproofs, ran across the yard and pounded on Mac's door. Mac was already by the Aga having a cup of tea.

"Come in, have a cup of tea whilst I put my oilskins on."

"We need to get going."

"It's an order. I don't want you keeling over with the cold. Have two sugars."

He should not have said that; Charlie's thoughts flashed back to happier times with Daniel in her flat and her heart dropped back two runs on the ladder of recovery.

They set off up the road and then slowly climbed the track to the fields where the Swaledale ewes were. The weather was atrocious. George met them at the old wooden gate and dragged it open over the snow, so they could drive in.

"The snow is not too deep here but it's drifting over the tops of the stone walls up agin the moor. Follow me," suggested George.

They managed to get to within a hundred yards and shone the Gator lights onto the wall. Or at least where it should be. They took their shovels and George probed the snow drift with his crook till he could feel a sheep. They dug in shifts, as it was hard work, but soon got down to the first group. Seven live sheep jumped out of the hole in the snow and ran off down the field.

"That's a good start," said Mac. "Where are the rest?"

"A bit further up near the broken wall. They might have been trapped for longer."

Charlie moved the Gator so the lights shone onto the new area of drifting snow. George and Mac dug into the snow, when the crook had done its magic. Charlie shone a hand torch into the hole. No sign of life.

"Let's try a bit further along the wall." More dead sheep. They leant on the shovels, depressed in the biting cold, snow clinging to their woolly hats.

"I think we will have to call it a day, George, the weather is setting in and the snow is relentless," said Charlie reluctantly.

They all squeezed into the diminutive cab of the Gator and headed home. Twenty-three dead, in-lamb ewes were pulled from the drift later in the day when the snow eased. Shepherding on the moor was a challenging job at the best of times and sometimes just heart-breaking.

March turned into April and the weather improved. Lambing started in the in-bye fields and the Galloway suckler cows were calving. Charlie liked helping with the lambing, scooping up the new-born lambs, spraying their navels with iodine and putting the tags in their ears. The mule gimmer lambs would be sold in the autumn sales at Hawes market, owned by William and Paul, who were such good sports at the Boxing Day flush.

Charlie still rode Darley on some days up to Masham Moor and she slowly managed to get to the end of the ride without crying. The day riding out with Daniel, when she fell off and he kissed her for the first time, was so special she did want to lose the memory – ever.

One day in July she was riding up past Tom's farm near Bramley Grange, where she and Daniel had stopped to say hello to Tom who was having his hunter shod. She noticed there were two police Land Rovers parked in the yard. She assumed they were doing a routine check of some sort – poachers, shotgun licence etc., and continued on her ride in the warm sunshine.

When she got home and was having lunch with her parents in the kitchen, she happened to mention the police vehicles in passing.

"It's a bit odd there were two vehicles?" queried her father. "Sergeant Pickles usually does that sort of thing on his own; unless he is training a new constable? I'll give Mac a quick ring. He knows all the local gossip."

Edward came off the phone looking very upset.

"A walker found Tom dead this morning up in Hutt's Wood. It looks like he shot himself."

"That's terrible Edward. We have known him for years and he has always been such a nice man," lamented Elizabeth.

Charlie was very distressed and a tear trickled down her cheek.

"I only spoke to him a couple of days ago and he seemed fine then. Have we any idea why he did it?"

"Mac did not know for sure but they had to slaughter all his beloved Limousin cows and calves last week. They had reacted to TB caught off the badgers in the sett near Wreaks Beck. I guess the loss got on top of him. His whole life revolved around those cows since his wife left him five years ago."

"What will happen to the farm?" asked Elizabeth.

"Well, there are no children to take it on, so I guess we will add it on to one of the neighbouring farms, Mummy. It really is too small to be viable on its own. It only worked for Tom because it was his life's dream to have his own herd and live in the country. He had a good pension from the RAF so he could make ends meet on his own. He didn't spend much. Just loved living in the Dales and being one of the community. Does Mac know when the funeral will be yet Daddy?"

"No. But we will all go obviously," replied Edward

"If there is no family, I would like to read the Eulogy," added Charlie as she left the room, struggling to cope with the desperate situation and her painful memories of Daniel's death.

"You know what that's about?" said Elizabeth to Edward.

"I know, but it might help her come to terms with things. She has been doing very well really. I am proud of her," consoled Edward.

* * *

Two days later, just before lunch, Sergeant James Pickles drove into the kennels yard in his white, slightly muddy Land Rover Defender. He knocked on the kitchen door. Mac opened the door.

"Mr Mactaggart? I am investigating a complaint that somebody has been interfering with the badger setts in Haggs Wood and the adjacent locality in contravention of the protection of Badgers Act 1992."

"You better come in Sergeant. How can I help?"

"It appears that all of the badgers in that vicinity have disappeared without trace and some nature lovers from Harrogate are concerned what has happened to them. A red pickup vehicle was seen in the area on Tuesday night about midnight. Have you seen anybody acting suspiciously in the last few days?"

"You mean like going in the wood and shooting themselves because of what the badgers have done to his life's work?" suggested Mac angrily.

"That's not helpful Sir. Could you tell me where you were on that evening between 11 pm and 2 am the following morning"

Mac thought for a moment. "In bed with my wife Sally."

"Mrs Mactaggart, can you please confirm that."

"Yes. All night Sergeant."

Sergeant Pickles closed his small black police notebook, secured it with the attached black elastic band and placed it slowly on the table.

"Thank you for being so cooperative Mr Mactaggart. That completes my formal investigation and this line of enquiry is closed. Put the bloody kettle on Sally and get me some of that delicious fruit cake you make!"

"Have you got the results of the postmortem yet?" asked Mac.

"Yes. I am afraid it was sadly as we expected. He put the gun in his mouth. He knew what he was doing; there was nothing on the tox. report. The funeral is next Wednesday at 11 am at Kirkby Malzeard Church. I think there will be a good turnout. He was much liked by everyone and the circumstances of his death are tragic. I think we should all feel a bit responsible, but that's life... and death I'm afraid. Have you got any of that sugar beet pulp left, I could do with some for the Ryeland tup I am going to take to Wensleydale Show?"

"I think there is a bag left in the garage next to the pallet of VetSpec dog food. Just help yourself."

"Thanks Mac. See you at the funeral."

* * *

The cars were queued from Galphay in one direction and Grewelthorpe in the other; it was going to be a good turnout, as Sergeant Pickles had predicted.

The sun was shining, with only the odd fluffy cloud drifting slowly across the clear blue sky. The men were all in dark suits, some more Saville Row than others, but all with black ties, as is the tradition in Yorkshire and many other counties in England. The ladies were all wearing a variety of hats in respect. Charlie and her parents arrived early and after much sombre shaking of hands and pleasantries, they took their places on the plain wooden benches, typical of the less affluent parishes in the Dales. Muffled conversations pervaded the small nave and the vicar shuffled his papers in readiness.

The black limousine purred gently to a halt outside the lychgate and the black silken undertaker orchestrated the removal of the simple oak coffin from the hearse. Mac and Tim had organised that they, and four members of the hunt, would carry the coffin adorned with a single wreath of wild roses. They lifted the coffin onto their shoulders and moved in-step down the aisle to the Adagio from Mozart's Clarinet Concerto. They rested the coffin on two plain trestles, and took their places in the congregation. The vicar stepped up to the lectern to give his welcome. Charlie was already crying; her mother held her hand and gave it a gentle squeeze.

The address was fairly short and was followed by Alexander's famous hymn 'All Things Bright and Beautiful'. It was then Charlie's turn to give the Eulogy.

"Tom was gentle, courageous and a giant of a man. His love and knowledge of the countryside was boundless. His loss is a terrible chasm in all of our hearts. Will we ever forgive ourselves for not coming to his rescue in his hour of need? But we are just simple human beings, leading our own lives and without our families to support us in those dark hours, we too could be lying in his resting place. Tom had no living family and he lived on his own without that loving care and understanding around the kitchen table. No one to see the cracks appearing or the pain unfolding.

"Tom was born near Leyburn in 1976. His father was a veterinary surgeon and his mother a primary school teacher.

He was an only child, with a passion for wildlife and spent much of his childhood watching the animals and birds that share our daily lives in this beautiful countryside, in which we are privileged to reside. He went to Durham University and got a first-class honours degree in Geography and then joined the RAF as a trainee pilot. He proved to be brilliant at flying and rose rapidly through the ranks to become a Squadron Leader. He flew Tornados in Afghanistan on Operation Herrick and later became involved in the introduction of remotely piloted Reaper aircraft. When he left the RAF and took on his farm, he loved watching the Hawk T2 trainers flying up and down the Dale, reminding him of the exciting, if dangerous, years he spent helping to protect our freedom from the aggressors, far away from our lands.

"The love of his spartan life on the farm was his small herd of pedigree Limousin cows, which he built up with great skill and knowledge, as with everything he tackled in life. His skill as a breeder was recognised by being invited by the breed society to become a judge and his year officiating at the Great Yorkshire Show, was the pinnacle of recognition by fellow breeders. The loss of his herd to TB, ironically caused by the very wildlife he adored, had a devastating effect on him, to a level those of us in this church will hopefully never suffer.

"We will always remember his happy smiling face, his willingness to help those in need and a man with integrity, intelligence and true love of the countryside.

Charlie walked slowly back to the safety of her mother's arms. Her tears falling to the cold stone paving of the church floor.

The congregation said the Lord's prayer and then Mac, Tim and the others lifted the coffin and carried it out to the grave, dug in the corner of the graveyard under the old yew tree. The vicar read out the committal and, as the coffin was slowly lowered into the grave, the ever-increasing roar of Rolls Royce Adour engines grew over Grewelthorpe moor. As the dull thud of the coffin met the Yorkshire clay, all eyes were lifted upwards as five Hawk jets in T-formation appeared slowly over the horizon until they were overhead.

Squadron Leader to flight: "Go vertical. Full thrust. Now."

The five jets headed towards the heavens, with the Adours' thunder showering over the graveyard.

Squadron Leader: "And roll left. Now."

With that, the five jets disappeared over the horizon.

Edward looked at John standing next to him, smiling.

"Just coincidence," said John quietly.

* * *

After the burial, Charlie slipped away, having made sure her mother and father would be staying to represent the family for the traditional tea and sandwiches in the village hall. She felt emotionally exhausted after the service, but strangely that some of her own grief had been shared in some way. She drove back to the Hall on her own, made herself a cup of tea, changed into jeans and jumper and decided to take the dogs for a walk in the warm evening air. The gimmer lambs were growing-on well now, in the home pastures, ready for the autumn sales. The silage fields were lush with second cut and the fruit trees in the orchard were set with a bumper crop of swelling produce for Elizabeth and Sally's pies. Charlie felt at peace with the world for the first time since Daniel's death and she was ready for a new challenge.

Two weeks later, Charlie was riding up the drive on Darley in the evening sunshine, when she saw John's old Series II Defender parked outside the front door. John was in the kitchen talking to Elizabeth and Edward about his forthcoming trip to the NATO summit at Bretton Woods in New Hampshire.

"Hello Charlie. How are you?" He stood up and gave her a godfatherly hug.

"I am good thank you. What's this about another taxpayers jolly," she joked.

"I was telling your parents about the forthcoming NATO summit in New Hampshire that I have to go to in early October and I was wondering if you would like to come with me? Not to the conference of course. That will be as boring as hell, but it's not far away from Lake Chocorua and the autumn colours up there will be stunning then. I have a friend who owns a house near the lake, with a live-in caretaker and his wife, so you would not be on your own. I am there for about a week so we can fly up from Boston, which will only take a couple of hours, and then I can pick you up after the conference and we can fly back. What do you think? You can bring your camera and enjoy yourself without any pressure."

"Crikey, that sounds amazing but I have got to run this place."

"I think we can struggle on for a week Charlie. We know you are superwoman but us mere mortals can probably hold it together till you get back," laughed her father.

"Err! OK then you're on. That's fantastic John. You are the best godfather in the whole world. Ever." With that she threw her arms around his neck and gave him a big kiss on the cheek.

"Great. I will organise all the flights etcetera. All you will need is your passport and a bag. We will probably get a flight from Newcastle so it will be an easy trip. Right, I better get moving. I will email you all the details in a couple of days."

The old Land Rover rumbled off down the drive. Charlie looked at her mother across the kitchen table with a worried expression on her face. Elizabeth smiled back and prevented the second thought.

"It's too late now Darling, you have said 'Yes'. John will be mortified if you let him down. You will be fine. It's only a week and you will enjoy getting the old camera out again."

"Better start polishing my lenses then," she joked tentatively.

CHAPTER FIVE

Chocorua – New England – The United States of America

The flight to Boston was uneventful after the usual security issues at the airport with large heavy camera bags. At Boston, Charlie and John jumped onto a local flight up to Portland International and then hired a car to drive across to Bretton Woods, dropping Charlie off at Chocorua Lake on the way.

The scenery travelling up the Pequawket Trail just blew Charlie away. The trees were losing their summer green chlorophyll and turning into a blaze of vivid yellows, reds and oranges. Charlie wanted to stop every ten minutes to take pictures but John insisted on pressing on, assuring her there were even more stunning landscapes to capture when they got to Chocorua. When they got to Conway, they turned down onto the Chocorua Mountain Highway, passed Iona Lake and down to the bridge between the Chocorua Lake and the aptly named Little Lake. From the bridge, Mount Chocorua was silhouetted against the azure sky with the lake in front, surrounded by a sea of vivid autumn colours. A million photographs have been taken from the bridge of this stunning landscape but Charlie was determined to make it one more.

Lake Chocorua

They drove a little way around the Lake and came upon some impressive black ornate gates hanging on large white stone pillars with golden eagles perched on top. Bit better than our gates Charlie thought. Better get some eagles.

John pressed the entry code and the gates slowly swung open. He inched the car through the gates and stopped as they closed silently behind them. Before them was an immaculate estate. Money was obviously not a problem here. The golden gravel drive swept its way down through acres of mown grass and specimen maples from around the world. The white colonial-style mansion stood on a slight rise in front of the lake, set against Mount Chocorua in the distance.

"So, this belongs to your impoverished friends then?" joked Charlie.

"I never said they were impoverished! Shall we get out and enjoy the view?" replied John, with an ulterior motive.

They both got out of their air-conditioned haven, into the warm fall air and leant on the bonnet.

"I have got something I want to tell you. It's very personal and complicated," advised John. "I know your life has been hell for the last six months and, as your godfather, I am so sorry you have had such an awful time. I need your help and I have got a proposal for you that will significantly change your life."

"Sounds exciting. To be honest I need something to focus on. Since Daniel was killed, all my dreams were shattered after just a few days with him. And although I have made a huge effort to move on, I'm a bit of a lost soul I'm afraid."

"Well, this might be what you are looking for then. But it's like opening that gate and shutting it behind you. From this point you cannot go back."

"Let's go for it. I need a challenge," said Charlie inquisitively.

"It will certainly be that."

"Go on then."

"Just come and sit down with me for a minute," asked John, leading Charlie across to a rather lovely old bench, where she sat very still and listened intently. He cleared his throat and slowly began. "This is about Daniel."

Charlie took a deep breath, "Go on."

"Daniel is actually still alive," continued John slowly. "He is alive and living here in this house. He was very seriously injured in Columbia, but is making a good recovery now. It was touch and go for a very long time."

Charlie looked absolutely shocked, grabbed John's arm in disbelief and went pale. She shifted her position on the bench, to look at John directly. "I don't understand. Everybody said he was dead!"

"I don't know if you saw it on the news back in February but there were two massive explosions that killed some of the leading coca growers at a meeting in Caquetá. They also destroyed a central clearing warehouse for drugs destined for Mexico. Unfortunately for Daniel, there was a malfunction of a software detonator switch on his laptop and he got caught in the warehouse blast. He managed to crawl into the nearby forestry and was there for days with no communications, and his medical condition was deteriorating rapidly. By some miracle, one of his software team managed to locate his damaged laptop remotely and they got him out. God knows how."

"I still don't understand, I thought he was a businessman, something to do with restructuring companies."

"He certainly restructured theirs!" laughed John.

"You know when we were in Greece, there was an explosion that blew up a house and killed a load of Chinese ivory smugglers. You don't think……?"

"No idea. He makes his own itinerary. He doesn't work for anybody."

"Now I am even more confused. So, he is not CIA or anything like that?" asked Charlie, struggling to make sense of it all.

"No. He is much too dangerous for them," he smiled.

"Does he know I am coming?"

"He has talked about nothing else for weeks. Well, what do you think? Are we going down the drive or back out the gates?"

"I think you know the answer to that," answered Charlie with her heart beating at three times its normal rate.

They climbed back into the car and swept down the gravel drive and parked in front of the marble palace. Very American and very impressive.

"I am not coming in. I will give you a ring at the end of the week to arrange travelling home. Anne Marie will look after you."

With that, John drove back up the drive, leaving Charlie with her bags standing with trepidation by the huge shiny front door.

The door opened and a very young attractive woman wearing denim shorts and a check cotton shirt came down the steps and shook Charlie's hand, vigorously.

"Hi, my name's Anne Marie. I'm looking after Daniel. Can I help you with your bags?"

The hall had a white marble floor with twin mirrored staircases curving their way to the next floor. A beautiful display of blue vervain and mountain mint flowers took pride of place on the central table.

"We can leave the bags here for now and I will take them up to your room for you later. Let's go through into the garden and find Daniel."

They went through the enormous French windows and out into the bright sunlight. The lawns were immaculate and the flower beds were bursting with colour of every hue. Daniel was lying on a sun lounger and when he heard the footsteps, he eased himself up cautiously.

"I was just passing and I thought I would call in to see you."

"Have you fallen off any horses lately?"

"I thought you were dead?"

"So did I."

Charlie threw her arm around him. He flinched; his shoulder was still painful but he held her tight next to him.

"I've missed you."

"Missed you too. Please come and sit down. How are your mother and father? How's everything on the estate? Has Mac shot any badgers lately?"

"They are all fine, including the badgers. So, are you going to tell me what happened to you?"

"Fell off a horse?"

"Very funny. What really happened?"

"Not now. I might tell you one day, but for now I fell off a horse."

"OK, ignoring that, how are you, what have you broken?" asked a very concerned Charlie.

"Pretty well everything. But it's all slowly coming right. No long-term damage. Nature is a wonderful thing."

"Who owns this lovely house, the gardens are amazing?"

"It belongs to a friend of mine."

"You seem to have lots of friends."

"Lucky, I guess. How long can you stay?" enquired Daniel.

"John is picking me up on Friday so we have a few days. I've brought my camera. Are you well enough to show me the local landscapes?"

"Try and stop me."

"Anne-Marie has prepared us supper by the lake. She does awesome lobster salads."

"Are you and Anne-Marie…………?"

"Why?"

"Just wondered. She seems very attentive."

"She works for my friend who owns this house."

"She wears very short shorts."

"Hadn't noticed."

"Liar!" – she laughed. "Let me go and change first; It's been a long day."

"I will take you upstairs and show you your room."

They climbed the curved ornate staircase up to the spacious landing on the first floor. Two sofas faced a picture window giving a panoramic view of the lake and mountain. Charlie's room, or rather suite, was enormous and had the biggest bed Charlie had ever seen, even compared with her mother's standards. The bathroom was wall to wall marble with mirrors on every wall, magnifying the dimensions. You could have held a dinner party in the shower.

"The towels are in this cupboard here. If you need anything else just press the silver button by the bed and Anne Marie will come and look after you."

"Do you use the silver button in your bedroom much?"

"At least twice a day," smiled Daniel. "I'll see you out on the terrace for a drink about six. No rush – when you are ready."

* * *

When Charlie came down to the terrace Daniel was already there, sitting in a white cane chair next to an Italianate table. He was wearing soft blue denim jeans, fraying at the bottom and a wide American leather belt. His open-necked shirt had a Texas look about it. Charlie decided to put Anne Marie in the shade and wore her favourite white silk shirt with nothing underneath. She was not sure if her flared linen trousers were in fashion or not, but she did not exactly come prepared to impress a man. Daniel stood up carefully and gave her a kiss on the cheek. He felt that tiny spark of life again, that he had felt at the reservoir in Yorkshire.

"Wow you look stunning Charlie. Definitely worth getting killed for!"

Daniel took two flutes from the sideboard (and a rather ostentatious bottle opener) and handed Charlie a bottle of chilled Californian Chardonnay to carry, as he led her from the table.

"Let's wander down to the small lake at the bottom of the garden and we can eat supper there," he suggested.

The cane chairs had magically appeared by the small lake where there was an impressive variety of Koi swimming around. A pine table was laden with a delicious salad that Anne Marie had prepared. The fresh lobster looked exquisite, the maple-infused dressing had a wonderful aroma and the blue cheese and pears were arranged to perfection.

As the evening shadows lapped the edge of the lake, the conversation turned to the past.

"You are a very mysterious lady, Charlie. You are an incredibly beautiful young woman, fantastic company, have a great sense of humour and are super intelligent. So why aren't you married to some prince and have ten children?"

"It's long boring story and a painful one so I don't talk about it. It's best buried and forgotten."

"Sorry, you haven't been seriously ill and can't have children?" replied Daniel quickly, thinking he may have caused a faux pas.

"No, nothing like that. Just personal stuff. Anyway, if it comes to that why aren't you married with eleven children?"

"It's a long boring story and a painful one so I don't talk about it."

"Touché!" smiled Charlie. They sat for a while in silence looking into the lake watching the koi swim gracefully to nowhere.

"I would genuinely like to know what happened to you, that was so awful, it has clearly affected your whole life," asked Daniel sensitively. "Not out of morbid curiosity but I want to get to know who you really are. I keep getting sparks but they fall extinguished in the mists of the past. Of course, I noticed that you dressed up specially for me tonight and it is really nice that you want to, but that confuses me a bit?"

"Well, I am glad you noticed kind sir! It took a lot of courage but you may have noticed I am quite competitive! Anne Marie is a very sexy young lady and she knows how to exploit it. I half fancy her myself."

"You're not……?"

"No, no, nothing like that. Not that there is anything wrong with being a bit Sackville-West."

"Who was she …. or whatever?"

"Just ignore me. No, I prefer handsome young men, particularly those that like getting blown up." Daniel leant across and kissed her on the cheek. "I was hurt by someone at university and it screwed me up psychologically," she added.

"What happened exactly. Did he rape you?" he said bluntly.

Charlie felt a bit shocked by the word and found it very difficult to relate the event that had had such a dramatic impact on her life.

"No. It sounds a bit pathetic now but a group of us had been out partying, as you do, and this American boy seemed to genuinely like me. I guess I was flattered because he was president of the student's union and he came from a very wealthy family and could basically have any girl he wanted. On the way home we were crossing the campus through a small group of trees and he pinned me against a tree and started to kiss me very roughly. I sort of went along with it for a bit, but then he got aggressive and forced me to the ground and ripped my nice blouse that Mummy had given me. He then pulled up my skirt but was too drunk to do anything, muttered some expletive about me and staggered off leaving me alone on the ground with my clothes in tatters. As ridiculous as it sounds, I was more worried about my blouse and what Mummy might think of me than anything. It was only when I got back to my digs that I broke down and went completely to pieces."

"Did you tell anyone what had happened or report him?"

"No. He was very popular and I was worried people would think I led him on and I deserved it; and his family were big donors to the college. It just seemed the wrong thing to do at the time. It was a different era of course. I hope you understand that it has affected me badly and I haven't felt close to anyone since. I guess my body shut down and I threw myself into work and my photography. I love landscapes. There is such beauty out there and it cannot hurt you."

Daniel felt an overwhelming urge to protect Charlie from such a hurtful encounter. "That's horrendous. Is this bastard still alive?"

"Yes. He seems immune from reality and floats along on a sea of political connections and an ocean of money. He has an intelligent, beautiful young wife, three lovely children and a cockapoo. He has a terrible taste in dogs! Four houses in the US, one in Monaco and one in Mayfair. A private jet and is just in the process of buying the biggest yacht from Perini you have ever seen."

"How do you know all this stuff? Are you stalking him?" Daniel smiled trying to lighten the moment.

"Not exactly! There just happened to be an article on him in the in-flight magazine on the plane coming over. I tried to ignore it but it's a long flight. Since he attacked me, his golden lifestyle has just floated on regardless of the psychological effect it's had on my life. I am sure he will have forgotten I even existed and probably wouldn't even remember who I was or what happened. I suppose some people just lead a charmed life and are completely divorced from the real world."

"Catharsis is what you need."

"Does it come with a nice wine?"

"We will have to ask you father which is the most complimentary vintage."

"Anyway, that's enough about me, and why I am a screwed-up spinster of the parish. What's your excuse? You seem to lead a pretty nomadic life? Do you have any roots?"

"I met my wife, Elizabeth, at Oxford University. It was love at first sight, I guess. I was reading chemical engineering and she was studying to be a doctor. She always wanted to be a paediatrician. She loved children, but she miscarried our first child and couldn't have another of her own."

"Where did you live?"

"We never really settled down. We moved around a lot after Oxford with our careers and never got round to buying anywhere. She ended up working with the World Health Organisation and travelled abroad a lot, running various health programs, and I was always away on business. We were very lucky. It was one of those magical relationships that no matter how often we were apart or whatever problems we had; we were just one. I miss her terribly." He swallowed and took a deep breath before adding. "Sorry, I've never talked about it to anyone before."

Charlie put her hand on his arm and smiled sympathetically. "I am so sorry I was flippant. I just had no idea that you been through grief of that magnitude."

"She was working near Nairobi in Kenya and was taking a break from work one weekend with a girlfriend, who was a doctor she worked with. They decided to go up to Nakuru to photograph the black rhino. She never came back." Tears poured from his sad eyes as he struggled to hold back the years of grief.

"The rangers found their bodies, dragged into the scrub by Somali poachers. They were hacked to death with machetes, near a carcase of a rhino whose horn had been cut off with a chainsaw. The rangers assumed that they came across the poachers and probably confronted them. These Somalis are highly organised, ruthless and well-funded. It's a very lucrative trade to China via Cambodia. I have since found out that one of the Swiss banks is laundering the money generated by the gruesome trade."

Charlie could feel the pain and anger Daniel had in his voice relating the event that had changed his whole life.

"Did they catch the poachers?" asked Charlie.

"No. A local farmer saw them in a Mercedes Unimog at a filling station heading north. I managed to get a copy of the CCTV footage and the local police identified them as known poachers. I tracked two of them down in Somalia but I do not know what happened to the third one."

He paused. "I think it's time for a glass of that wine."

Daniel opened the 2018 Russian River Valley and poured it carefully into the flutes. Charlie served the lobster with maple syrup dressing and they sat back to enjoy the Anne Marie special.

"Cheers. Here's to the future."

"Cheers."

They sipped the wine and had second helpings of the pear and cheese.

"I thought I would take you riding tomorrow." Daniel proposed. "Very slowly! Over that hill in the distance there and down to Chocorua Lake. There are a couple of places we can stop on the way where you should be able to get some lovely landscape shots of the trees around the lake. What do you think?"

"Are you sure you are OK to ride?"

"I had a practise a couple of days ago with Anne Marie and I managed OK. I am a bit slow at dismounting because my leg gets stiff."

"That could be interpreted in many ways!" smiled Charlie.

"She was amazing!" joked Daniel. "So attentive."

They walked slowly back up to the house carrying the empty crockery and took them into the kitchen. They loaded the dishwasher – very domesticated Charlie thought.

"It has been an amazing day, Daniel. This morning I thought you were dead and I was coming to some house with strangers and was worried how I would cope. Now you are alive. We have bared our souls to each other and had a wonderful evening together. I am terrified I will wake up in the morning and it has all been a dream."

Daniel took Charlie in his arms and kissed her passionately on the lips. Her response was electric. "You have an incredible effect on my heart rate."

"The feeling is mutual," said Daniel. "There is no rush in the morning. Just come down when you are ready. The weather looks good all day so we can take our time."

For fun, they walked up separate staircases, came together at the top and kissed again. She felt his body against hers and they then went their separate ways to bed. Both happy to retreat to the status quo. For now.

CHAPTER SIX

Flames in the Fall

Charlie came down late for breakfast, having slept really well after the long flight. No one was around, so she helped herself to fresh orange juice and a bowl of oat flakes from the breakfast bar and wandered out onto the stone-flagged terrace. The rays of the autumn sun escaped the odd passing cloud and it was surprisingly warm for an October fall morning. Further along the terrace Anne-Marie was doing some physio on Daniel's back. He was lying face down with a towel over is bottom half and she was working on his shoulders. Every now and then he winced when she accidentally touched an unrecovered muscle.

"Good morning Charlie. Did you sleep OK?" asked Daniel.

"Like a log."

"I'll believe you this time!"

"Would you like a cup of Earl Grey?" offered Anne Marie. "We like to make our guests feel at home."

"That would be lovely thank you."

They sat and had breakfast enjoying the view. Charlie thought the view of Daniel without his shirt on was exceptionally enjoyable. He was surprisingly fit considering everything he had been through; if a little battle-scarred in places.

"Jake will bring the horses up at about ten. Have you ridden Western before?"

"No, but it looks very comfortable for mountaineering," replied Charlie half joking.

"He is bringing three so you have a pack horse for your camera and gear. We can also put an 'Anne Marie lunch' in the saddlebags."

The quarter-horses arrived with Jake, as if by magic, out of the trees on the edge of the garden. The buckskin was for Daniel to ride, Charlie's was a beautiful chestnut and the pack horse was a palomino. Very colourful.

Charlie collected her things from her room and loaded them into the capacious saddlebags. The packed lunch was carefully tucked away along with a bottle of wine and ice packs.

"What sort of wine have you chosen?" Daniel asked Anne Marie.

Pack horses

"Columbian red," she replied, smiling wickedly.

"Very funny. Go and do something useful like dusting or something."

"Yes master!"

"She has got those shorts on again," Charlie whispered.

"Didn't notice."

They made their way slowly up through the sea of flaming fall colours to the first ridge, which looked down on the house and lake. Charlie turned her horse so she could take some photos from its back, as a memory, and then they hacked over the ridge towards the valley below. The views were amazing with endless waves of reds, ambers, yellows and greens. In the valley bottom, a crystal lake doubled the palette of colours, only broken by the occasional osprey skimming the mirror.

Halfway down the track a stone outcrop made a great place to set up the tripod, so they dismounted. Daniel's leg, still stiff from the accident, was glad of the rest. Charlie locked her camera onto the tripod and scanned the view.

"I think this will be special. The light is fantastic."

"Only because you're here," said Daniel trying not to smile.

Surprised. She lifted her head from the camera. A strand of autumn coloured hair fell across her face. She stepped lightly across the rocks. Took his hand and kissed the back of it.

"Thank you for bringing me to such a beautiful landscape Daniel."

Charlie took a range of panoramic shots, changing lenses, filters and settings to fill her RAW folder. She recorded the GPS location and backed up the files on her Seagate hard drive.

Daniel watched her move professionally around the camera, like a hummingbird searching flowers for nectar. He could not take his eyes away from her. He felt a serenity from decades before, that had been buried with the never-ending escape from grief.

"I think that will do for here. Can we move down to the edge of the lake for the next shoot before the surface is broken by a breeze?"

"Of course." With that, they mounted up, untied the reins from the branches and made their way slowly down the gravel path to the lake side.

They arrived at a small clearing right next to the lapping water's perimeter. The trees around the edge of the lake, flaming red maples, golden birches and maroon northern red oaks were doubled with their reflections. The air was so still that the surface of the water echoed the clear sky. Charlie unloaded her camera and tripod from the saddlebags and set them up right at the water's edge.

"I'll get some preliminary shots whilst the water is still and then perhaps, we can have some lunch?"

"Good idea. I will get Anne Marie's luxury lunchbox out and open up the mystery wine. We have even got crystal glasses wrapped in bubble wrap."

Daniel laid out the green plaid picnic rug on the grass and poured out the wine. He held it aloft and read the label. Domaine Carneros Brut Rosé from California. Anne Marie seemed to like Californian wine.

Charlie was happy with her first few landscapes – they would need very little editing with such a perfect canvas to work with. She sat down next to Daniel on the rug and sipped from the sparkling glass, which was refreshing after a long morning's work.

"Do you actually get paid to do this? Go to beautiful romantic places all over the world, take a few photos, and then while away the afternoons drinking an excellent wine with a handsome young man," wondered Daniel.

"Not sure about the young!"

He rolled over, tickled her sides and they collapsed in a giggling heap. He ended up on top of her and kissed her softly and gently on her lips.

She wriggled away laughing and said, "I think we better have lunch before the salad gets cold!"

The salmon was softly cooked, the spinach and lemon dill dressing perfect and the minted peas as fresh as spring. Anne Marie had excelled herself again.

"Is there anything she is not good at?" asked Charlie, with a hint of jealousy.

"Not so far, but I am increasing the challenges daily. She will break at some point!"

"Look the ospreys are back. They're magnificent birds, aren't they?"

"Not sure the fish would agree," pointed out Daniel.

"On that conservation conundrum, I am going to try and get the reflection of some of those clouds on the water, with the mountain in the background."

"Sounds very creative. I am going to have a sleep whilst you slave away over a steamy camera."

Charlie got to work trying this lens, then that filter. Daniel watched her for a while and then fell asleep on the rug. The perfect afternoon.

After an hour or so Charlie had exhausted all the possible landscapes and sat next to Daniel, who was still fast asleep. She poured herself another glass of rosé and lay back on her elbow looking at him, wondering how this was all happening and where it was all going. He slowly opened his eyes and saw the sunlight streaming through her hair and her infectious smile.

"Hello stranger do you come here often?" asked Charlie.

"Only when I am looking for damsels in distress."

She leant over and kissed him, which developed into a longer embrace than she had intended but enjoyed it even more for it.

"Thank you for bringing me down here. I adore the lake, the atmosphere and all the different colours in the trees. If heaven turns out like this, I shall be very happy."

"We have got to struggle through the rest of this life first and we have only just found each other. I have had enough of near-death experiences for one year thank you," he chuckled. "I think I need another kiss to ensure this is all real."

Charlie willingly obliged. Prolifically.

"Definitely alive now. How about a real American barbecue when we get back? Shall I invite Anne Marie and Jake to join us? Jake cooks a mean steak."

"That's a great idea. As long as she doesn't wear those shorts!"

They loaded up the saddlebags and made their way back up the hillside. At the first stony halt they had made in the morning, they stopped for a minute to look back at the lake, to absorb the view and store it in their memories for eternity.

When they got back to the house, Jake took the horses and Anne Marie planned the barbecue with Daniel. "OK, first beers at seven then." And they returned to their rooms to freshen-up.

When Charlie came down, she went into the kitchen to see if Anne Marie needed a hand. She was busy making the salads with one of her trademark dressings.

"Hi, can I help carry the food out?"

"Sure thing, thanks. Can you get the tray of steaks out of the fridge and take them out to Jake? He has got the fire pit going over by the trees."

Charlie picked up the tray with half a cow on it; how is Anne Marie so slim she mused as she carried it across to Jake. The hickory logs were well alight and a plume of grey smoke drifted through the tree tops and disappeared from trace. The heat from the fire was welcome, as the temperature had dropped considerably from the daytime. Daniel had set a trestle table up near the pit covered in assorted bowls of delicacies and bottles of wine and beer. No Black Sheep.

Jake carefully placed four steaks on the metal grill over the red glowing logs; the smoke having died down a bit. He painted each steak with a special sauce which had been passed down the generations of his family, with minor amendments and additions from each kitchen genius along the way. Daniel arrived looking very Western including a large Stetson.

"Where is the lasso?" asked Anne Marie smiling.

"In my room. I'll tie you up later if you behave!" She looked willing.

Jake pretended not to hear but clearly wished he might be there too. He brushed more sauce on the steaks and put an array of other culinary specials over the grill including corn on the cob and lobster tails.

Daniel poured out the Smuttynose beer for everyone and they all toasted the Fall.

Charlie got chatting to Jake and asked him all about his quarter horses. It turned out his family had bred horses for over a hundred years and had won many championships around the US circuit. Charlie told him about her mother's Arabs and, like all genuine horse people, he was eager to learn all about the bloodlines she was using. He was amazed at the showing techniques and tack used with Arabs, especially the fines you got if they got loose in the show ring. A bit different to calf roping.

"Right, steaks are ready." Jake forked them off the grill and handed the plates out. "Help yourselves to all the extras." They all loaded their plates and sat down on the grass to eat. Charlie made sure she was next to Daniel whilst Anne Marie got her plate.

"This is absolutely delicious Jake. What's in that special sauce?" asked Charlie.

"I'd have to shoot you if I told you that."

As the sun went down, the conversation drifted from barrel racing, to the new mirrorless cameras and line dancing. The beer flowed, the half cow shrunk to a quarter and they slowly got colder.

"I think we better clear up before we all freeze to death," observed Daniel. "Can you put the grill to bed, Jake and we will take the pots back up to the house? Thanks for bringing over the hickory – it always makes the best steaks."

Charlie and Anne Marie collected up the leftovers and plates and Daniel carried the residual beers. When they got back to the kitchen, Anne Marie put things away and wished them 'goodnight'. Charlie and Daniel made coffee and sat on the kitchen sofa overlooking the garden.

"I thought we would go up Chocorua Mountain tomorrow so you can take some photographs from a higher elevation, as you look down on the lake with all the colours around it. What do you think?"

"That sounds really good but what about your leg? It's far too far to go on horseback," suggested Charlie.

"Yes, I think you are probably right. I'll try and organise some transport in the morning."

"Thank you for a lovely day Daniel. It's been such fun and I have enjoyed being with you so much. Honestly, it's been years since I have felt so chilled out and relaxed. You have a good effect on me."

"I'm pleased about that. The feeling is mutual Charlie. Now, what about tomorrow? Do you think we should leave early in the morning, so you can get the best of the light? Are you OK to leave about six?"

"Sounds like a plan. Will you give me shout about five?"

"I will bring you a cup of tea in bed. Anything for a lady," he smiled.

They climbed the separate staircases again – it was becoming an 'in' joke between them – kissed briefly at the top of the stairs and walked back to their rooms. Daniel was very tired after the long day, having not done that much riding since the day up on moors with Charlie, back in Yorkshire. He slept well.

* * *

Daniel knocked on the door. "Room service. Tea and toast for mademoiselle."

He threw back the curtains. Charlie was clearly still asleep and peeped, bleary eyed, from under the voluminous eider-duck duvet. Daniel walked towards the bed with the tray and she sat up forgetting she was naked and partly revealed her left breast.

"Oops!" She quickly retrieved the duvet and her modesty.

"I will have to bring you breakfast in bed more often!" he smiled. "It's just gone five. Will you be ready for six if I order the truck?"

"Sure thing. I will just grab a quick shower and meet you in the kitchen."

"Ok don't be late," he smiled again. "Off for a cold shower."

* * *

Charlie came down at five to six and Daniel was already in the hall with all the equipment in a neat pile.

"You will need a warm coat – it's still pretty nippy out there. I'll borrow one of Anne Marie's for you, she won't mind."

They stepped outside just as a Bell Jet Ranger helicopter landed on the front lawn.

"I thought you were ordering a truck?" exclaimed Charlie in surprise.

"They had run out of trucks so we will have to make do."

The pilot, who called himself Maverick – but no one was convinced – carefully stowed all the equipment and chivalrously helped Charlie into her seat. Daniel climbed aboard and the rotors spun into life, as Maverick filed his flight plan.

"Where are you allowed to land on the mountain?" asked Daniel.

"Technically nowhere, but if I hover three inches off the ground, I reckon I have not landed, so where do you want to go?"

"Charlie wants to take some photos of the lake, so can you land fairly high up on this side."

"Know the perfect place. It's a bit steep so be careful. You will get a *National Geographic* from there," said Maverick confidently.

Maverick did in fact land – so he could get the lady out safely he said – on a small ledge with a perfect view of the lake. He instructed Daniel to just give him a Bell – in joke with helicopter pilots – when they wanted to go back to the house.

"Have a fun day." And he was gone.

"What do we do if he doesn't come back?" asked Charlie.

"Lose weight?"

Charlie set up her tripod and fitted the camera to it, this time with a tether lead to her laptop, so she could check the shots in more detail, in case she missed something on camera. The sun was still low in the sky and reflected wonderfully on the lake. The colours of the trees just looked phenomenal in the rich early morning sunlight. The magic hour photographers call it; and it was. The laptop was a good idea because Daniel could see what Charlie was capturing and she was trying to explain some of the technical stuff to him. For example, how she used the settings on the camera to get round things like 'burn out' due to the direct sunlight shing into the lens. He was really enjoying being with such a clever, beautiful young woman in such an isolated and romantic location.

"Why can't every day be like this?" he sighed.

"I think you might get bored sitting on the side of a mountain every day."

"With you? Never."

Charlie leant down and gave him a kiss. "Shall we have some coffee?"

"Good idea" Daniel opened the rucksack and pulled out a flask and two plastic cups. "Not Limoges, I'm afraid."

"I am sure we will cope. Is there any cake, I am starving, for some reason."

"Raspberry macaroon or apple linzer tart?"

"The apple sounds good."

They sat, leant back against a rock, and took in the splendour of the endless, multicoloured landscape.

"It's so easy in life to be too busy to sit back for a while and enjoy how beautiful the world is." Charlie looked into his eyes and rested her head on his shoulder for a while. After about half an hour she noticed that the sky was changing again. "Those clouds are reflecting really nicely in the water at the moment. I think I will try and catch them."

Charlie stood up, stepped forward to the tripod, caught her foot in the camera tether and slipped, disappearing over the edge of the mountain. Daniel jumped to his feet and rushed to look over the edge. Charlie fortunately was just five feet lower on another outcrop, but flat on her back. He cautiously clambered down to her rescue. Again!

"God. Are you OK?"

"I think so. My hip hurts where I landed. Is my camera all right?"

"Don't worry about the bloody camera, you could have killed yourself. It's a long way to the bottom."

"I think I am in one piece." Charlie sat up looking a bit shocked. "Help me up please."

Daniel put his arm around her waist and lifted her to her feet. "I'm fine. Just a bit bruised that's all." She climbed back up to her camera and checked it over. "Thank goodness the quick cable release functioned properly or I could have lost two day's work."

"That would have been a disaster. We would have had to go to the lake and do all that kissing thing again."

Charlie kissed him briefly and smiled. "We don't have to go down to the lake to recreate that."

"You're getting quite good at falling off things. We will have to do less dangerous exploits in future! I think I better bell the Bell, and get you home."

Daniel rang Maverick and within half an hour he was hovering overhead. He landed gently on the ground, albeit illegally.

"Hi folks. Did you get the golden shot for *Geographic*?"

"It was brilliant thanks to you Maverick. It was the perfect location. I am really grateful that you risked your licence to get us here."

"No bother. Piece of cake. *Terminator 2* – Now that was a real challenge!"

With that, they were regaled about his stunt work on the film all the way back to Anne Marie's house. It was obviously the highlight of his flying career.

"Arny was a great guy. Did all his own stunt work. I flew the Bell to within one foot of this building. Had to bank away hard left. All the warning lights were screaming at me. James Cameron thought I was amazing. It was brilliant. Arny was such good fun. I like Arny a lot."

They landed at the house, having heard a complete synopsis of all his exploits in the film world.

"Thanks Maverick. You are a superstar. Take care," shouted Daniel over the rotor noise.

The helicopter took off, glided gracefully over the trees, and disappeared.

"I think I will go for a soak in a hot bath before lunch, to ease my hip," said Charlie, limping slightly.

"I think that's a good idea. I will get Anne Marie to make us up a light lunch in the sunroom, now that breeze has got up."

Anne Marie offered to give Charlie a massage before lunch to help ease her hip so they agreed she would go up to Charlie's room when she pressed the silver button. Daniel had some phone calls to make, so he disappeared into the study.

About an hour later he was sitting in the kitchen having a quiet cup of coffee when Charlie appeared in jeans and jumper, looking much recovered if a little flushed.

"Hi. Are you feeling a bit better after your bath?"

"I think I am gay!"

"You enjoyed the massage then?" laughed Daniel.

"She is wonderful. What she did to my body in half an hour was amazing. She woke up parts of it I did not know I had!"

"Does your hip feel less painful?"

"Did I have a hip problem?"

Charlie sat next to Daniel on the sofa and gave him a soft kiss. Anne Marie appeared, grinning happily.

"What have you done to my friend Anne Marie? You're a naughty girl."

"Just doing my job Master. Anyway, it made her forget about her hip!"

"Mmm. And the rest."

"She has a very sensual body, Daniel. You are a very lucky man. Wish she was mine."

"Well, you can't have her."

"So, I am confused Anne Marie. Are you gay?" asked Charlie hesitantly, not knowing which answer she wanted to hear, but quite enjoying being fought over.

"You two have got overactive imaginations, I am off to serve a very late lunch," said Anne Marie winking at Charlie.

Charlie looked at Daniel and shrugged her shoulders. "I think I like New Hampshire; it's a bit more exciting than Masham."

Anne Marie made a Canadian salmon pie with fresh dill and red pepper salad for the late lunch. Complimented with a Roederer sparkling wine from the Anderson Valley in California.

Tomorrow was their last full day together because John was coming to pick Charlie up at ten on Friday morning, to head home to the UK.

"I thought we'd take the truck, not the one with the rotors this time, and head on up the Kancamagus Highway to the Sabbaday Falls. If it stays fine, we can drive up to Mount Washington in the afternoon. You can drive all the way up to the summit at this time of year and you should get some spectacular landscapes from there."

"That sounds great; I can get some final shots for my files."

"OK that's a plan. What would you like to do this evening?"

Anne Marie interjected with enthusiasm. "How about I turn up the hot tub, out on the terrace, and you two can relax and watch the stars? I will make you a nice supper and fetch it out to you."

"That's really kind of you Anne Marie," said Charlie.

"Sounds a good plan, Anne Marie. Well done!" agreed Daniel.

"The only problem is, I didn't bring my swimming costume." Charlie pointed out shyly.

Anne Marie smiled. "Love her, she is so English! I will lend you one Charlie. I have one or two that Daniel likes."

Charlie naively thanked Anne Marie. "That's wonderful thank you. Can you pop it on my bed?"

"Will do. Tub should be ready for about six."

"I think I'll go and get a shower and have a rest for a bit," said Daniel. "I will see you in a while Charlie." Daniel got up and headed upstairs, still a bit stiff from the previous day's exertions.

* * *

When Charlie came down, Daniel was already sitting in the tub with the steam condensing in the cool evening air around him. His muscular shoulders shimmering in the spotlights adorning the terrace. She pretended not to notice.

Charlie was wearing a long white towelling robe and looked a bit sheepish.

"Aren't you going to join me then?"

"It's a bit embarrassing really. The swimming costume Anne Marie left for me is rather small. Minute actually. It consists of three tiny triangles of silk held together, hopefully, by fine gold chains. I think it's an Anne Marie special and I am sure she looks wonderful in it but it's a bit daring for me."

"It's my favourite, and she knows that," revealed Daniel. "Come on, jump in."

Charlie dropped the robe and took Daniel's breath away. "Wow, you are amazingly beautiful Charlie; you look fantastic. Please come in with me."

Daniel stood up, took Charlie's hand and helped her step into the traditional wooden hot tub. It was lovely and warm but Charlie felt very vulnerable in her costume, or rather, lack of it.

Anne Marie appeared carrying a tray of salads, with watermelon, mixed greens, pickled red onion and feta cheese.

"Charlie, you look very sexy in my costume. Can I come in too; I promise I will be good!"

"No, you can't! Go and polish the stairs. Anyway, there's not enough of it to call it a costume," joked Daniel.

When Anne Marie had gone, Daniel looked a bit serious after all the good humour. "Charlie, I don't want to bring it up, but you are going home on Friday and we need to have a story for your folks back in Yorkshire, so they don't query how I managed to rise from the dead! I think the easiest story is if we perhaps stick with – I went riding in the countryside, I fell off, hit my head and lost my memory. I was rescued by a local tribe until I got my memory back and then, the company I was working for collected me and sent me here for convalescence."

"It might work. We're good at falling off horses," agreed Charlie.

They lay back on the edge of the tub, enjoying another bottle of the Roederer wine and eating Anne Marie's salad. The sun was setting and the shadows lengthened across the well-manicured lawn. The temperature was also dropping but the tub was warm and they felt cocooned from the outside world. The wine was working its universal wonder and Charlie was laughing and joking with Daniel about falling off the mountain and Anne Marie's magic physio. Daniel accused her of being gay and she splashed water in his face. He grabbed her arms and swung her around so she was facing him. She leant over and kissed him sensuously. He responded and she put one knee each side of him on the seat and sat in his lap. She kissed him again. And again. She put her arms around his neck, looked directly into his eyes and smiled.

"Look, I know we both have difficult pasts and problems with intimacy. You because of poor Elizabeth and me because of the bastard but let's just enjoy being together and it will come right one day, I am sure of it. I am afraid I am getting very strong feelings for you, even after this short time. We seem to enjoy the same things, have a similar outlook on life, and even have the same stupid sense of humour. What have we got to lose if we just enjoy being together? We don't have to be intimate."

Daniel smiled. "You know how I really feel about you. I am still screwed up about being with someone else properly and I know it doesn't make any sense but it would give me great pleasure just to make you happy."

"Well cover me in sandalwood bubbles before I call Anne Marie for help."

Daniel laughed and rubbed mountains of the sandalwood gel on the rough sponge and he started to slide bubbles all over Charlie's hands, arms and down her spine. Charlie loved the feel of his hands on her skin and as the sponge glided over her body it came alive. She ran her fingers across his chest making use of her nails to good effect.

"Is that nice, tell me what you like?" she asked.

"Keep going and I will let you know."

Daniel concentrated on the small of her back and massaged the sponge up and down her spine. He kissed the side of her neck. Gently. He loved her response. She was so good at letting him know what she liked with tiny moans. Her top was now totally wet and left nothing to the imagination. Daniel had noticed. The evening was a pleasurable circle in a spiral of sensitivity. As darkness fell, Charlie lay back in his arms in an ocean of pleasure under the Chocorua stars.

* * *

The next morning, they met for breakfast in the kitchen at about ten and discussed the plans for the day. Anne Marie served the Earl Grey and then helped them pack the equipment into the pickup. They headed north on the Chocorua Mountain Highway, passed Iona Lake and then turned onto Kancamagus Highway at Conway. The road followed the Swift River passed Falls Pond. The autumn colours were a symphony of reds, ambers, yellows and greens. Mile after mile of sensory delight. When they got to the Falls, they were lucky that no one else was around. Daniel explained that it was quite a popular place for tourists to see in the summer but it usually got a lot quieter in the fall, so they had picked a lucky day.

Charlie set up her camera at the bottom of the Falls and took several shots at normal speed to capture the sunlight glinting on the droplets as they cascaded down to the crystal-clear pool below. She then set the camera up to a much slower shutter speed to 'blur' the water into a fine ethereal river of water falling over the lichen covered rocks. As on the first day at the Lake, Daniel was happy just sitting there watching her at work.

"You were very sensual last night. Your kisses were magical," he remembered.

"I think I drank too much fizzy wine."

Charlie bent down and gave Daniel a quick peck on the cheek.

"Coffee and cake?" asked Daniel.

"Just coffee, I think. Black!"

"Did you give Anne Marie her costume back?"

"She brought me a cup of tea in bed this morning and said I could keep it to remind me of her. It actually reminds me of what you did to me but I was polite and accepted her offer. Not sure I'll ever have the courage to wear it again."

"I am sure we will find somewhere suitable one day."

"We are planning to meet again then?"

"After last night, I think there is more chance of all the stars falling out of the sky than us not meeting up again one day."

"Are you coming to the UK in the near future?"

"No, nothing planned."

"So, are we just hoping I will get robbed again somewhere exotic and you will just happen to be passing?"

"It worked last time."

Charlie tickled his side. He grabbed her arm. Rolled her onto the grass and lay on top of her. At exactly that moment two children and their parents appeared right next to them on the path.

Daniel looked up in surprise. "Err, sorry we were just practising the kiss of life."

The wife smiled. "You can practise on me if you like!"

Charlie and Daniel quickly packed up their bags and headed back to the car giggling like young lovers.

"That was embarrassing."

"I thought she was rather attractive." Daniel teased, earning another tickle.

They headed back to Passaconaway and then took the remote Bear Notch Road, which is impassable in the winter snows, towards Bartlett. The autumn colours were unbelievable as they swept along in a wave of Fall patterns. When they had gone over Douglas Brook, Daniel finally gave in and pulled over so Charlie could take more photographs.

"It's going to be a big file?" said Daniel jokingly.

"I may never come back, so I want to catch all the images I can whilst I have the chance. I have missed so many good opportunities in the past thinking that I would go back to places and of course, life takes over and you never do."

"The colours of the leaves are particularly intense this year, so you are right not to miss the opportunity of a lifetime."

"I think you are inferring what I am thinking Mr Daniel. I am not as rustic as you think," she grinned.

"Enough of this literary symbolism Miss Charlie. We need to be pressing on before it gets dark on the Mountain!"

They grabbed a quick sandwich at the Shannon Door Pub on Pinkham Notch Road and headed for Glen House where you cross the Peabody River to pick up the Mount Washington Auto Road that ascends the 6000-foot climb to the top of the mountain.

They stopped halfway up so Charlie could get some panoramic pictures of the trees and, once they got above the tree line at the summit, she set up the tripod to capture the enormous views in every direction. The Presidential Range of Mt Jefferson, Mt Adams and Mt Madison swept to the north; and Mt Lafayette and Bretton Woods, where John was attending his NATO summit, to the west. The endless vistas, from this lofty perch looking down on the millions of coloured trees dressing the landscape for hundreds of square miles, was breath-taking.

After Charlie had finished, they just sat there for an hour, and took in the moment. Daniel put his arm round Charlie's shoulder and together they absorbed the beauty and the silence of the millennia that had created such a remarkable landscape.

The afternoon was drifting on and Daniel suggested that they call in at the Notch Grill at the foot of the mountain and have a meal before driving home. Charlie was hungry after the physicality of the day's creativity and loved the idea.

They found a table outside, in the autumn sunshine with a view of the mountain. They went for the crab cakes, roasted bell peppers and spicy remoulade for a starter and pan-seared scallops with asparagus, sweetcorn puree and citrus salsa for a main. Charlie was desperate for a cup of tea afterwards so they gave the wine a miss. They talked about the day's locations, the kiss of life and Hydra; shared experiences that couples have for a lifetime.

When they got back, Anne Marie was as attentive as ever and brought onto the terrace tumblers of iced elderflower for the last time. They sat and watched the sun sink down behind the golden trees, holding hands across the table between them.

"I think I will go up and grab a shower and get changed out of these mountaineer clothes," Charlie said, squeezing Daniel's hand.

"Good idea. I will do the same. Why don't you come along to my room when you are ready and I will get us a glass of malt each to round off a lovely day together?"

"That sounds a good plan." They walked up the same set of stairs together. The first time they had done that.

"See you in a while."

Charlie debated what to wear for the malt and decided on her simple white towelling robe from her bathroom. It was long and sophisticated with a small gold emblem, and not at all suggestive. She was naked underneath but Daniel need not know that unless he wanted to. She knocked politely on his door.

"Hi come in. There's no need to knock." He was wearing an identical dressing gown and she immediately wondered if he was in a similar state of undress beneath. Charlie was staggered by what she saw in the room. One wall was completely covered in photographs of people of all nationalities, surrounded by yellow sticky notes containing various hieroglyphics. Pieces of different coloured strings joined some of the photographs to a map of the world.

"This all looks very technical. Who are all these people?"

"They were all involved in Elizabeth's murder."

"That's awful Daniel, but I thought you said that she was killed by three Somali poachers?"

"They actually committed the act but all these men and women are the trash that paid for their obnoxious trade in rhino horn and ivory."

"Why does this string go from Thailand to Switzerland and this sticky note with a question mark?"

"I am not sure who the financiers are yet but I will track them down like I tracked the Somalis. They will not get away with what they did, however rich and influential they are."

Charlie felt a little bit uneasy about his passion to be jury and executioner. But she knew the reality was, that these people act outside the civilised world and across international borders to escape prosecution 99% of the time.

"I understand why you need to do this Daniel and if I can help in any small way then please let me. The only thing I don't understand, is how your job in Columbia fits in with all this?"

Daniel smiled at last. "It doesn't. That was a simple commercial operation I did for money."

"So, you blow people up and occasionally yourself for a living?"

"Something like that, but only really nasty people."

"But who pays you?"

"Now you are asking too many questions Miss Charlie. Can you please pour us a malt from the bottle on the side there, whilst I just finish this email?"

"Is it another hit job?" she smiled. "It's sort of quite exciting."

"No, I am ordering a pizza!" he said sarcastically.

She brought the drinks over to his chair and leant over to kiss him. As she did so her dressing robe fell open accidentally, so he could see she was naked under it. He put his hand behind her neck and kissed her softly.

"Anything for you."

Charlie stood behind his chair and started to distract him. She put her arms around his neck and kissed his hair. She then slowly slid her hand down inside his robe and started to tease him with her fingers. He pretended to ignore it, so she probed a bit further.

"If you carry on doing that, I will blow up the wrong people!"

"I'll stop if you like?" slightly withdrawing her hands.

"Don't you dare. Please carry on. It's really relaxing."

Charlie did as he asked and he slowly lost interest in killing people.

Daniel swung round on his chair and guided her onto his lap facing him. He gently pulled the robe apart and kissed her breasts. Her body responded instantly and the passion she had felt the previous night returned in ever increasing waves. He looked up at her and smiled.

She returned the smile. "You are very good at that sir. Can I have more please?"

Daniel complied with her wishes. He could feel her thighs tighten against his. He teased her with his tongue, slowly increasing the rhythm as she closed her eyes. She did one of her little moans which he enjoyed so much.

She could feel him under her and leant back. Her hair falling free. He moved against her and kissed her passionately. Her whole body felt wave after wave of sensuality until she fell into his arms. Charlie lay on his shoulder and he rested his head on hers. They clung together at the start of their long pathway to mutual catharsis and consummation.

Daniel carried her to his enormous bed and lay Charlie next to him under the white linen duvet. She looked into his eyes and saw her future.

* * *

When Charlie woke up, Daniel was already dressed. He opened the curtains, knelt on the bed and gave her a kiss.

"Was that a dream?" asked Charlie.

"It was the best dream I have ever had," he smiled.

"I've pressed the silver button. What would you like for breakfast?"

"Tea and some fresh fruit please. What time is it?"

"Ten to nine."

"Crumbs! I better get a quick shower. John is coming at ten."

With that, Charlie resumed her modesty and carefully put on the robe keeping her body hidden under the duvet. She took her shower in his bathroom. It seemed appropriate.

* * *

Anne Marie brought Charlie's bags down for her and made a neat pile by the front door. John arrived promptly at ten. Charlie and Daniel met him on the front steps.

"Now then you two. Have you had a nice, relaxing few days together?"

"Very revealing," said Daniel. Slowly adding. "I have learnt a lot about focal length and filters. How was Bretton Woods?"

"Lots of learned discussions and well-meaning rhetoric but I doubt it will change the world."

"Did you get some interesting landscapes, Charlie?"

"Daniel has been a wonderful host and taken me to some fantastic locations. I have really enjoyed the break. Thank you so much for suggesting it."

"Well, that's great. We had better be getting on the road or we will miss our connection down to Boston."

Daniel took Charlie in his arms and gave her a kiss and a big hug. "I will give you a ring."

"Preferably this year!" smiled Charlie.

They swept up the drive to the large white pillared gates and were gone. Daniel stood alone on the front drive in the sunshine, wondering where life would go next.

Anne Marie appeared with a towel.

CHAPTER SEVEN

Hvar – Adriatic Sea – Croatia

"**H**i! Did you have a good flight back?" Charlie was in her loft studio sorting out her RAW files from New England when the phone rang, and the call caught her completely unawares.

"Hi. Yes, great thanks. No issues. John seemed to be able to override any problems with some sort of special pass. Are you OK?"

"Yes fine. Are you happy with all the landscapes you took? I miss your body."

Charlie smiled. "Miss yours too. What are you up to?"

"The planning for my trip to Thailand is going really well and I am hoping to leave at the end of November. The reason I am really ringing is to ask you if you would like to meet me in Croatia at Hvar, on about the fifteenth of December and spend a few days with me there? There are some beautiful shorelines along the Adriatic coast which you can photograph."

"That would be wonderful Daniel. I have never been in that part of the world before. I will just have to check with Daddy that there is nothing pressing at this end, that he can't cover for me. I am sure it will be fine. I can't wait to see you again."

"That's great then; I will make some provisional bookings for your flights and hotel room. So, all you will need is your passport and bags."

"Are you working in Hvar?"

"Just one meeting about my mountain gorilla project in Rwanda. Shouldn't take long and it's not dangerous, so you can come along if you like?"

"Funny place for a meeting about gorillas?" asked Charlie suspiciously.

"You will enjoy the meeting. It will be fun. Well, I better go or I will be in trouble with Anne Marie. She sends her love by the way."

"Tell her I miss her too!" she laughed.

"I will. Have a fun day."

October turned into November and the leaves turned into a pale shadow of their North American friends. Daniel and Charlie spoke a few times on the phone but it was not really an electronic relationship. The elegant blue-faced Leicester rams were being turned out with the Swaledale ewes and the Limousin suckler cows and calves were brought into the fold yards bedded in deep, soft barley straw. The rooks were calling in the back fields aloft the bare oak trees and the shooting season was in full swing. The Russians did come with love and drank copious amounts of vodka; so most of the grouse lived for another day.

Charlie's Hydra photos were a great success both financially and artistically. She won an award in the landscape section of the Greek Photographic Circuit and they appeared in several tourist brochures and websites.

She had her usual long chats with her mother over cups of coffee in the great kitchen, but for the first time in her life

Charlie felt she did not want to share everything, keeping it corralled with Daniel and her special space.

"So, when are you seeing him, assuming he does not fall off his horse again?" asked Elizabeth.

"He has invited me to Croatia in mid-December. He is over there on business and he says there are lots of picturesque places to see and photograph. That's assuming you and Daddy can manage without me for a few days?"

At that point Edward strode in for lunch. "What's this about another holiday. You have only just got back from the last one!"

"Edward. Shut up and stop teasing her. Of course, you can go my darling and stay as long as you like. It will be a marvellous experience, as long as you are careful. I don't know any Croatians but I assume they are reasonably civilised."

"Most of them I think, Mummy."

"That's settled then. You must go into Harrogate and buy yourself some warm clothes. I can come with you and help you chose them."

"Thank you. That's very kind of you. We can have a nice day out together and go to Betty's for lunch."

"What about me?" asked her father in jest.

"I'll leave you a cheese sandwich in the fridge!"

The start of December was unusually cold in the Dales, with snow on the higher ground but not enough to drift and cause problems for George's sheep up on the moor. He did, however, start to take them some big round bales of haylage so they had some good food inside them, for the lambs they were carrying.

John and Julia came round for supper on the first Saturday in December so Edward could raid the wine cellar and try his 2006 Château Rayas Châteauneuf-du-Pape. It was worth the long wait for it to mature.

Elizabeth roasted some lamb shanks with an onion gravy and followed it with her signature apple pie along with homemade custard. After supper, they retired to the blazing oak logs in the great hall and sank into the sofas to enjoy the conversations.

Julia and Elizabeth shared recipes, whilst John and Edward's discussions were far ranging, covering world politics, international finances and the front bearings on the Land Rover. Charlie sat patiently waiting for a quiet word with John. When her father set off for another bottle, she moved next to John and whispered, "Have you heard any news from Thailand lately?"

"No. Very quiet over there. Oh, apart from a massive explosion killing nine people and destroying one of the most valuable houses in Lampang. Gas leak they think."

"Sad that. Gas can be very volatile," said Charlie. John smiled knowingly.

"I hear you are off to Croatia soon for a holiday. Anywhere nice?"

"Just around you know. See how it goes," replied Charlie vaguely.

"Good girl. You have fun but take care. This one is off-piste."

"Everything seems to be off-piste with Daniel!"

* * *

The next day an email arrived:

Dear C,

Please find attached your e-ticket for flight from Manchester to Split. I have arranged for a car to pick you up from home, a week on Friday at six am, to take you to the Airport. Sorry about the time but there are only limited direct flights and changing planes might be stressful with all your camera stuff. I have booked a hotel for six days but it is open-ended if you would like to stay longer. The return ticket is also flexible.

Th. went well and mission accomplished. I will be back in Croatia a few days before you, to sort some things out, so don't worry if you do not hear from me until a couple of days before you fly. Looking forward to seeing you again. Bring some warm clothes!

Whatever xx

Charlie got that tingle again.

Dear Whatever,

That sounds wonderful. Can't wait. I will look forward to getting the ticket. I have plenty of warm clothes, and one that isn't, which you might like!

Charlie xxx

Charlie's plane landed at Split, on time and she negotiated the baggage merry-go-round and customs without any problems. She emerged into the real world, scanning all the expectant faces for Daniel, but he was nowhere to be seen. She had no idea where she was staying or even in which town, so she felt a bit lost.

"Hi darling. How are you? Did you have a good flight?" A glamorous young lady, in a very expensive long trench coat, approached with open arms and overgrown sunglasses.

"Hello," said Charlie hesitantly.

The lady dipped the shades. It was Anne Marie.

"Well, that's a nice surprise. What are you doing here?" asked Charlie, confused.

"Daniel doesn't like airports so he asked me to pick you up."

"I suppose you just happened to be passing through Croatia?"

"Good God no! Daniel's life would be chaos without someone to organise the detail. He does a million things at once and is twenty steps ahead of everybody else but forgets someone actually has to make the plans happen."

"Err. Well, where is he actually?"

"I have no idea! He left the hotel last night, in the dark, and I haven't seen him since. Don't worry he will turn up. In the meantime, you have got me to keep you happy," she smiled. "Right. Let me grab the trolley and we will head for the boat."

"Boat?"

"Yes, you know. One of those things that lets you travel over water!"

"But I thought… Oh hell! I will just go with the flow."

"Best idea when you work with Daniel."

The Van der Valk motor yacht was moored by the dock and Anne Marie efficiently loaded all the bags into the cabin. She gave Charlie a hand to get onboard, holding her hand slightly longer than necessary.

"Where are the crew?" asked Charlie, looking around.

"I am the crew; I know I am only a woman but I can steer a boat!"

"A very capable, attractive one though," observed Charlie, playing the game.

"You've made my day. Glad I came now." They both laughed and took off at great speed. Anne Marie was clearly enjoying herself.

"Daniel has borrowed it from a friend for the week, so we can get around the coastline and you can take some landscapes."

"Very thoughtful of him but it's freezing," mused Charlie.

"Don't worry, it's got three cosy cabins, I can keep you warm!"

"Where are we staying?"

"Near Hvar, at a place called the Little Green Bay. Lovely country hotel. Nice and secluded."

When they arrived at the hotel quay, a very smart young man appeared and helped them with the bags through to reception. Anne Marie had checked in a few days before so she knew her way around. Charlie had got her own room which she felt comfortable with, given the circumstances.

"Dinner is at seven. Would you like me to book you two a table?" asked the receptionist.

Charlie looked at Anne Marie and before she could speak Anne Marie said 'yes' and defined which one. In the corner overlooking the boats at the quay side. Daniel's boat was the biggest. It was just gone five, so they had time for a rest and shower before dinner.

The hotel was a small converted farmhouse with only fifteen rooms so it had a unique rustic charm blended with Parisian design. It was warm and friendly and off the beaten track so a good place to work from.

Charlie arrived in the bar first and ordered a gin and tonic. She was wearing her blue denims and her new jumper which she had bought in Harrogate with her mother. Safe she thought. Anne Marie arrived a few minutes later carrying a file with potential landscapes for Charlie to photograph. She was wearing denim jeans and a near identical jumper to Charlie's.

"Snap!"

"Great choice Charlie. Daniel will love it!"

"Have you heard from him yet?"

"Not a thing. He'll be buried in some plot or other. Don't worry, he will turn up when he is ready. He asked me to look after you until he returns and I am very happy to satisfy your desires whatever they may be?"

"That's very kind of you Anne Marie, I look forward to spending some quality time with you, starting now. Cheers!" They clinked glasses.

"I have put together some possible locations we can easily reach with the boat. Weather permitting, I thought that tomorrow we could go island hopping up to the Zadar Archipelago. Saharun Beach on Dugi Atok looks beautiful with white pebbles against the turquoise-blue Adriatic waters and there are some dramatic cliffs, at the other end of the island, falling into the sea.

Anne Marie continued enthusiastically. "The winter sun on the ancient Veli Rat lighthouse could work really well from the boat too. Anyway, there are plenty of potential landscapes to keep you happy, whilst I supply you with hot coffee. The forecast is good for the next few days but it will be chilly, so if we wrap up warm it could be fun. I know Daniel wants to take you out for a meal on Saturday evening at Hvar harbour, overlooking the boats in the port, so we have a couple of days to get some photography in. You can teach me how you take those amazing photos. I was looking at some on your website; the one of Chocorua Lake you took with Daniel has fantastic colours on all the trees."

"Flattery will get you everywhere Anne Marie."

"That's what I am planning on. Shall we have another drink and order some food. I'm starving."

"Can I have another G&T please and I think I will go for the tuna tataki with jasmine rice. How about you?"

"I am going to have the grilled octopus with the rosemary fried potato wedges." The attentive waiter took the order and brought more drinks.

"How long have you known Daniel? You obviously have a very close relationship?" asked Charlie.

"He tried to kill me about ten years ago in Morocco, along with a few other really nice people. I managed to outwit him and escape his pathetically implemented plot, so I think he thought he would rather have me on his side!"

"I didn't think he targeted nice people for money?" queried Charlie; but was interrupted.

"Don't listen to her. She is just trying to ingratiate herself to you so she can get you into bed!" Daniel had arrived. He went straight to Charlie and kissed her cheek ignoring Anne Marie.

"I am so sorry I was not here when you arrived Charlie, but I had a small technical issue with the meeting about gorilla conservation on Saturday and I wanted it to be perfect, as you will be there as my guest."

"It's not a problem honestly. I am just glad you are here and I can see you again. Pull up a chair and have something to eat. Did you come over to Croatia with Anne Marie?" asked Charlie.

"No, I had to come over earlier but I stayed in Dubrovnik, so this is my first night here. Are your rooms, OK?"

"It's really comfortable and the people are so welcoming and friendly. We already feel at home. Don't we Anne Marie?

"Yes, it's cool. I picked up the boat from your friend's yard yesterday as instructed. It's a really powerful Van der Valk with a nice warm cabin. His man said we can keep it for as long as we need to because his boss is away in Moscow for a few months on business."

"Anne Marie was very proficient at being captain. I felt very safe."

"She ought to be. She crewed in the America's Cup last year!"

"You never told me that!" said Charlie in astonishment.

"I like to be a bit mysterious."

"You are certainly attractively mysterious to me," smiled Charlie. Anne Marie glowed.

After they had eaten, Daniel ordered Anne Marie to bed. "Charlie and I have lots to talk about."

"Just a slave, that's all I am," and she reluctantly drifted off to her room.

Daniel kissed Charlie again. "Shall we go onto the terrace and have a drink out there?" They sat on a sofa together, covered with a large Arabic throw to keep themselves warm. Charlie updated Daniel on all the news from the estate in England and Daniel briefly told her about the success of the Thailand mission.

"Do you feel better now you have destroyed that part of the ivory supply chain. I know it means a lot to you."

"Well, it was an important link but until I can sort the financiers out and locate the third Somali in either Kenya or Somalia, I will not feel I have purged the cloud that hangs over Elizabeth's death."

"I know you want to complete the job. Have you made any progress in identifying the bankers?"

"It's the hardest part of the whole thing," reckoned Daniel. "Finding intelligence about criminal activity is relatively easy because there is always some minion who will sell his soul to the devil for a fistful of dollars. But banking has always been based on confidentiality and there are so many layers of secrecy and intercontinental electronic transfers that go on these days, even the tax authorities in most countries have no idea what's going on where. However, my good friend, called Sebastian in the Cayman Islands, is a software genius and it is unbelievable the things he has found out for me. With the information he has uncovered about this and other things, I have enough work for the next ten years!"

"You're impossible! Don't you ever stop work?"

"Only when I am with you." Daniel leant across and kissed her gently on the lips. Charlie felt that special feeling again and responded with a lingering return.

"What time are we setting off in the morning?" asked Daniel.

"I am not sure actually. Anne Marie has suggested that we go up to Zadar Archipelago, which sounds really exciting. Will you be able to come with us?"

"Yes of course. I am all yours now, for the next few days. Shall we all meet for breakfast at say eight o'clock and then she can tell us what she has got planned for the day?"

"That's great. Shall we get back inside and have a night cap?"

They had another drink in the bar and Daniel escorted Charlie back to her room. They kissed again by the open door but it was as though America had not happened, and he went off to his room leaving Charlie a bit bemused. She thought he was probably tired after a busy day's work and retired alone.

* * *

Charlie got down to breakfast first and ordered an Earl Grey. It was the sort of establishment that would have it, naturally. Daniel and Anne Marie appeared together and Daniel pulled her chair out for her. He then kissed Charlie on the cheek and asked her if she had slept well.

"Yes, fine thank you. The bed was very comfortable and it's so peaceful here. Just like home."

"Except you have bottle-nosed dolphins rather than Swaledale sheep!" observed Anne Marie.

"Not as easy to round up I assume!" joked Charlie.

"Shall we all help ourselves to breakfast and then we can discuss the photography plans?"

* * *

Anne Marie had organised flasks of hot coffee and a picnic basket for lunch which she stowed away in the galley. She carried out her pre-sailing checks on the boat and contacted the coast guard to file the planned route and get the local weather forecast, which looked clear and dry all day. Anne Marie helped Charlie on board but left Daniel to his own devices.

* * *

The sun was quite warm for the time of year but the wind chill factor was high, as Anne Marie pushed the boat along at maximum knots. The hot coffee was soon resourced and was welcome for warming the hands. They passed Otok Zirje and then cut up between the islands of Kornati and Zut. The views were amazing and Charlie had to keep asking for the boat to stop so she could get good images, of the rugged terrain of the multitudinous islands.

When they arrived at Dugi Otok, the sun was shining and the crystal-clear waters were still, in the bay; perfect for some good shots. Charlie set up her tripod on the deck and affixed her new Canon R5 camera which she had been lent by her local camera shop to see how she got on with the new technology. Anne Marie was despatched to the galley, like Cinderella, to unpack the picnic, whilst Daniel was fascinated watching Charlie work out the new controls.

"So why is this camera so much better than your other one?"

"It costs more, so it must be better!" said Charlie cynically.

"No seriously, I am interested because it looks pretty much the same and although I am not in your league, obviously, I do sometimes have to use a camera for my work."

"I guess the main benefit for you would be that it is a lot lighter to carry around. It doesn't have a flip-up mirror mechanism, like current SLR cameras, so it's probably more robust too. It is sealed against the weather and dust so it will be good for cross-country stuff. I wanted to try it today on the boat because it has what's called image stabilisation built into the camera, so it should help to take a good sharp landscape, even though the tripod is moving slightly."

"Is it working then?" enquired Daniel.

"Difficult to say until you get it up on the computer back home. I didn't dare bring the tether after what happened on Mount Chocorua!"

"It's a bit cold to fall in the water today! Talking of which, how about a break in the galley and get some lunch?" They descended into the warm galley where Anne Marie had laid out a banquet from the hotel.

"That looks delicious, but there is enough to feed the whole island!" marvelled Charlie.

"Don't worry, Daniel can eat like a horse. I am sure he will do it justice. Coffee for both of you?"

* * *

When they were replete, Charlie packed away the picnic, whilst Anne Marie programmed the below-deck autopilot to take them around the island to Veli Rat Lighthouse.

They stopped at various, unmissable landscapes on the way there. Charlie was very pleased with the technology of the R5 and the more she played around with the possibilities, the more excited she got.

Daniel and Anne Marie were amused by her enthusiasm, but were just enjoying a day away from the pressures of their daily existence.

They finally reached the lighthouse and Charlie decided that they should have a go with the camera, to see who could get the best shot, judged over dinner that evening.

"I am going first whilst the sun is shining," claimed Anne Marie competitively. So, she took over and clicked away in auto, whilst Charlie took the planned opportunity to sit next to Daniel. He put his arm around her shoulders and gave her a peck on the cheek, smiling. He realised what Charlie was up to, but played along. When Anne Marie was satisfied with her creations, she invited Daniel to do better.

"Come on then Mr Superman, show us what you can do." Having seen what Charlie had done, she sat next to her, put her arm around her and kissed her. Quick as a flash, Daniel took a shot of them.

"I think I have the winner!" he laughed.

"We have much better ones of us together, but we're not showing them to you!" Anne Marie said, putting her tongue out.

"I think I better have the camera back before you two get out of hand!" smiled Charlie.

Charlie took a few more landscape shots which looked really good as the sun was getting lower in the sky. The contrasting shadows across the towering cliffs were a dream sequence that she would later use to great commercial success.

They arrived back at the hotel at about half eight, as the sun was setting low on the horizon. It had been a long day on the boat, so they had a quick bar meal and delayed the judging of the photography competition till breakfast. Charlie was a bit disappointed but did not let it show.

When she got back to her room alone, she took a long hot shower and climbed into bed. After ten minutes there was a tap on the door and Charlie thought it was Anne Marie, so ignored it at first, but the knock persisted. She got out of bed and opened the door. It was Daniel in his bathrobe looking tousled and rugged.

"I was just passing and wondered if I could persuade you to put my shots first in the competition? he smiled.

"You better come in and try."

* * *

At breakfast the following morning Daniel won the competition, after excessive protestations from Anne Marie that the judge had been bribed. She promised to seek her revenge at the earliest opportunity.

That day, Anne Marie had planned a trip to the Blue Cave in Balun Bay on Biševo. It was only about five degrees, when they set off and bitterly cold with the windchill on the speeding boat. They set the autopilot and took it in turns to go below to keep warm. Although very cold, it was a bright sunny winter's day and when they arrived at the tiny island, a small inflatable craft met them, lying offshore. They transferred, with Daniel carrying the camera equipment for Charlie. The cave is a big tourist attraction in the summer months and can become overrun with small boats, but in December it was deserted and with the sunlight streaming through the crystal-clear water the luminous blue light was ethereal.

"What do you think then Charlie?" asked Anne Marie.

"It is absolutely beautiful. I am so glad we came. It is not a classical landscape but a microcosm of our blue planet from space. I don't think I will need the tripod thank you Daniel; this new fast camera will take an excellent photograph in this light."

Charlie happily clicked away for about twenty minutes and captured every angle and colour, including the light pink pebbles shimmering beneath the waters. The pilot of the inflatable then took them outside and Charlie took some more general shots of the cliffs and cave entrances.

"I think we should get back to our boat and have a hot cup of coffee. I am freezing!" stuttered Anne Marie jokingly.

They headed back and Daniel courteously helped both ladies aboard. Anne Marie paid the pilot of the inflatable with a handsome tip, as he had turned out specially on a cold winter's day. After coffee they circumnavigated Biševo so Charlie could photograph even more rugged cliffs and caves.

After the previous day's long excursion, they returned to the hotel by mid-afternoon so they did not freeze to death. Daniel suggested that they met in the bar at seven and had a long restful evening meal, to plan what they would do on Saturday. He had an ulterior motive because of the primate conference in the evening.

Daniel arrived first and ordered a Gemišt cocktail on the recommendation of the hotel owner, who was manning the bar. It was nice and warm in the bar after the chill of the day at sea so Daniel took off his jumper. At that moment

Anne Marie appeared wearing black, tight, silk trousers and a royal blue deep V-necked lantern satin blouse. And high heels – dressed to kill.

"You are looking very sensual, Annie," whispered Daniel in her ear.

"It's a long time since you called me Annie."

"Sorry, I forgot our pact on that. Just slipped out. Better revert to Anne Marie for the rest of the evening."

"You really like Charlie, don't you?"

"I do, I'm afraid, but you know that you and I will always have a special relationship."

"I hope so, after everything we have done together but it won't stop me wanting her too."

"I know, but I get first pick," Daniel laughed.

Charlie came into the bar and looked straight at Anne Marie. "Wow, you look amazing Anne Marie. I didn't know we were going out on the town."

"I dressed especially for you Charlie. Please call me Annie." Daniel nearly choked on his drink.

The waiter appeared with the menus and Daniel ordered them all more of the Gemišt cocktail. They all enjoyed the local speciality as a change from gin.

"Now then, what are my two favourite ladies having for starters?"

"Well, I am having the beef carpaccio with lemon caviar and Parmigiano cheese," declared Anne Marie in her most sophisticated voice.

"How can we choose anything else after that introduction?" smiled Charlie.

After the main courses, the conversation turned to the trip to Hvar the following day.

"I suggest we leave about eleven and cruise around to Hvar and tie up in the harbour. Anne Marie, can you book a berth because they might be busy on Saturday night?" planned Daniel.

"Already done Master."

"I told you she was efficient Charlie."

"Efficient and beautiful. That's a powerful combination," Charlie winked at Anne Marie.

"Can I come and work for you please?" Anne Marie asked Charlie.

"That would be wonderful but you might get bored with farming in the Dales. It's a bit mundane after your life with Daniel!"

"True but at least I would be appreciated and loved properly."

"We can discuss it later when Daniel's gone to bed," smiled Charlie.

"All right you two, that's enough of your fantasising. What do you want for pudding?"

"I fancy the watermelon with mint," chose Charlie.

"I'm having the crème brûlée. What about you Daniel?"

"I'll go for the apple tart. Coffee for both of you?"

The waiter hurried away to get the food.

Changing the subject, Charlie asked about the gorilla project in Africa.

"Don't start him on gorillas or we will be here all night. If you think he loves you, wait till you see him with his favourite female gorilla!"

"Just ignore her. She has no idea about conservation. There are basically two types of gorillas, split into four or five subgroups depending on which scientist you talk to.

All the groups are in trouble, mainly because their habitats are slowly being eroded by increasing human populations needing more land for agriculture and for timber extraction. They are also very susceptible to human diseases, mainly respiratory, so we have to be careful with tourists and keep them at a safe distance from the families."

"So how many are left in the wild?" asked Charlie, genuinely interested in the project.

"I suppose nobody really knows because we are talking about vast areas of land, some of which is heavily forested, but the best estimates are about 100,000 western lowland gorillas which are the ones you see in zoos and wildlife parks. The mountain gorillas are the most severely endangered and there are only about 1,000 of them left, so they are the ones we are trying to protect."

"Where do the mountain ones live?"

"Mainly in the high montane forests of Rwanda and Burundi. The group we are trying to help are in the Virunga Mountains in the north of Rwanda, to the west of Lake Victoria. There is a silverback male and seven females, some with youngsters, which is really good. The main problem is poachers who try and take the babies, which they can get a lot of money for as pets. They just shoot the mothers if we don't get to them first."

"That's horrendous, but how do you protect them in such a remote area?"

"We use a lot of modern technology but maybe I will take you there one day so you can see them for yourself and see how we try to look after them."

"That would be amazing. Could I take photographs of them?"

"Only if you ask their permission! I think we better change the subject again before Anne Marie falls asleep," observed Daniel, looking at Anne Marie's heavy eyelids.

* * *

They all had a lazy start the following morning and wrapped up warm for the short boat trip around to Hvar harbour. It was a lovely sunny morning and unseasonally warm for the time of year, but still chilly on the boat.

The harbour at Hvar looked beautiful in the morning sunshine with its pristine yachts bobbing up and down on the glistening sun-kissed ripples of water. Anne Marie tied-up at the pre-booked berth near the harbour-front cafes, which were busy serving coffees, croissant, and French toast with strawberries. They found a seat and ordered coffee, whilst enjoying the view of the imposing white-stoned town hall with its fifteenth-century loggia and the locals bustling around the businesses in the square. Charlie took some photographs of the historic buildings and walked back to the harbour-front so she could get a landscape shot of the town, with the ancient fortress perched high on the hill behind.

"I'm off shopping whilst you two have a wander round on your own. I will meet you at Divino's for lunch at about one, if that suits you?" And Anne Marie strode off purposefully, down a shadowed side alley and disappeared.

"That was a bit odd to suddenly disappear like that?" queried Charlie.

"Don't worry. She has probably seen something exotic on the internet and wants to buy it on her own. There is a lovely old cathedral just around the corner. It might be a good one to have in your file if you want to do a Dalmatian coast portfolio?"

Charlie and Daniel walked across the square and he took her hand in his. Charlie enjoyed that and felt secure with him. Charlie liked the imposing St Stephen's Cathedral – from the outside anyway – and took some shots. It was bright light, so she had not bothered to bring her tripod because it was another thing to lug around all day. Besides, her new Canon camera was coping beautifully with its built-in image stabilisation. The cathedral's square renaissance bell tower, shone with a white radiance against the blue-sky seeping through the structure of narrow arches. They held hands again and wandered through the shadows of the historic narrow streets, stopping occasionally to look in shop windows. Daniel bought Charlie a long artisan necklace, of no specific value, except the love with which he clasped it around her slender neck.

"Shall we find Divino's? I think it's down here somewhere," suggested Daniel, looking down a narrow passageway.

"There's Anne Marie clutching a mountain of shopping bags. Looks like her trip was successful. Hi Annie. What have you bought?" said Charlie, utilising her new permission.

"Lots of lovely soft silk dresses and blouses. I will give you a mannequin parade later."

The restaurant was as good as its reputation and they enjoyed a relaxing hour drinking Pošip and eating the fruits of the Adriatic. After lunch they wandered over to the Franciscan monastery on a small headland near the harbour so Charlie could take some more photos. They sat in the sun in the gardens surrounded by rustling cypress trees, that had been there for centuries.

"When does the gorilla meeting start?" wondered Charlie.

"Oh! much later. They will not start without us," replied Daniel casually and rapidly changed the subject – "Shall we go across to the Palace Elizabeth for afternoon tea? It's rather grand, but very civilised. They might even have Earl Grey," he smiled.

They wandered across the square again and through the architectural loggia and found a table over-looking the soporific bay. They ordered a light meal, having indulged themselves all day in the culinary delights of the island. And they did serve Earl Grey.

After about half an hour, a large party of American businessmen arrived en masse and parked themselves across the loggia, pulling several tables together. They were laughing loudly, and generally changing the atmosphere, to one of a baseball competition. They ordered copious amounts of expensive but not particularly good wine, and treated the place as though they owned it. When the waiter returned to get the food order, they were particularly denigrating to him and one could see how slavery was ingrained in the psyche.

Charlie was looking uncomfortable but she had Daniel on one side of her and Anne Marie had deliberately sat on the other side, so she felt safe. The leader of the pack started to talk about a party that night for his fortieth birthday and that Croatia would never have seen anything like it before. It soon became apparent that he had paid for all the acolytes to fly over to Hvar to help him celebrate. They were suitably sycophantic and obsequious.

"I am feeling a bit uncomfortable with all of this. Can we go please?" mumbled Charlie quietly.

At that point, the leader stood up and proposed a toast to himself. "I would like to thank you all for coming to help me launch my new eighty-metre yacht tonight. It will be the biggest and most expensive yacht, all eighty million dollars of it, permanently moored at Martha's Vineyard and I think I deserve it," he bragged arrogantly. The acolytes suitably agreed. "We will start with champagne and fireworks at seven, so make sure your wives stop spending your hard-earned payroll and are here on time for the spectacular. The pyrotechnicians did the New Year display at Sydney harbour last year so it will be a world class event. Cheers!" They all sang 'Happy Birthday', which was ingratiating in the extreme.

Charlie gripped Daniel's wrist and looked into his eyes. He could see a tear in her eye and she had turned very pale. Her hand gripped tighter and started to shake.

"It's the bastard from university that attacked me," stuttered Charlie, struggling to hold back the tears.

"Are you one hundred percent certain we have got the right man?" queried Anne Marie suspiciously.

"Yes of course, but what do you mean – the right man?" asked Charlie. Daniel remained silent, quietly contemplating his empty glass. At that point, Charlie's attacker walked past their table, not acknowledging them, and disappeared towards the gents' toilet. Daniel winked at Anne Marie and followed him. Anne Marie looked puzzled. "He's gone off-piste again. I can't trust him to do anything right."

"What's going on?" asked Charlie.

"God only knows," retorted Anne Marie.

Ten minutes later Charlie's attacker staggered back into the loggia, clutching his chest, and a dribble of blood ran from his broken nose. His acolytes surrounded him, probably more concerned about their revenue stream than his medical welfare. One shouted for the waiter to bring a towel and another called the police on his mobile. A waitress brought the bastard a drink of water, which he rudely cast aside. Meanwhile, Daniel had not reappeared and Charlie was starting to panic with all the confusion, when Anne Marie's phone rang. She shook her head in frustration.

"Right, we're off to the gorilla conference," she exclaimed, as she put a thousand kuna under the small flower vase on the table."

"But where is Daniel?" fretted Charlie.

"Just put your arm around me and pretend we are lovers. Don't worry, we will find him." They left as one and made for the cathedral entrance. They found Daniel leaning nonchalantly up against the sacred wall with a glass of wine in his hand. He raised his glass "To catharsis for my beautiful English princess!"

It was slowly dawning on Charlie what might have happened. She threw her arms around his neck. "Are you OK? What happened?"

"I am not sure. He tripped and fell head-first into the urinal. Twice," he laughed.

Anne Marie was not amused. "You could have ruined all my careful planning you idiot. Bloody men and their hormones!"

"Oh, go on he deserved it after what he said to the waiter. Anyway, he will remember this evening every time he looks in the mirror, which he probably does at least once an hour, with his vanity level," promised Daniel.

Charlie felt as though she was floating along in some sort of dream, not knowing what was going to happen next. And she was right.

"OK. I am off to Switzerland," chimed Anne Marie. "You two enjoy the conference. Have a good Christmas." She kissed Daniel on the cheek and Charlie passionately on the lips. "Look after him my darling. He's insane." With that she was gone.

Daniel took Charlie's still trembling hand and they walk slowly down one of the colourful side streets lined with small shops. "Did you do that for me Daniel?"

"Being a genuine bastard, I can't stand imposters... Right, are you game for a long climb to the conference?"

"At this point, if you said run naked along Downing Street, I would. Where to my gallant knight?"

Daniel took her hand and they set off up the thousand steps to the top of the Tvrđava Fortica that has protected the town for millennia. As they ascended, the lights on the boats in the harbour twinkled in the trembling waters and the town shrank away into a toytown of miniatures. When they reached the plateau on the highest terrace, they leant on the old stone walls next to the canon embrasures and looked out across the Adriatic vista as the Greeks, Romans, Ottomans and Turks had done before them.

It was five to seven and Daniel opened his bag and took out two fine glass flutes and a bottle of Pol Roger's Winston Churchill champagne. He carefully removed the cork and poured the pale golden liquid into the glasses. He placed them on the wall as his mobile rang.

Hilltop Fortress above Hvar harbour

"What is the temperature of the iceberg? OK."

Charlie looked mystified.

"Are all the penguins off the iceberg Max?"

Charlie looked even more mystified.

Daniel's other phone rang. "Hi Sebastian. Did the transfer go OK? Brilliant. I owe you one. Thanks."

"Who is Sebastian and what has Max got to do with penguins on an iceberg?" mused Charlie, even more mystified.

There were cheers seeping up from the town below, as a spectacular fireworks display started on the bastard's gigantic new eighty-meter yacht, moored offshore.

"I love you for giving him a bloody nose, but as I said in New England he just floats along above reality and us poor mortals."

"But you have forgotten my mountain gorilla project. Look, this is Abraham my silverback male." Daniel showed

Charlie a picture of the gorilla on his mobile. "He controls everything that happens. He is very powerful."

"I am starting to think Anne Marie was right about you and the gorillas," Charlie laughed.

"I give you a toast to Abraham," said Daniel raising his glass. "Stroke his back – he loves that" said Daniel offering the phone to Charlie.

"Anything for you tonight." With which, she touched the gorilla on the phone face, smiled at Daniel and they clinked glasses.

The fireworks subsided down in the town, there was ten seconds of dark peace in the Croatian night sky and then a massive explosion lit up the giant yacht. Then another, then another, then another. A huge mushroom cloud of light lit up the whole Adriatic Ocean. Shattered debris flew into the air as the yacht listed. It rolled to starboard, gradually sinking slowly below the turmoil in the water. The churning sea quickly settled consigning the bastard's yacht to the depths.

"Now that's what I call real catharsis!" said Daniel, raising his flute to Charlie.

"Christ. Did I do that?" said Charlie, looking at the phone she was still holding. Did I kill anyone. How?… God that is the most amazing feeling in the world. Did I really do that?"

"You did. All on your own. Well, with a bit of help from Abraham of course. It was a gorilla attack!"

"Do we need to run now? What happens next?" Charlie started to panic.

"No rush. Just enjoy the moment. Anyway, we have got to finish the Winston first." They sipped their drinks as steam and smoke issued from beneath the Adriatic waters. Police sirens and fire engines appeared, to no avail. There was much running and screaming below, but only American egos were crushed, as they watched in dismay, towards the wreckage strewn across the bay.

When they had emptied the bottle, they made their way back down to the thronging crowds that had gathered at the water's edge, to ogle at the spectacle. Hand in hand, they slipped down a side street and Daniel opened a car door for Charlie to get in.

"What happened to *our* boat?" asked Charlie.

"Anne Marie stole it to go to the airport. We thought an old Fiat, with lovers in, would be more discrete."

"I like the lover's bit," Charlie grinned.

They arrived back at the Little Green Bay Hotel and sat on the terrace for a peaceful drink after all the excitement. Charlie lay back in Daniel's arms desperate for him to kiss her and be with her. "Will you sleep next to me tonight please? I need you to be near me to feel safe."

"Your room or mine?" he smiled. "I want to hold you safely, forever."

Charlie felt an overwhelming desire to kiss him and took the initiative. She felt empowered to shape her own destiny at last. Daniel stood up and took her hand and as he turned, he casually threw his Abraham mobile over his shoulder into the Adriatic. Its secrets to be dissolved for eternity.

Back in Charlie's room, she stepped into the shower to wash away the dust of the day. As the warm water caressed her slender body, Daniel stepped in behind her. She had never shared a shower before and felt a wave of pleasure following the flow of water over her breasts and down her thighs. She turned and felt his muscular body against hers. They embraced passionately, their lips teasing each other. Daniel gently ran his fingers through her long hair and massaged her head with the sandalwood shampoo. Charlie threw her head back under the spray and the scented bubbles floated down her back. Daniel put his strong arms around her waist and kissed her neck. She felt she was losing control of her body and wanted more. She didn't want control, she wanted his hands on her breasts, between her thighs and his kisses everywhere. She made her little moans that he loved so much, to direct his passions. She felt herself floating away, as her body reverberated with sexual satisfaction and collapsed into his arms. He lifted her up and carried her to the bed and lay her down gently on a soft white Egyptian cotton towel. He dried her body slowly and deliberately, and she drifted into a sea of fulfilment. He lay next to her for an hour or so and she eventually opened her eyes and looked into his. "You are wonderful, wonderful, wonderful," she smiled.

"I know," he laughed, "and I can blow up yachts!"

She playfully punched his chest as she had done in New England.

"Can we do this forever please?"

"Whenever you like my darling. I adore being next to you," he smiled.

"I worry that you cannot be with me properly and I cannot do the same for you."

"I just love being with you, and your reaction to my caresses tonight was magical. Maybe one day my head will let me, but Elizabeth just floods my mind when we get close to being intimate and my body shuts down. One day maybe?"

"You are wonderful."

"I know, you have already told me," He smiled again.

She kissed his cheek. Where is our next decommissioning trip?" asked Charlie.

"You're my assistant now are you?"

"Partner actually! I am fully qualified!"

"OK, as long as you stand half the costs," proffered Daniel.

"I have never been so excited before. The adrenalin rush is pretty addictive."

"There is obviously a lot of preparation and planning to do and things don't always go as planned."

"As in Columbia?"

"No comment."

"There might be a project coming up in Switzerland in a couple of months and you could come with me if you would like to. You could take some alpine landscapes and maybe take in some skiing? The job is too dangerous for you to be actively involved in, but you can help me with the cover operation."

"Do I get paid?" she smiled.

"Only with a seduction."

"It's a deal." She kissed his cheek again and lay on his shoulder.

He stroked her hair and kissed the top of her head.

"I suppose it's back to boring old Yorkshire tomorrow?" said Charlie sadly.

"You know you love the Dales and the green landscapes of home; and your parents will be desperate to see you and catch up. Just don't tell them anything about this evening. That's just between us, for ever I am afraid."

Charlie thought for a moment. "Just one thing. Won't he just claim on the yacht's insurance and get another one?"

"It was just not his day. Sebastian's friend, at Lloyds in London, deleted his insurance policies from all their databases yesterday."

CHAPTER EIGHT

Verbier – The Alps – Switzerland

Eagles would definitely look pretentious, decided Charlie, as she drove through the old stone pillars of the Hall off the Leyburn Road. She had been back in Yorkshire for a couple of days and, as Daniel had accurately predicted, she was enjoying the green and pleasant land of the Dales landscape. The winter was being kind so far, with no snow and the estate looked pristine in a rustic sort of way. She liked that. One of the old oak trees next to the drive had finally succumbed to the easterly gales in November. It was being diced into logs, by the forester with a screaming Stihl chainsaw; to be used by the mysterious ghost that kept the fires burning in the Hall.

Charlie parked in the stable yard, walked through the stables, gave Darley a pat on the way past and climbed the creaking stairs up to her studio. There was an email waiting in her inbox.

Hi C,

Hope some of the partridges have escaped and that the badgers are all well. I love you. (That was the first time he had referred to Charlie in that way and her tummy turned over).

Plans are going well with our skiing holiday and I hope to have the lodge booked shortly. Can you ski? It might help on this sort of holiday. I will organise all the tickets etc. and I have a friend who can lend us all the equipment out there, to save looking 'Home Counties' on the way out. Probably best to buy your own jacket and salopettes, whatever they are, because you will want to choose your favourite colours, style and all that ladies' stuff.

Not sure of timescales, as it will depend on when our colleagues can join us but I would think early February would be a good guess if you need to organise things your end. I know how useless everyone else is on the estate without you! I trust that your parents are well and that all the plans for Christmas are in place. I wish I could be with you again this year, but I am in the middle of planning the next two business ventures and they are exceptionally complex this time round. I hope you win the Flush again this year. I am sure you can find another lucky amateur to partner.

Whatever xxx

Charlie felt like a teenager whose un-requiting classmate had just smiled at her. 'I love you' and three x's at the end. She needed to be next to him – soon. Her hormone control systems had melted away.

Hi Whatever,

Love you too! I actually went skiing in St Moritz every year, when I was at boarding school, and got quite good but I might be bit rusty now. I guess once I get there it will come flooding back. I will buy some bright colourful ski clothing so you don't lose me on the black runs. Early February would be good for me as the shooting season is coming to a close and we will not have started lambing then. I know you will be busy but if you could give me a quick call on Christmas Day, I would love to hear your voice. I know you cannot tell me where you are but please take care of yourself.

C xxx

Charlie put their Mozart on, made a mug of coffee and sat on the sofa hugging a cushion.

She decided that she needed to get some practice in to impress Daniel, as she was sure Annie was almost certainly an Olympic skier at the very least. She booked a short course at Castleford Snozone and decided to go into Leeds to buy some professional clothing, so she looked the part. She then decided she was being stupid; but five minutes later booked it anyway.

The preparations for the Christmas Eve party were well underway in the kitchen and Elizabeth had a new cookery book open on the old pine table, surrounded by jugs and bowls of delicious smelling orchard produce. Charlie never understood why her Mother had to try a new recipe for the same meal every year but she was grateful that she did. Her father had been to the wine merchants and ordered a case of 2015 Château Ausone Saint-Emilion Premier Grand Cru for Christmas to go with the venison – in 2025!

The party was its usual big success but not vintage for Charlie whose mind was filled with Stetsons, giggles and sinking yachts. She had the most exciting stories in the room but could tell no one. Maybe others were in the same situation and there were a thousand stories that could not be shared. Who knows what lies beneath the surface of other people's lives?

Tim was keen to double check that Daniel was not going to appear over the horizon at the last minute, like some Western movie, so he could regain his title but Charlie was able to assure him that he would not be coming this year. Tim smiled and walked away so Charlie said "But I have got the world skeet champion coming instead." Tim spun round but realised she was having him on. "Look, I had enough trouble with Sundance last year without Butch coming as well." He had watched the old film since last year's defeat.

Charlie managed to have a quiet word with John but they danced around the situation, each not knowing what the other knew, or was meant not to. But she found it strangely reassuring that he knew something, even though she did not know what it was. He quietly wished them well and was so pleased he had made the offer to take her to New England. The candle was burning again.

Daniel rang on Christmas Day as promised, when Charlie was up in her studio and on her own. "Happy Christmas my darling. I'm missing your mother's delicious festive meals and your father's cellar. And you of course. What are you up to?"

"Hiding from the rain. It's starting to get bitter here, so I am in my studio Photoshopping some files. How about you?"

"It's about 23 degrees here so very pleasant. Plans are progressing well but having to tiptoe through the politics."

"I assume you are not where I thought you were?"

"Probably; but I will explain when I see you. Are you still OK for February? It looks like the second week at the moment but I will send you more details shortly."

"I can't wait to see you again. Miss your touch."

"Miss your smile. Better go now. Enjoy the flush tomorrow."

"I will. You take care."

There was so much Charlie wanted to say but found relating on the phone difficult. Where was he, that was so warm in winter? What was he planning now? Was Annie there? She decided she was getting paranoid and busied herself with her RAW files.

Was Annie perhaps wearing an even smaller version of the swimming costume she had given to her?

* * *

Charlie partnered George, the young shepherd, in the usual Boxing Day flush. They came last. Tim and Annabelle won the malt and everyone was strangely relieved that normality was restored. That's the way in the Dales.

The dreaded New Year came and went, but Charlie looked at it differently now. It was a year nearer being with Daniel again.

* * *

The snowflakes were starting to float from the leaden skies one Wednesday afternoon in mid-January, when Charlie's emails blossomed again.

Hi C,

Hope you are getting lots of skiing practice in your snowy winter wonderland. Arrangements for our trip are now in place and I would like to meet you in Nice on the 3rd February. I will send you the e-tickets and I have arranged for a taxi to pick you up from the Hall at eight-thirty am. When you get to Nice, the Hotel concierge will meet you at arrivals with a board saying Mrs Day. He will take you to the Hotel Negresco and just check in as Mrs Day. They will not ask for your passport – I have told the very nice clerk you are my mistress.

Whatever xxx

Charlie was rather hoping he would be Mr Day but decided to play along.

Hi Whatever,

Snow not quite deep enough for skiing yet but looks promising. That all sounds great and the plans are good this end to manage without me for a few days. I thought Nice was in France but I am sure all will become clear in due course. Can't wait to see you again and be your mistress.

C xxx

The snow did not settle and skiing practice was limited to the artificial slopes in Castleford. Not quite St Moritz; but the sheep were happy.

Charlie's bags were bulging with a colourful array of clothes for the slopes, along with all her miscellaneous camera equipment. Excess baggage was a certainty but she knew she had to be prepared for variety of situations when she was with Daniel.

The plane touched down in Nice only ten minutes late and the concierge was waiting with his little board and a big smile. Did he know about the mistress bit Charlie wondered? He was very attentive and scooped up the voluminous bags onto a trolley and led her out to the Negresco Mercedes right outside the entrance, parked in VIP. She felt a bit like a film star but there were no paparazzi, who were fortunately hunting the real thing somewhere else.

A very smiley young man took the bags up to the room and the smiley clerk checked the mistress in without a problem. The actress bit was growing on her. When she got to the room, she tipped the young man generously. Her father's advice was always to tip heavily on arrival if you want a good stay.

The room was beautifully furnished and the paintings, tasteful but not extravagant. The view of the Mediterranean was spectacular and the bathroom had a very handsome man leaning against the marble sink.

"You're ten minutes late."

"Mistress' privilege."

Daniel took Charlie in his arms and kissed her passionately for what seemed like two weeks.

"Missed you."

"Missed you too. Lots."

"How are things back home. Are your parents fit and well?"

"Yes, they are fine. Mummy had a bit of a scare after Christmas but she had a scan and she has got the all clear, so that's a massive relief. How are all the plans going and why are we in Nice. I thought we were going to Switzerland?"

"One of the problems with this business is that you always have to go somewhere else first, but you do get to meet your wife in some lovely cities and spend some money."

"Wife! That was a quick marriage. Did I miss something?"

"For the purposes of this trip we are Mr and Mrs Day when we cross over into Switzerland. You said you wanted to be my partner."

"I meant business partner but I am happy to go with the trial marriage to see how you work out!"

"I'll try my best dear! Right let's get washed up and I want to take you out to a shop on Rue Lamartine and then have a meal later on Rue Lascaris which is nearby."

The breeze coming off the sea was chilly but they wrapped up warm and walked the fifteen minutes to Caralys, one of the best dress shops in France. Daniel wanted to buy Charlie an elegant evening dress for a surprise he had in store for her. All the clothes in the shop were beautifully handstitched and the materials were amazingly soft and sensual to touch. Charlie tried several long dresses on but when she put on the azure blue velvet number there was no contest. It fitted like a glove and the pink silk lining highlighted the lowcut neckline, but in a sophisticated way. They both loved it and Daniel secretly paid for it so Charlie did not see the price. Whilst the lady was carefully wrapping it up in endless matching tissue paper Charlie gave Daniel an excited kiss on the cheek.

"It's absolutely wonderful. I will so enjoy wearing it for you my darling husband."

Clutching an enormous glossy Caralys bag, with the dress lovingly folded inside, they made their way to Jan's Michelin star restaurant for a romantic evening together.

* * *

The next morning Mr and Mrs Day were up early and had breakfast in their room. They checked out with the smiley receptionist and the young man took the bags to the waiting car outside, a Ferrari 812 GTS Spider.

"Very discrete!" said Charlie smiling.

"It is, down here; everybody has one, so you are invisible."

"I'll believe you. I suppose you borrowed it from a friend?"

"No, I bought it for you. Jump in, you're driving."

* * *

Getting all the bags into the limited boot space was a challenge but they managed with two square centimetres to spare. Charlie slid into the luxurious leather driving seat, pressed the ignition and the roar of the V12 engine lit up behind them. With only a slight wheel spin they were off to Monte Carlo.

They drove down into the heart of Monaco with the roar of the Ferrari bouncing off the tall buildings reaching for the expensive sky above. Daniel was right and there were more Ferraris and Lamborghinis than Fords – a surreal world. They stopped for a cappuccino at Le Parc de la Roseraie and watched the rich and famous come and go into the heliport adjacent to the sea. After half an hour they slid back into the luxurious leather and drove back up onto the main highway, crossing the border into Italy at Grimaldi, the new Mr and Mrs passports not required.

"Where are we going?"

"We are staying at the Fortezza Viscontea in Cassano d'Adda near Milan. Do you know the way or shall I map read?"

"I love this car and I am sure it will have a satnav somewhere!"

"You better put your foot down if we are going to be ready for tonight."

"Not another gorilla meeting?"

"Not sure if gorillas like Mozart."

Charlie smiled, pressed her right foot hard down and the kilometres disappeared behind them in an adagio of noise. They arrived at the thirteenth-century fortress, perched high on the banks of the river Adda, in the blink of an eye. Such is Ferrari magic. Their suite overlooked the river through ancient mullioned windows and the room was a cocoon of Italian romanticism.

Daniel had booked a box for the evening at La Scala in Milan, just another car's blink away. Charlie slipped into her long blue gown, put on the bracelet Daniel had given her, and he fastened a fine gold chain with a solitaire diamond around her slender neck. Charlie kissed him gently on the lips and he took her in his arms and held her tightly.

"I love you my darling. You look amazingly beautiful in that dress. Will you accompany me to the opera?"

"It will be my pleasure my handsome prince."

Daniel held Charlie's hand and they descended the stairs to reception. The wife of another couple going up the stairs smiled jealously at their obvious love for each other.

They arrived at Teatro alla Scala and had a drink of Veuve Clicquot champagne before taking their seats for *The Marriage of Figaro*. Charlie had not seen it before but she adored Mozart and knew the music well. After the performance they stopped at Café Trussardi for supper and reviewed the opera.

"I think I like the 'Sull' aria the best but it's very difficult not to think of the prison yard in *Shawshank Redemption*!" observed Daniel.

"My favourite is definitely Cherbuino's 'Voi che sapete'." said Charlie. "Do I need to?" she smiled.

* * *

Daniel drove them back to the Fortezza in the warmth of the Ferrari, insulated from the cold night air.

"I love operas with happy endings and the arias were sung beautifully. It has been such a lovely evening. I want it to last forever. Thank you so much for the dress, it made me feel a million dollars and the necklace is just perfect. You are spoiling me and I will not want to go back to Yorkshire."

"That's my plan. Tell me what love is," he said referring to the aria Charlie loved so much.

They lay on the bed together and Daniel held Charlie in his arms. He made no move to caress Charlie and she knew how difficult he found the physical side of things. The next few days were going to be very challenging as he completed his catharsis from Elizabeth's murder.

She was just so happy to be with him, lie next to him and feel a man next to her. The longing her body screamed for could wait for another day.

* * *

The next day was a crisp February morning with ice crystals glinting in the trees. They set off in the Ferrari for Verbier and vowed to come back to Fortezza Viscontea one day. They never did!

Daniel briefed Charlie as he drove towards the mountains.

"We are Mr and Mrs Day on a normal skiing holiday. We have been married for ten years. No children. You are a photographer writing a new book and I work in computers. We have not been to Verbier before but usually go to St Moritz every year. You can look up where we stay. In Verbier we are staying at a shared lodge with a group of unknown fellow skiers. The best place to hide is in a crowd, however tedious that is. Try not to talk much about us and ask lots of questions. People love talking about themselves. Try not to yawn too often."

"I didn't know you could ski?" queried Charlie.

"I can't. Snow is wet, cold and dangerous. I will always be too busy to ski because of meetings etc. This is a working holiday for me."

"Any questions so far?"

"What happens if it all goes wrong? How long will we get inside?"

"Don't even think about it. It will not happen. We have contingency plans in place if it goes off-piste, note the topicality. If it does get complicated it is important that you do exactly what I say quickly and efficiently, no matter how ridiculous it sounds. I would not have brought you here if there was the slightest risk of it going wrong. This is a civilised country with nice people. Apart from ten bankers that is."

"It's all very exciting!"

"Try and act normally. Be calm and relaxed. You are on holiday – just enjoy the ride."

They pulled into Verbania next to Lake Maggiore at the foot of the Alps. Daniel pulled out his iPhone, looked up an address, and drove into a business park. He drove around for a while and when he had located a deserted warehouse, pressed a key fob on the dashboard of the Ferrari. The roller shutter door squeaked its way skywards and he drove in. In the darkness at the back of the building was a Land Rover Discovery complete with skis on the roof rack.

"This is where we lose the Ferrari; we don't want to get it stuck up a mountain. I'll just transfer the bags."

"I love the Ferrari. It will get lonely in the dark all on its own."

"Don't worry we will get it back one day. I will put it on a trickle charger so it does not die whilst we are having fun." They drove out of the dark cavernous warehouse and into the bright sunlight. Daniel lowered the squeaky door and they headed for the mountains.

The journey through the Parco Nazionale della Val Grande took Charlie's breath away as they headed for the Rhône Valley on the Swiss side of the border. The alpine slopes rose majestically to the heavens and the snow-capped summits beckoned. Charlie insisted on stopping at Varzo to take some photographs but Daniel's mind was focussed on other things flooding his head.

They left the Rhône at Martigny and started the long switch back climb up to Verbier itself. Charlie was glad they mothballed the Ferrari in favour of the all-wheel drive of the reliable Land Rover. As they drove into Verbier town they passed endless huddles of multicoloured skiers, carrying snowboards, skis and broken legs. The wooden lodges nestled on the mountain sides, covered in festive snow and with après ski lights beckoning. They drove up the hill to the Alpine Estate with its luxurious, traditionally designed chalets, catering for every desire and delicacy one aspired to. Daniel had booked the best room, obviously, a master bedroom suite on the top floor with a private balcony, over-looking the sparkling town nestling in the surrounding wall of snow-dressed mountains. Charlie collapsed on the bed whilst Daniel scanned the room for any hidden bugs out of habit, and necessity.

"I am starving. Shall we go and get something to eat. What do you fancy – cheese, cheese or cheese?"

"Well I suppose we should eat as the locals do. I will go for the cheese!"

They went down to the communal eating area, bedecked with a vast array of local delicacies, including Raclette with cheese and Älpermagronen with cheese. Fortunately, the wine was cheese free and was actually very good being a Petite Arvine from Valais. There was a blazing log fire in the grate and a steady flow of young wealthy skiers arrived in chatty groups, to replenish the calories burnt off on the slopes. Some were quiet and reserved and others adrenaline junkies coming down from their Black Diamond exploits, but they seemed a happy lot and enjoying their winter break.

"Hi. This is my partner Jenny and I'm Shane, we are from Oklahoma, where are you guys from?"

Stunned silence as they had not discussed that. "We are from Devon, near Exeter," said Charlie creatively. "What line of work are you in?"

"We are into social media and designing apps for companies to sell their wares online. It's a big growth area in the States and Shane is brilliant at it." Jenny grinned at Shane adoringly and was clearly besotted with him.

"And how long have you guys been together?" asked Daniel.

"About three weeks now Shane isn't it? We are a match made in heaven. We just like all the same things and are very compatible in bed." Too much information thought Daniel and tried another tack. "When did you both learn to ski?"

"Yesterday!"

"That's great, so how is it going so far?"

"Our personal instructor, Hans, is amazing. He has trained all the great rappers in the US. He thinks we will be on the black runs by the end of our second week. He has got an amazing app on his phone which tells you which runs are powder and which are busy etcetera. It's cool. Wish I'd thought of that."

"So, have you found any good restaurants whilst you have been here?" asked Charlie hopefully.

"We went to La Channe last night and the cheese fondues were amazing. We love all the night life here. Lots of evening entertainment, live bands, beer on tap and a cool mosh pit."

"Sounds like Charlie's dream night out, we will have to call in later in the week," replied Daniel seriously.

Charlie choked on her wine.

"Well, we are off for an early night. Double Black Diamond tomorrow," said Daniel seriously.

"Wow you guys are cool. So, pleased to meet you. Maybe we could have a night out together."

"Have fun tomorrow with Hans!"

Charlie and Daniel got back to their room and collapsed on the bed laughing. "I will have to look mosh pit up on Google," said Daniel. "I think I feel old!"

"So, what are the plans for tomorrow?"

"I thought we would go sightseeing, so you can get some snowy landscape shots. It will also establish a good alibi. If we get the heli-ski up to Mont Fort, you can get fantastic views from up there. It's over 10,000 feet so you can see for miles and if it's a reasonably clear day, you will be able to see the Matterhorn and Mont Blanc. We could then hop across to Lac des Vaux which is a beautiful place to photograph. How does that sound for day one?"

"Brilliant. I can't wait. What are we doing next.?"

"Well, I have got to go out for a few hours and do some reconnaissance, so why don't you have a nice long hot relaxing bath, as it's been such a hectic day, and get an early night? I will try not to wake you when I get back."

"I suppose we are working! Please take care out there at night. It is dangerous."

"I'll be fine. Just checking out some stuff I did a couple of weeks ago, to make sure it is all where it is meant to be."

"When do the bankers arrive? I assume you know where they are staying?"

"Yes, all taken care of. Sebastian made them a chalet offer they could not resist. Tight bastards these bankers. It's nicely out of town and under a snow cornice higher up the mountain near the Savoleyres Lift, above Tzoumaz, so it should make my life easier – and their's terminal. The snow is pretty unstable up there and if I can fracture the weak snow layer under the sintered slab near the staunch-wall I should be able to cause an avalanche that looks like a natural seismic event. That's the plan anyway."

"It all sounds very technical. Where did you learn all this stuff?"

"Kindergarten!"

Daniel donned his waterproofs, kissed Charlie on the cheek and disappeared. It wasn't the evening Charlie was hoping for but she was getting used to Daniel's determination to revenge his wife's death in every quarter and was just glad to be near him. She had the long hot bath he suggested and felt sensual as she climbed into the huge bed but soon fell asleep and did not hear him return.

When she woke up he was still asleep and she watched him next to her and felt safe and secure. She slid quietly from under the eider duvet and took a quick shower washing her long auburn hair under the torrent of mountain fresh water. Charlie turned off the shower with the touch screen and turned to grab a towel. Daniel handed it to her smiling.

"How long have you been there?" she asked.

"Long enough," he replied, "to admire your beautiful body."

"Thank you, kind sir. Are you coming in?"

Daniel dropped the towel from around his waist and stepped in next to her, deliberately pressing his body against hers. The sensuality from the previous evening came flooding back. He put his hands around her back and drew her tightly against his muscular frame. The water cascaded over them and they kissed passionately. Charlie looked into his eyes and began to see a sparkle she had not seen before. Maybe their relationship was coming to fruition at last.

"We better hurry up if we are to catch the heli-ski." Evidently not yet!

"I want you Daniel."

"You can seduce me tonight," he smiled and grabbed a towel for her and one for himself.

"You're on!" Charlie laughed.

They got dressed and Charlie put on her new bright green ski suit. She checked her Billingham camera bag and put on her new snow goggles. Daniel's outfit was much more reserved but at least it wasn't camouflaged.

The helicopter pilot was much more professional than Maverick in New England, but less amusing for it. When he learnt Charlie was a professional photographer, he took a detour around the 'Four Valleys' so she could get some spectacular shots of the mountains from the air. She clicked away very happily for half an hour and then he dropped them off on top of Mont Fort, agreeing to pick them up around lunch time.

It was a beautiful clear sunny day to be on top of the world with the man you love. The never-ending sea of snow-capped mountains projected to the horizon in every direction. The valleys below, dived down in a sheer white multitude of acute angles, dotted with skiers that looked like coloured ants. They left slalom tracks as they sped to the base, only to gondola back up for another adrenaline descent.

Charlie stood in awe of the landscapes with Daniel's arm safely around her. She did not want to move; in case she woke up alone in her bed in the old stables.

"Are you going to do any work today?" joked Daniel after a few eternal minutes.

"It's so beautiful and peaceful up here, above the rest of the world scurrying around their daily lives. How can I possibly capture that with a simple camera?"

"Well you better have a try or we will not be able to afford the trip. Why don't you set your camera up on the timer and take a picture of us conquering the world?"

Charlie loved the idea and set the camera up with the circular polarising filter to reduce the glare from the snow and set the remote timer. Daniel stood in front of the camera so Charlie could get the focussing right and with the mountain ranges as a backdrop. She then came round to the front of the camera and stood next to Daniel who put his arm around her back and looked lovingly into her eyes. Charlie pressed the remote, hidden in her gloved hand and captured a photograph that would adorn her bedside table for the rest of her life.

She spent the next two hours recording the 360 degree-winter wonderland. A pair of golden eagles soared over Cleuson Lake in the valley below the Glacier du Mont Fort, and it reminded Daniel of the less spectacular red kites they had seen at Gouthwaite in Yorkshire.

The heli-ski arrived on schedule and lifted them off the mountain and flew them on the short trip to Lac de

Golden Eagle

Vaux. One of the highest lakes in the Alps at over 8000 feet, it was frozen over in February. Fed from melting snow on the sheer surrounding slopes each spring, the waters were always extremely cold but that did not stop young enthusiastic skiers diving in to impress their friends, probably after a night in the mosh pit.

"I think we better make a move?" asked the pilot who had kindly stayed on to eat his sandwiches whilst Charlie took some shots. "The forecast is for a big dump of snow tonight and we don't want to be caught in a white-out here."

"Thank you. That's good advice, and anyway my shots are fairly limited here at this time of year," agreed Charlie.

They quickly packed up Charlie's equipment and headed back to Verbier. It was a good call because even in the short flight to town the snow flurries had started to drift from the darkening skies. Daniel looked happy.

When they had left the helicopter, Charlie asked him what was so amusing.

"A big dump of snow was just what I needed to make the avalanche look more natural. Manna from heaven!"

"God must approve of your plan and decided to give you a hand!"

"Let's hope it all comes off OK. Shall we have a coffee in the lounge and a Swiss roll. Always wanted one in Switzerland."

They settled down on a huge sofa by a roaring log fire and enjoyed the cakes and coffee. They were soon joined by a party of residents that had abandoned the slopes, as the flurries turned into a blizzard.

"Good afternoon. We have been trying our hand at snowboarding today. Have you had a go yet?" asked a very polite German lady in impeccable English.

"Not yet," replied Charlie. "Is it good fun?"

"It was hilarious. We spent more time horizontal on our bottoms than standing up. It is much more difficult than skiing. Sorry, can I introduce my husband Franz and I am Rowena. We are from near Konstanz on Lake Constance in southern Germany. Are you from England?"

"Yes. This is our first visit to Verbier and we are hoping to go skiing for the first time tomorrow, if the snow is not too deep."

"I would not worry. They are very good at grooming the pistes here and the powder runs should be great fun. We will definitely ski tomorrow. We have been coming every February for over twenty years and we know all the slopes very well. As long as you stick to the main runs you will be fine. The off-pistes could be a bit tricky and you might start an avalanche!" she laughed.

"We wouldn't want to do that," said Daniel smiling. "Do you always stay in this lodge when you come?"

"Yes, we really like it here. We have tried others in the past but it is nice and quiet here and the facilities are excellent, so if you cannot ski for a day or two there are plenty of things to do. Franz is not as interested as me in skiing so he stays here some days whilst I go out with an instructor from the Ski Centre up the road. He is brilliant and knows all the slopes in great detail and never pushes you too far but does test your skills."

"Perhaps you could give us his number and we will see if he is available to go out with Charlie on the bunny slopes."

Charlie gave Daniel one of her playful punches on the arm, "Hey I am not that bad. At least I can manage a red run."

"Can you recommend a good restaurant where we could get a nice meal tonight?"

"It depends what you are looking for but we like La Cordee restaurant. It has an excellent French chef and they serve a superb menu for all tastes."

"That sounds right up our street thank you. Well, hope to see you around and we will let you know how we get on."

Daniel and Charlie went back up to their room for a rest before they went out for the meal. Daniel was on the phone most of the time, whilst Charlie had a shower and prepared a surprise for Daniel which she had promised him earlier.

"I have organised a ski instructor for you tomorrow from the place those nice Germans recommended and he will pick you up from the room at ten in the morning. I have got to disappear for the day on business but I will be here for dinner tomorrow night as usual!"

"Thank you darling, that's very thoughtful of you. Is he handsome?"

"Three-foot dwarf, I think! I am off for a shower too."

Whilst Daniel was in the shower Charlie put on some revealing sky-blue silk underwear that she had brought specially, hoping he would like it. She wore a warm white rollneck jumper and tweed button skirt, quite short and long brown leather boots which came up to her slim thighs. She completed her outfit with a full-length Holland and Cooper Marlborough trench coat in camel. When he came out of the shower his eyes lit up.

"Wow that will stun the whole of Verbier. They are only used to the regulation romper suits here!"

The falling snow had slackened a bit, but it was still deep and crisp and even in the streets, as they made their way to La Cordee. They were not disappointed on arrival. The restaurant had a warming ambiance and the staff were very knowledgeable from a culinary perspective. Daniel ordered a bottle of Clos de Tsampéhro. The waiter recommended the Rillette de fera du leman so they both ordered that for starters and went for the Noisette d'agneau en croûte d'herbes for the main course. Charlie was a bit worried about eating Swiss lamb when she reared thousands of prime English lambs at home, but Daniel pointed out that she was doing market research and therefore the whole trip was tax deductible. That appealed to Charlie's farming roots, as Dale's farmers never pay any tax unless they are due for a tax audit, in which case they declare a few pounds.

Charlie's thoughts kept drifting to her plans for Daniel later and she felt herself getting aroused by her thoughts.

"Another glass of wine?"

"Er. Yes please."

"You were miles away. What were you thinking?"

Charlie thought for a moment and decided to take the risk.

"You said I could seduce you tonight so I was making a plan."

"I thought you might have forgotten that?"

"No chance. I need you to want me my darling," said Charlie, suddenly aware that she was probably pushing her luck.

"I always want you; you know that. It's just…"

"Let's just enjoy being together. I love you and just want to be with you and please you."

"What are you wearing?"

"A white sweater and skirt."

"I know that. You know what I mean. I saw that glint in your eye."

"That's for you to find out later."

"Shall we skip the coffee," they both said at the same time and laughed.

When they got back to the lodge Daniel received a phone call and indicated for Charlie to carry on upstairs and he would be up shortly. She went up to the room, took off her coat and quickly removed her jumper and skirt. She then put the coat on again over her silk underwear to give him a surprise. Daniel came into the room smiling.

"Is everything OK?" asked Charlie.

"Yes, all fine. Just confirmation from Sebastian that the targets are in place and we are on schedule for tomorrow night."

"That's good, at least I will get one day's skiing!"

"I will stoke the fire up. Shall we have a glass of champagne to celebrate the plan so far."

"Sounds good to me."

"Well are you going to take your coat off – it's getting hot in here?" Daniel passed Charlie a glass and they toasted the plan. Charlie then slowly and deliberately put down her glass and started to undo the buttons on her coat from the top. Daniel's eyes took in the slow revelation of Charlie's lovely body clad only in tiny pieces of French silk.

He took her in his arms and gently kissed her neck. "You are incredibly beautiful Charlie. I love it that you want me so much."

"Please explore my body. I have been desperate for your touch since Hvar."

They kissed passionately and Daniel started to gently move his hands down her back, his fingers massaging every tiny muscle along her tense spine. She turned around and rested her hands on the mantle over the fire, her body glistening in the flickering light from the flaming logs. She was getting hotter and hotter, the flames and his hands teasing her body. He slid his fingers inside the flimsy silk covering her breasts, and delicately rolled the tips of her erect nipples between his fingers and thumbs. Charlie made one of the little moans he loved so much that indicated he was doing what she yearned.

"Please do that a little firmer. You are wonderful. I want you so much."

Daniel carefully followed her leads and her body became taut and she trembled with desire. His careful fingers found; and she cried out in ecstasy as her body melted in a cascade of sensuality. She turned around and collapsed into his arms.

"You are amazing, wonderful and a sensational lover my darling," whispered Charlie.

"I know," he smiled, with a hint of arrogance.

He scooped up her glistening body and lay next to her on the soft eider duvet. He stroked her damp hair from her brow and kissed her softly.

"I have never felt anything like that before," said Charlie looking into his eyes, "But I was meant to be seducing you!"

"I just want you to lie in my arms. We can worry about me another day."

Charlie kissed Daniel again and lay on his shoulder. Silently now, but sure another day would come with the passing of time.

* * *

When Charlie woke up the following morning Daniel had already left, so she had a lazy start, waiting for the ski instructor to collect her and take her up the lift to the first run. She was a little apprehensive as it had been a while since her last practice on the dry run back home and years since she had skied properly. She hoped he would be sympathetic to her trepidation.

At exactly ten o'clock there was a firm knock on the door.

"Good morning ma'am. You look amazing!"

"Max! what are you doing here? …….. No, don't bother to answer that. This is a nice surprise. I had no idea you were in Verbier. Can you ski?"

"Greek national champion. Well I would be if it snowed enough. Right let's go. I've got the skis outside."

Charlie and Max had a fabulous day laughing and joking on the slopes. Charlie fell over on some particularly bumpy moguls. Twice. Max was trying to show off with a jump turn on some steep terrain and likewise ended up in an undignified heap. They found some virgin powder snow and completed a wobbly figure eight and photographed it on Charlie's iPhone for posterity. After spending most of the day on the red runs accessed from the Médran gondola, they ventured higher, on the more difficult black runs, and as Charlie's confidence grew, they managed a very fast simulated downhill which pushed her adrenalin into overdrive.

"That was fantastic fun Max, I am so glad you just happened to be passing!"

"My pleasure ma'am. I know it's colonial, but I enjoy saying it to you because you are such a beautiful English lady."

"You are incorrigible," admonished Charlie grinning.

"I know, but you like it really. Right, I will walk you back to within a block of your chalet and then disappear. We had better not be seen together this evening. Daniel should be back just after seven, so get packed and ready to run."

"Sounds exciting."

"It won't be if they catch you. It's very cold in Swiss gaols! See you around."

* * *

At seven o'clock that evening Daniel checked the camera traps at the Swiss banker's chalet, to confirm they were all at home and enjoying their après ski. He drove the Land Rover back into Verbier and pulled up in a random hotel car park and waited for a car to leave. Two couples came out of the hotel laughing and enjoying the prospect of a fun evening on the town. It was about to get more fun than they anticipated. Daniel pressed the GPRS detonator on his phone to ignite the gas/oxygen cylinders he had positioned to start the avalanche. A huge rumble could be heard from the valley above Verbier as the snow gathered pace down the mountainside engulfing the banker's chalet; terminally. He walked casually passed the couple's pickup and threw the phone into the back amongst the ski boots and salopettes. The pickup set off in the direction of Riddes, which was a lucky break, as it would be a good distraction if the phone was tracked. It was. And the two couples had a very interesting evening at Verbier police station.

As Daniel drove back to meet Charlie, the streets filled with skiers flooding out of the chalets and bars to see what was happening. There was much pointing and mobile phone flashing as they observed the spectacle. Emergency vehicles appeared from everywhere with lights colourfully illuminating the snow-covered urban sprawl. Sirens screamed to add to the chaos and a helicopter droned overhead with search lights blazing.

When Daniel got back to the room, Charlie had packed the bags ready to leave.

Charlie put her arms around Daniel and kissed him.

"What happened to the bankers. Did the plan work?"

"Let's just say their assets are frozen. I am going to have to leave on my own I am afraid; it's got too dangerous for you to come with me."

"I will need to come and look after you then," smiled Charlie.

"If you insist, but you will have to do exactly what I tell you and don't argue!"

"Everything is packed ready."

"Great. Unzip your ski suit and take your bra off."

"Why?"

"You are arguing already, and we are not out the door yet!"

"OK. OK. Whatever."

They exited the chalet via a side door and jumped into the Land Rover.

"Put your gloves on and grab a phone out of the box on the back seat whilst I set the satnav."

"There are about ten phones in here, which one?"

"Any of them. Just press send and throw it out the window into that pile of snow, so they can't track it."

"You get through a lot of phones in this job."

"It's OK. I have got shares in Vodaphone."

They drove slowly through the thronging streets, with police Land Cruisers everywhere. They headed to the south of town and were doing fine until they hit a roadblock manned by two large policemen with H&K submachine guns.

"Just relax and smile. We are going to a friend's party in Sarreyer. Undo your zip."

Charlie obliged.

"A little more."

Charlie grinned and put on her irresistible seductive pose.

Daniel rolled down the window on both sides of the car. The policeman on Charlie's side was a woman!

"Good evening sir. Can I ask where you are going this evening?" asked the male policeman.

"We are off to a party in Sarreyer with some skiing friends from England. What's going on?"

"There has been a serious avalanche up the valley and we think several people in a chalet might have been killed. It looks like the avalanche might have been started deliberately."

"God that's awful. This is a holiday resort. Is it some sort of terrorist thing?"

"We have no idea, but we are just checking for suspicious people."

The lady policeman could not take her eyes off Charlie's cleavage. "You look as though you are in for an exciting evening dear. Have fun."

With that, they were waved on their way.

"Powerful distraction a lovely cleavage. I think she fancied you!" said Daniel.

"I wouldn't want to be handcuffed in her prison!" confided Charlie, with a smile.

They picked up the old Route du Soleil which winds its way down to Sarreyer. Daniel put his foot down and the tyres squealed as they took the bends on the switchback road. Just before the village, Daniel pulled onto a track into the forest out of sight. Two minutes later a rusty Mercedes pulled up next to them. It was Max.

"OK Charlie grab the bags. This is where we swap cars," instructed Daniel.

Daniel and Max had a brief discussion. Max was going to hide the Land Rover in a barn, high up near a remote farm. The farmer would strip the car and sell the parts for his trouble.

"Is Dimitri on his way?" asked Daniel.

"All sorted. He will be waiting for you, but he can only be there for five minutes, so don't stop for tea… or anything else," he said, looking at Charlie's cleavage.

"Oops sorry!" said Charlie, rezipping to restore her modesty.

"Oh, don't apologise. I like a nice landscape," he laughed.

Daniel and Max shook hands, as civilised gentlemen always do, and wished each other well.

The rusty Merc was not a good choice for narrow country roads. It rolled like a whale on the corners, left a fog of semi-digested diesel, and creaked like Charlie's staircase. But no one was looking for an old farmer's car. They hoped. They passed by Morgnes and picked up the Route de Mauvoisin. The headlights flashed along the trees picking out the odd deer risking its life on the road, nearly as much as them. Daniel had his foot hard down. One of the phones rang.

"Can you answer that? Do not say anything – just listen," said Daniel calmly.

"It says the Swiss Airforce have put up a Tiger II scrambled from Payerne and its coordinates are crossing us at Fionnay."

"Shit. Take the card out of the phone and throw it into the forest. Get another phone and press send. When it's answered by a woman just say 'Put up the drones'."

"I know, and then take out card etcetera. I am getting the hang of this. What do the drones do?"

"They are just to confuse the air traffic control and give them something else to think about, in the north. We have also leaked some info to the DW News Channel and they will not be able to resist putting up their helicopter camera, which will add to the mix."

"Where are we heading?"

"That depends on the Tiger II but hopefully a reservoir."

Just before the intersection point near Fionnay, they turned off the road into the forest and turned off the lights. Daniel opened the window and listened. Nothing. They waited five minutes for the Swiss Airforce Tiger. But still nothing.

"Let's hope the drones worked." Daniel restarted the Merc and set off at even greater speed to make up for lost time.

The roads got worse and the car cried in pain as it made life-threatening turns that were not in the manual. They passed through the village of Mauvoisin leaving a cloud of dust and fumes and descended the track down to the dam of Le Lac de Mauvoisin. The concrete radius arch of the dam fell away 850 feet below them, and in front of them, floating peacefully on the water, was a de Havilland Otter Floatplane with a handsome pilot standing on one of the floats.

"Privyet! You are late again Mr Daniel. Your car is a heap of shit. Can't you afford a decent one!"

"Hi Dimitri. Is this the eight-thirty to Cavallo?" joked Daniel.

"Do you have a ticket?"

"Just load the bags, you Russian idiot, and let's get out of here."

"And who is the beautiful lady, Mr Daniel?"

"This is my boss, Charlie – so watch out. Have we got everything before I ditch the car?"

"Yes all in." Dimitri climbed into the pilot's seat and started flicking switches.

"No!" exclaimed Charlie. "We have forgotten my dress in the boot."

"I will buy you another one. Let's go!" retorted Daniel.

"No, that one is special I am not going without it."

"For Christ's sake we will probably get killed."

"He never understood women. Now, Russian men are much more attentive to ladies," smiled Dimitri.

Daniel retrieved the dress, carefully folded in the hanging bag Charlie had stolen from the chalet. He took the handbrake off the Merc and pushed it down the ramp into the deep cold waters of the lake. It gurgled and hissed as it sank to a deserved burial at sea. Dimitri started the plane and skimmed along the lake at ever increasing knots until he could rotate and head skywards.

"Strap yourselves well down. It will get a little bumpy in between these mountains. I need to stay as low as possible to avoid being tracked. I have no satnav or flight recorders so you will have to navigate Daniel. Try and avoid the mountains if you can. Is your dress creased Charlie?"

"Dimitri, you are a womanising Russian idiot. Just fly the bloody plane."

"Where is Cavallo?" asked Charlie nervously.

"It is a very nice place for a holiday," proffered Dimitri.

It was bumpy – very, but Daniel managed to navigate them out of the Alps and hug the hills north of Turin. They then cut down to cross the coast south of Savona to avoid the flight path into Nice Cote d'Azure Airport. Once over the Med, Dimitri could fly very low over the sea to avoid detection. They flew down the east side of Corsica and came into land on the sea, just off the southwest tip of Cavallo, a small island almost deserted at that time of year.

"What happens now?" asked Charlie, slightly nervously.

"We will wait here till daybreak and see if there is any noise about us on the airwaves. Dimitri will monitor the radio and look out for any unusual aircraft activity."

"There are some very good homemade prisuttu sandwiches in the bag behind the back seat and a bottle of Vermentino di Gallura from Sardinia. I like to enjoy the local produce when I am visiting nice places," bragged Dimitri with a wink to Charlie.

"That's very thoughtful of you Dimitri and have you organised a band for us to dance afterwards?" asked Daniel.

"I risk my life for you, fly you through the dangerous mountains and avoid military jets covered in missiles and all I get is criticised."

"I think you are wonderful Dimitri and very thoughtful of you to bring the sandwiches. I am sure we will all enjoy them, won't we Daniel?" said Charlie firmly.

"Don't encourage him or he will start rambling on about his royal ancestors who ran Russia before the Bolsheviks took over."

"I am very pleased you mentioned my glorious ancestors Daniel…"

"Dimitri. Shut up and listen to your bloody radio!"

It was a cold night but by dawn there was still no sign of anybody looking for them. Daniel decided to take a risk and fly straight to Avignon Caumont, a private airport near to the ancient walled city. Dimitri checked the plane over and fired her up.

"Book a landing slot, Dimitri and say you have picked up some wealthy people from a broken-down yacht in Corsica and hopefully we will avoid customs."

Daniel made a couple of calls on a new phone and threw it in the sea.

"You forgot to take the card out," reprimanded Charlie.

"It's OK the fish like the chips," joked Daniel.

"Oh, very funny Mr Daniel. You must be tired… I know, just fly the bloody plane!"

The skies were clear and the flight up to Avignon was only a couple of hours. Charlie tried to make herself look more like a wealthy person, instead of a skier on the run, which was difficult in the back of an Otter with no mirror. She managed a miraculous transition, which left Dimitri spellbound. They landed safely at Avignon and were met by a very helpful young lady who helped them into the VIP area of the small terminal building. Dimitri waved goodbye and disappeared into the sky, not to be seen again for over a year, but it was that sort of business.

"Are you on holiday?" asked the nice young lady.

"Yes, we are on honeymoon and staying at the Hotel d'Europe for a few days," said Daniel casually.

"That's very romantic. I hope you have a very happy stay in our lovely city. Your car is waiting outside with key in the glove pocket. Can I help you with the bags?"

"That's very kind of you but we will be fine. Thank you so much for your help."

They walked out into the sunshine and there, waiting in the VIP car park, was the Ferrari they had left in the dark warehouse in Verbania. Charlie was lost for words for once. Well, almost.

"How did the car find its way out of the warehouse and drive itself to Avignon when we only knew we were coming here two hours ago?"

"I know. I was wondering that too," replied Daniel. "Well jump in – it's your car, you can drive."

"Look, it's a beautiful car and I love it but you can't give me a present worth half a million pounds plus. I thought you were joking in Italy."

"I never joke about Ferraris. Enzo would not be pleased."

"Who is Enzo?" Charlie looked quizzically at Daniel, who was laughing. "I know. Just drive the bloody thing!"

The V12 engine purred into life and growled louder as they headed for the most romantic city in Provence.

CHAPTER NINE

Romantic Landscapes –
The Loire Valley – France

They drove through the arched stone city wall, as a million travellers had done before them, and pulled up at the large iron gates that protected the Provencal courtyard with trees and climbers bathed in winter sunshine. Named on the insistence of General Bonaparte, Hotel d' Europe has a very long history and boasts one of the most sophisticated guest lists of anywhere in the world, but Charlie would be fascinated by that later. Both exhausted by the adrenalin, the stress and the travelling, all they wanted to do was collapse and sleep.

Charlie woke up a few hours later and tried to drag her location from the confusion of images that filled her mind. There was no sign of Daniel but he had obviously had a shower, from the chaos left in the bathroom. She wasn't sure if she was a wife, a mistress or a deserted partner, but not one for musing for long, she showered and did the wifely thing and tidied up the manly mess. She had no idea what to wear, where they were going or when, or even if he would return. She pulled on a pair of denims and her favourite Ryeland wool jumper and ventured out onto the roof garden. The view across the weathered ochre roof tiles to the Palais des Papes, topped with a gold statue, was stunning in the low, early-evening sunshine. The ancient narrow streets below were empty, apart from the occasional cyclists pedalling their undergraduate, basketed transport to their destinations, somewhere in the historic maze.

"I don't normally expect to be cleaned up after," said a voice behind her. "I just wanted to let you sleep." Daniel put his arms around Charlie's slim waist from behind and kissed her long auburn hair that shone iridescently in the evening light. "Are you feeling OK now you've had a good sleep?"

"Much better thank you. Have you had any feedback on whether we were successful?"

"Yes. I have just been talking to Sebastian and all the newsfeeds are concentrating on why terrorists would pick a group of apparently successful bankers. He has got some of his more dubious friends to use social media to implicate them in financing international criminal groups, including the illegal transport of rhino horn and ivory to China. He will leak our evidence through third parties and the Swiss police will not want to get involved. With a bit of luck, it will all run into the sand, or rather snow drifts, over the next few weeks."

"You are a genius and I love you."

"I think we were lucky and although I take the micky out of him, Dimitri did a fantastic job risking his life for us, so we owe him one. Now what do you want to do tonight?"

"A quiet little restaurant somewhere would be great. Just you and me and no gorillas."

"You are starting to sound like Anne Marie! You had better wrap up warm – it's pretty chilly out there."

Charlie changed into a rollneck alpaca top, which looked more suitable for dinner and put on her trench coat, which now had scintillating memories for both of them. Daniel smiled approvingly. They came down in the lift, past the incongruous jewel encrusted crocodile in reception and headed out onto the cobbled streets. Daniel took Charlie's hand, as lovers often do, and she felt his strength surround her with safety. She wondered if he had the H&K in his belt but decided not to check. They walked through the narrow, deserted streets where only local artisans were heading for their sandstone houses. Charlie stopped occasionally to look in the windows of the sophisticated dress boutiques not found in England, with the possible exception of Cheltenham, where she liked to wander around after the Gold Cup. Daniel pretended to be interested and make positive noises about the ones she liked, as a gentleman would. He offered to bring her shopping the next day to buy a trouser suit that she particularly liked. He would have rather been wrestling the Khmer Rouge... but anything for a beautiful lady.

"We're looking for the Fou de Fafa on the Rue des Trois Faucons which is somewhere down this end of town behind the Musée Angladon. I could look it up on my phone but that seems too much like work somehow," Daniel suggested.

After walking round for five minutes he gave in to Google maps. They were literally only a few yards from the tiny restaurant which is one of the best in France.

They were welcomed warmly by the wife, who runs the front of house, and shown to an immaculately laid table with crystal and flutes glinting in the candlelight.

"Could we have a bottle of the Veuve Pelletier champagne please?"

"Of course. Have you been to Avignon before?" asked the wife.

"No. This is our first visit. We are on honeymoon and are touring around France," said Daniel obviously enjoying extending the cover story. Charlie smiled approvingly.

"I will leave you with the menu whilst I get the champagne. The duck breast with raspberry and orange is exceptional tonight. We purchase the duck from a local farmer and he has never let us down." And she disappeared into her husband's domain.

"She speaks very good English. This place has a really nice ambiance with its original yellow stone walls and oak beams. How do you always manage to find such unique places for us to eat?"

"Just luck I guess," smiled Daniel.

With the champagne served, they caressed their flutes and went with the owner's recommendation. They talked about the estate in Yorkshire and Charlie's plans to expand the forestry with more diverse species of trees and how they might encourage more animals and birds to make it their home. The red squirrels project had been a big success by increasing numbers, whilst generating extra income from photographers wanting to capture the perfect shots in the wild. The conversation naturally drifted to Africa and Daniel's conservation projects for white rhinos and mountain gorillas.

"How do you manage to run the projects when you are always somewhere you shouldn't be and incommunicado half the time?"

"The secret is to have people who are younger and cleverer than you on the project. Consultants are a waste of time. You need enthusiastic and passionate young people who will take risks, make mistakes but succeed through sheer determination to make things better. I would love for you to meet them sometime."

"There is nothing I would rather do than go to Africa with you. I don't know what it is about Africa but it's like a genetic magnet that makes you yearn to be there. Maybe it's because it is the birthplace of mankind or because of Karen Blixen, who knows, but to go with you would be amazing and meet your team. I am sure it would open up new horizons for me."

"I thought you might be worried about going, with Elizabeth's death and all my emotional complexities entwined with the Tsavo landscape?"

"I feel that it's part of me too, now." She paused and ran her finger around the edge of her glass. She took a sip and looked intently at Daniel. "I can't explain but I love you and with love comes mutual happiness and pain. I understand now why you have sought to do what you have done and I am part of the retribution. I need to help you complete the elimination of these people because, in reality, nobody else will and they are vermin of the world and need to be exterminated like rats, to make it a better place for our children's children."

Daniel covered her hand with his and a tear trickled down his cheek. "You are an amazing person Charlie.

You have changed my life from anger and destruction to a glimmering light at the end of a very dark tunnel. I have just one more quantum of revenge to expedite before I can feel total solace."

"The third Somali?"

"We think we know his location and I am due to travel to Africa in April for my biannual visit, so I am going to track him down and complete the task. If you would like to meet me in Tsavo, I can show you around and you can get that fancy new camera of yours out."

"Are you sure you want me to come – I will understand if you feel it's too difficult for you."

"Yes, I definitely want you to come and meet everyone. You will enjoy their company and their wicked sense of humour. Anyway, we need to spend more time together when we are not on the run!"

Charlie got up and gave Daniel a big hug. "I can't wait. It will be fantastic to see Africa together."

"Sorry to interrupt. Any desserts?" interjected the wife politely.

"Can we have a selection of the sorbets please and two spoons so we can share it. You speak very good English," said Charlie.

"That's probably because I am! My husband is French and we have lived in France for a long time. We own and run this place on our own. Visitors seem to come back every year so we must be doing something right."

"Well, we have had a lovely evening and the food has been exceptional. Please pass on our compliments on to your husband. We will definitely come back one day."

They wandered back in the cold night air, where the occasional tumble of partygoers spilled onto the otherwise silent streets from candlelit eateries. With Daniel's arm around her waist, Charlie felt the happiest she could ever remember. They stopped to look up at the chiming clock in the Place de l'Horloge and kissed passionately as the sound resonated around them.

* * *

Waking early the next day, they decided to have breakfast in a tiny patisserie they had passed the previous evening near to the hotel. They sat outside in the early morning sun, muffled against the chilled air. The croissants were, well, French – as good as it gets – and the hot café au lait was perfect for the cool nonchalance of café culture. They watched the world steadily increase momentum as the inhabitants went about their daily chores. Others walked their canine loved ones on designer leather leads.

"Let's go shopping!" said Daniel enthusiastically.

"I love you. I promise I will be quick."

They couldn't find the shop with the trouser suit, even though they could both navigate around the world. Such is the maze of Avignon. But there were plenty of other miniature Galerie to explore and Charlie slowly amassed a growing bulge of brightly coloured carrier bags containing the latest in Parisian style.

"How can the French and Italians create such sophisticated casual clothes when we have the same cloths and materials?"

"I am not party to such complex questions apart from how are we going to fit this lot into a Ferrari 812 GTS Spider?"

"We can ditch the ski suit and salopettes. I am definitely not going to Verbier again. The avalanches are too unpredictable!" laughed Charlie.

"Time for culture," said Daniel trying to terminate the shopping. "Let's drop this fashion mountain off at the hotel and go and have an alfresco lunch outside the Palais des Papes. Something to do with popes falling out; not that religious people ever disagree about anything or bear grudges for thousands of years and then murder each other. But it's worth a look!"

"Anything but shopping I think?"

"You could be right."

They found an empty sun-shaded table on the cobbled square outside the Palace. The citadel, with castellated walls, is flanked by ten large square stone towers which are buttressed by huge depressed arches 50m high, supporting the machicolations.

"You've got to be impressed with that, considering they didn't have a JCB when they built it," admired Daniel.

They decided to give the guided tour a miss, an easy decision, in favour of an unfinished bridge made famous in every English village school, including Masham. They climbed high up to the Rocher des Doms, the Palace's vertiginous gardens, so Charlie could take some panoramic landscape shots of the Rhone with the half-finished Pont Saint Bénézet, looking strangely lost.

'Sur le pont d'Avignon' is in every child's repertoire of favourite songs and perhaps the only French one they will ever know. The bridge was never finished because the fierce river Rhône, that floods under its magnificent arches, frequently swept away the foundations. They kissed standing at the termination of the bridge midstream. Charlie also took some photos, from the Saint-Nicholas Chapel which sits uniquely on the bridge, of the river sweeping gracefully down towards the flamingo'd Camargue.

They walked back over the wooden drawbridge with its ancient hand-forged chains and down through the narrow streets back to the Hotel, stopping only to buy a huge Marat d'Avignon tablecloth with a typical blue and yellow design, for Mummy's pine table in the kitchen. Charlie thought the bright blues and yellows would go well with the kitchen curtains.

"I think we will need a trailer," smiled Daniel.

They walked into reception passing the crocodile which looked ominously hungry, so they decided to eat in town. A small pizza restaurant nearby was full of Avignonians which Charlie decided was a good sign and they took a table tucked away in a secluded corner. Daniel ordered a bottle of Palette rose wine from Château Simone, to go with the French bread pizzas topped with caramelised onions, anchovies and black niçoise olives.

"Where are we going next?" enquired Charlie sipping the dry rosé.

"Where would you like to go?"

"I have never really seen much of France apart from the Alps and Versailles on school trips."

"I have always been intrigued by Versailles. What's it really like? It seems like a tourist playground but some of the photographs of it look stunning," asked Daniel in a slightly strange way, which Charlie would understand later.

"I suppose it is iconic and yes, it is always swamped in camera-hugging Chinese but it is so thought-provoking.

All the artisan workmanship that went into building it, its place in the history of France, and the sheer culture is overwhelming. I think one just has to go with an open mind, erase the grockles from your vision and see the pure elegance of the place. If we are crossing from Le Havre we could call in for a couple of hours because it's on the west side of Paris and not far off the route."

"I don't want to drag you round somewhere you have been before."

"You won't be. I would love to go again and anyway it will be different going round with you rather than with a gaggle of giggling teenage girls more interested in the lascivious paintings."

"It's a deal then, but you get to choose where we go tomorrow," offered Daniel.

"I have been having a sneaky look on the internet because I have never seen one of the great châteaux in real life, so could we head up to the Loire valley and stay there for a night or two and maybe visit a couple?"

"Never seen a château either. Have you sneakily found one you fancy?"

"Sneakily enough, how about Château Villandry? It's near Tours and then there is another one which spans the River Cher called Chenonceau which looks amazingly beautiful. We could stay in Tours and then go up to Versailles the next day?"

"Sounds a plan. I don't suppose you have a hotel in mind?"

"I've already booked us into Les Hauts de Loire at Onzain for two nights. Sneakily."

"How did you know I would agree to your impetuosity?"

"I still have my blue underwear in my bag."

"Well, if you put it that way, how could a gentleman say no! And actually, if we are going that way, I have always wanted to see the Chaîne des Puys at Clermont-Ferrand."

"And what might I ask is that, or them?"

"You will have to wait and see; but bring your camera."

"It's a deal. What are we having for pudding? I fancy les trois sorbets."

"I'll steal some of yours again."

Their breath condensed in minor clouds on the cold night air as they emerged into the empty streets. Daniel put his arm around Charlie's shoulder and they walked briskly along the cobbles passed the trouser-suit shop, which Daniel recognised, so he distracted Charlie with a hug. One day's shopping was enough for this millennium he mused.

* * *

The next morning, they added the hotel to their 'we must return' list, loaded the Ferrari with the skill of weaverbirds and headed for the Puys. The crocodile still looked hungry.

Having extracted themselves from the city walls, the Ferrari purred along the open road with the lovers immersed in their leathered cocoon and Mozart's Flute and Harp Concerto competing for the aural pleasure. As the road cleared of traffic, Charlie gently squeezed her right foot on the titanium pedal and the Ferrari overtook Mozart.

Orange, Montélimar, Valence, Lyon. The car ate up the miles in glorious comfort and power. They stopped briefly near Thiers, so Charlie could take some photographs of the Livradois-Forez for her French collection and arrived in Orcines at lunchtime. They stopped for fuel at the Ferrari's favourite filling station – Ferraris like filling stations, visiting them frequently. Charlie dashed in and paid, bought some baguettes and cheese from the boulangerie and a bottle of cidre for lunch.

They climbed to the top of Puy Pariou and sat down on the path circling the rim to eat lunch.

"Wow. A volcano! In France! That's cool," approved Charlie.

"It wasn't thirty-five million years ago when it erupted."

"I knew it would be something to do with explosions, as you were so fascinated by it"

Daniel tickled Charlie's ribs and she dropped her baguette.

"There is actually a whole chain of them across the centre of France which were created when the West European Rift was formed."

"How do you know all this stuff?"

"Misspent youth, I guess. Anything that that blew up was magic. Are you going to take some photos then?"

"As soon as I have finished my gritty baguette!"

After filling her memory card with the joys of a misspent youth they walked back to the car.

They took the scenic route through the Parc de la Brenne with its thousand bird-specked lakes and murky ponds with unphotogenic fish of every scale. The roar of the Ferrari probably did not amuse the ornithologists secreted in their drab hides, awaiting the rarest little brown bird to condescend to turn up for a fleeting moment. But the environmental assault was transient.

They turned into the forest near Onzain and drove up to the ivy-draped hunting lodge, squirrelled away deep amongst the mature deciduous trees. Les Hauts de Loire is an elegant country hotel, originally the relais de chasse for the Château d'Onzain, with a two-star Michelin restaurant. Charlie's sort of place thought Daniel.

The suite was enormous and sumptuously decorated. The furniture classical and the freshly cut flowers considerate.

"Shall we dress up for dinner, so I can try on some of the clothes we bought in Avignon?"

"Sounds a wonderful idea. You have one of their relaxing herbal baths for an hour and I will catch up on some work stuff. I will book a table for half seven."

Charlie emerged from the bathroom with a pure white towel on her head and the customary white bathrobe. She crept up behind Daniel who was engrossed in his laptop. She kissed his hair and put her arms around his broad shoulders.

"Hi. Those herbs smell nice. Do you feel relaxed, it has been a hectic, few days?"

"Wonderful thank you. You go and get your shower and let me get dressed into my new clothes."

Daniel came out of the shower with a towel around his waist. Charlie could not help secretly admiring his suntanned body with the scars now barely visible from the South American sortie. Charlie had put on her new turquoise satin blouse and white flared trousers. She was just putting in her favourite long gold earrings and wrapping the bracelet that Daniel had given her at the first Christmas in Masham, around her slim wrist, when he kissed her neck.

"You look lovely my darling. I hope you have my favourite blue underwear on?" he smiled hopefully.

"That's for you to find out later," she said with a grin.

The restaurant sparkled with crystal glasses and the finest silver cutlery. The antique French furniture had a wonderful patina and the oak-beamed ceiling had viewed the exquisite meals gracing the tables for centuries.

They started the meal with lobster flan and marine plankton, mainly because neither of them had eaten plankton before. It beautifully complimented the flan and fully justified the international reputation of the chef. They laughed and joked about the volcanoes, crocodiles and a certain heroic Mercedes car sleeping silently at the bottom of the lake. Charlie could see Daniel occasionally looking at the top two buttons casually undone on her blouse, an accident of course. Male hormones are designed to naturally tune a man's eyes into these things, and no matter how hard they try, the intrigue intensifies. She leant forwards so the gap increased slightly, smiled and caressed glasses filled with the Sancerre from the family estate of Domaine du Pré Semelé.

"Here's to a sunny day tomorrow to visit your châteaux," toasted Daniel. "I can't wait to see Chenonceau. It just looks amazing spanning the Cher."

They went for the guinea fowl with Touraine truffles as the main course and another bottle of the Sancerre. The guinea fowl was cooked to perfection and the roasted parsley was delicately structured to create a balanced plate. As the wine flowed and the conversation continued with passion, Daniel's hand covered Charlie's, which she had casually placed on the table. She turned her palm upwards and he caressed the palm with his index finger which made Charlie's tummy tighten. She knew what that meant.

"Shall we skip pudding?" she proposed.

"That sounds an excellent idea." With that, they thanked the attentive waiter and walked along the wide corridor with nameless portraits, by unknown artists, long resting peacefully in forgotten graves. Daniel closed the door behind them and took Charlie in is arms and kissed her gently on her open lips. Their tongues entwined and she wrapped her thighs around his waist. The passion intensified and the kissing become more sensual. Daniel sat Charlie on the wide raised end of the blue velvet chaise longue by the window. He fumbled with the satin buttons on her blouse and Charlie helped him with the last two. He pulled the satin from her belt to reveal her naked breasts already firm with desire for him. Charlie had decided he would like that. He did.

"You have the most beautiful body my darling. I want to kiss you all over." Daniel teased her earlobes with his tongue and kissed her neck gently. He gave her little teasing kisses down the centre of her chest. Charlie leant back and his lips found her erect nipples which he teased with the tip of his tongue. Charlie was losing control and let out one of her little moans. He followed the track down to her belt which he released and she could feel the leather sliding around her waist through the keepers. That stimulated her even more with anticipation and another catch of breath. Daniel carefully undid the trouser buttons and he lifted her so they slid to the floor. He covered her whole body with a thousand small kisses and teasing touches. Her body was taut with desire and he lowered her back onto the chair and orchestrated her crescendo of pleasure.

"You are wonderful to me," whispered Charlie, hardly able to speak.

"I know," said Daniel smiling. He pulled Charlie back up onto the end of the chaise longue, scooped her up in his arms and gently lay her on the bed. He lay down next to her and she rested her head on his shoulder.

"I want you so much my love. Is there anything I can do to make you want me?"

"Of course, I want you. Every time I look at you, touch you, smell your perfume next to me, my whole body aches for you. It's just my stupid brain will not let go. Please be patient with me, it will sort itself out."

"I know. There's no rush. I will wait forever for you."

* * *

They woke up the next morning with the sun's rays burning through the French windows. Daniel gave Charlie a quick peck on the cheek and looked out of the window.

"It's going to be a lovely day to be alive. Let's go châteaux hunting."

Charlie threw a pillow at him.

It was a beautiful morning, more like Spring, as Charlie wound the Ferrari up, down the north bank of the Loire River, towards the city of Tours, with its enormous Saint-Gatien Cathedral. Turning over the river and along the narrow, cobbled streets, lined by half-timbered houses, which echoed the music of the Ferrari exhausts, they made for Savonnières and then for Château de Villandry itself.

They parked the car and entered the gardens to the châteaux. Although it was winter, the structure of the Renaissance gardens massively impressed Charlie. She really appreciated all the toil and sweat that had gone into their construction because she had had to help her mother weed their humble vegetable plot back at the Hall when she was younger.

"Imagine weeding this lot!" exclaimed Daniel. "It must take weeks to trim all those hedges and when you get to the end you would have to start again."

"I think they might have a gardener or twenty."

"Capability Brown had the right idea. Lay it all to grass and let the deer do the work. Your father has worked that one out!"

"Oh, come on, you have to admit it looks spectacular and people come from all over the world to see it."

"I wonder if they have a Boxing Day flush?"

"You are impossible. Hold my hand and behave!"

They wandered around the formal pathways and Daniel mellowed as he pondered the organisation and architectural design required to construct such a masterpiece.

"The planning and execution of creating something like this must have been phenomenal without modern computerised surveying techniques. It always amazes me how they created these old buildings and castles with primitive tools and paper drawings. Seriously, I actually think it is really impressive how these structures survive all the wars and weather. I know they evolve and change with the times but they are still here many generations on. I think you are teaching me to absorb some culture. It's a miracle!"

"You are cultured, you like Mozart."

"I know but he was a genius. Let's have a coffee from that little shop over there."

They sat on a wooden bench and drank their coffees in the bright sunshine, absorbing the beauty of the garden and watching the little brown birds enjoying the visitors' croissant crumbs. They had become comfortable with each other's company and conversation was superfluous. They walked around the perimeter of the château but decided, as with the Pope's Palace at Avignon, to give the inside a miss. They decided that they were outside people and not curtain and carpet cultured. Charlie was pleased to have seen Villandry but probably would not rush to return. She would however tell her mother all about the magnificent potager gardens and a maternal visit would inevitably follow.

Daniel was much more interested in the Château de Chenonceau when they arrived, because not only is it built across a river, the Cher, but it had been blown up. Twice. Once by the Germans in 1940 because the French were using it to escape the Nazi occupied zone and once by the Allies because the Germans had moved in. It was now evidently owned by the Menier family, of chocolate fame, which may explain its chocolate box appearance.

Chateau Chenonceau

"At least they finished this one," observed Daniel.

"Go on then," said Charlie, humouring him.

"Well, the bridge in Avignon was only half built after hundreds of years and it only had a church plonked on top as an afterthought. Did you know that some of the statues from here were sold off to Versailles in 1720?" noted Daniel reading a noticeboard for tourists.

"We better go and see them tomorrow then to make sure they are looking after them properly," laughed Charlie, kissing him on the cheek and putting her arm around his waist. "Ferrari time!"

Charlie let Daniel drive to restore his interest in life and made a mental note to visit future châteaux with her mother.

"I really like your new car. It makes beautiful music."

Charlie did not know what the speed limit was but it was a lot slower than they were going.

* * *

The next morning, they headed north to Le Havre, via Versailles as planned. As they walked through the gilded gates of the palace, Daniel was unusually quiet. He held Charlie's hand – tightly – as they walked along the avenues and immaculate pathways, around Tuby's world famous fountain with Apollo bursting forth from the water in gilded elegance, and amongst the parterres and sculpted groves. The occasional tear, filled Daniel's eyes and touched his cheeks, before falling into the dust on the yellow gravel pathway that led to the statues of the gods. Charlie put her arm around him and hugged him tight. Versailles held a spirit for him that was too painful to share. She said nothing.

As they climbed into the car Daniel said "Let's go home to Yorkshire."

Charlie smiled and kissed him tenderly. He had said 'home' for the first time.

CHAPTER TEN

The North Yorkshire Moors – England

They pulled into the stable yard at home, at 2 am in the morning and climbed the creaking stairs into Charlie's studio. Her mother had kindly made a bed up for Daniel on the old sofa.

"You better ruffle the sheets up for Mummy's sake," said Charlie.

The following morning, they woke up exceptionally late, with strands of light on the bedroom floor from the small gap in the curtains. Charlie jumped out of bed, and realising she was naked, quickly grabbed her dressing gown from the peg on the door.

"Spoilsport. What time is it?" asked Daniel.

"Ten past nine. I haven't slept that well for years." Charlie opened the curtains. "I think we have some explaining to do."

"Why what's going on?"

"Daddy, Tim and Mac are circling the Ferrari like children around a new slide. I think they all want a go! I will have to get Daddy put on the insurance policy; he would love that. John will be mightily impressed – I bet he is here by lunchtime."

"I will need to change the number plates before you insure it."

"Why?" asked Charlie quizzically.

"They belong to some wealthy rapper in the US, he can afford the fines for speeding on the motorway last night!"

"You are impossible. I will give Mummy a buzz and we can go over and have breakfast with them and have a catch-up."

The teapot, already filled with Earl Grey, was sitting ready on the Aga and the home-cured bacon was sizzling in the pan. The brown, new-laid eggs were waiting for their turn. Edward was reading the *Yorkshire Post*.

"Good morning you two, what time did you land?" he asked.

Charlie gave her mother a good hug and Daniel shook Edward's hand.

"About two o'clock," replied Charlie. "We decided it would be better to drive up straight off the ferry, because there was no traffic and the weather was clear. What's all the news this end?"

"Somebody has parked a Ferrari in our stable yard and done a runner," joked Edward. "It's a beautiful car Daniel. How long have you had it?"

"Oh, it's far too flashy for my taste. It belongs to your daughter."

"Daniel bought it for me as a present and I don't think it's flashy at all. It sounds amazing and I think he is pretty amazing too!" Charlie gave him a conservative squeeze on his arm. Mummy was watching for signs.

"You are a very lucky young lady, Charlie. I hope she behaved herself skiing?" Edward asked.

"Most of the time. She needs to brush up on her mosh pit skills."

"What's that?"

"Just ignore him Daddy, he is teasing me."

"I have really missed your breakfasts, Elizabeth; this bacon is delicious," complimented Daniel.

"Yes, we like it. Our local butcher in Masham has found a farmer who keeps Gloucester Old Spot pigs fee-range and you can certainly taste the difference over hybrids. So, come on tell us all about the skiing. We heard there was an avalanche whilst you were there."

"Yes, it was a long way from where we were but it did cause some excitement in the bars and cafes. We had some fresh snow which made skiing great fun and there are so many different runs at Verbier, you could always find virgin snow to play in."

"Did you drive back up through Germany?" asked Edward.

"No, we decided to come back through France and visit a couple of châteaux in the Loire valley. Mummy, you must go Villandry and see the gardens, they are absolutely spectacular. You should go with your friend in the spring; the potager gardens with all the vegetables would give you lots of inspiration for your patch. So, what's been happening on the estate in my absence?"

"Well, there is some hot news but I am not allowed to talk about it," whispered Elizabeth.

"You are hopeless at keeping secrets!" muttered Edward. "Now you have let the cat out of the bag, I will explain what's happened. William rang me yesterday from the Auction Mart and they have been asked to market the estate next door in Wensleydale which we were hoping would come on the market at some point. It's been in the same family for 400 years Daniel, but the old man died last year and the three daughters cannot agree how to split it up and I think there will be a big mortgage to pay off too. It has a wonderful grouse moor, five in-hand farms and some mature forestry so it would fit in well with our estate. It also has a beautiful old house that's been well maintained but needs a bit spending on it to bring it up to scratch."

"That is exciting. What's the asking price Daddy?"

"They are talking about ten million but William thinks it could make more with the grouse moor attracting some foreign interest."

"So how does the selling process work with these big estates. Could someone come in and just snap it up?" asked Daniel.

"Well, it is possible but because I know William so well, I am sure he will keep me informed about what is going on."

"Do you think we can afford it?" asked Charlie excitedly.

"Your mother and I have discussed it and it's up to you really. It's your future. We have some other investments which we could cash in to help but it will be a stretch. I will have to talk to the bank of course but we don't have any borrowed money at the moment and the estate has been doing well for the last few years, so we should be a low risk for them. But you know what banks are like!"

"I suppose some wealthy oligarch from Russia could buy it and we couldn't compete with that," mused Charlie.

"So, Charlie, do you want me to do some initial investigations and then reconvene to make some decisions about what to do?"

"Yes please, Daddy. It would be wonderful if we could get it. Tim would be so pleased; he has been dying to get his hands on that moor since we thought it might come up."

"OK but don't get your hopes up too much. There's many a slip 'between cup and lip', as we say in these parts. So, Daniel, where are you off to next on your world travels? I hope you can stay a couple of days at least."

"That's very kind of you Edward. I have got to be in Washington early next week, but it would be nice to have a couple of days rest from travelling. Perhaps Charlie could show me where this new estate is and she can drive me around the Dales in her rosso corsa car?"

"She needs to give me a ride first," instructed Edward jokingly. "I've not been in a Ferrari before, apart from a very tame trip round Silverstone in my youth."

"Before we get into half shafts and gearboxes, how about a walk with the dogs and get some fresh air?" suggested Charlie, fearing a long mechanical discussion.

"Good idea. But we can talk about the spec later Edward," added Daniel.

They walked down the back lane, with the daffodils just starting to show their green shoots of spring. The ewes were heavy in lamb, gathered in the in-bye fields, with their multicoloured raddle marks, indicating which ram they had had a romantic encounter with.

"Good job men don't have to wear those or it could lead to some interesting conversations round the coffee machine," observed Daniel, smiling.

The black labs were enjoying their freedom from the kennels and were working the hedge-backs for any itinerant pheasant that had escaped the guns. The odd rabbit scurried a few feet and then dived back into the hedge for cover. The rooks were circling overhead looking for their next nest-building sites and the seagulls were covering the fields in a white, constantly moving blanket, devouring some unwary grub or other. The clouds were gathering and the daylight dimming as the sun's rays were occluded from the sky. They had just reached the stone tower in Meg's pasture, where the high pheasant stand was on Boxing Day, when the heavens opened. They dived for cover through the cobwebbed doorway, into the darkness. Two woodpigeons took exception to their human invasion and exited over Charlie's head, causing her to issue a slight scream. Daniel laughed and Charlie did her fake punch to his chest but he grabbed her arms and pulled her towards him and kissed her romantically on the lips. She responded positively and put her arms around his neck and extended the duration for several minutes.

"I love you," she said, looking directly into his deep blue eyes.

"I love you too."

They kissed again, even more passionately, for several minutes.

"I think we better get back before the pigeons get fed up with the squatters," Charlie smiled.

"We need to find Mac's labs first. I think they were embarrassed and went hunting on their own."

Charlie blew the horned whistle that Mac had given her as a present when she was eighteen and which she had cherished ever since. The two dogs obediently appeared from nowhere and rustled on ahead with their constant search for fresh scent. When they got back to the kennels

Mac had just got back for lunch and invited them in for a sandwich and a cup of tea. Sally had already got the kettle steaming away on the Aga and the behatted teapot was ready for the not Earl Grey tea bags.

They sat down near the roaring fire with the dogs drying off on the hearth rug.

"So, do you think we are going to buy the Wensleydale estate then?" enquired Mac.

"It's meant to be a secret," said Charlie quietly so the dogs did not hear.

"You can't keep secrets round here. The rumour is that some Russian has already bought it for thirty million pounds."

Daniel was intrigued how Mac had acquired such valuable information. "Who is in the know then?"

"The postman told me this morning. He thinks he knows everything but he is an idiot. Everybody knows it's an American."

"So how do you know about the American?"

"I can't say. I was sworn to secrecy, but it's a family involved in publishing with oceans of money."

"Well let's hope they are both wrong and a nice English family buy it. The last thing we want is a Disney World in Wensleydale," suggested Charlie.

"Nothing like a bit of gossip," said Sally serving a steaming bowl of rabbit stew for Daniel.

"Where do you find a wife like Sally, Mac?"

"They don't make them anymore." Mac winked at Charlie.

Sally wanted to know all about the holiday and was fascinated by the planting of the vegetable gardens at

Villandry. Mac wanted to know what size engine the Ferrari had and could he borrow it to go to the next gamekeepers' lunch to impress his fellows.

"I might swap it for a puppy from Bessie's next litter," laughed Charlie.

* * *

The next two days passed quickly, with long walks, much talk about the potential of the Wensleydale estate and with a growing depth of love between them. Daniel was impressed with the location of the Manor House and how well the farms were maintained and he thought the purchase was a good long-term investment for Charlie.

The morning of his leaving for Washington came all too soon for Charlie and she again found herself standing alone on the gravelled drive as another taxi took him away from her to another land. Hopefully this time it would be less traumatic. She returned to her father's study and they started work on the business plan. The bank had already agreed with Edward that, in principle, it was a good investment. Charlie was desperate to buy the place but her father kept her feet on the ground and tried to be more objective. After three days of spreadsheets, much head-scratching and a little bit of crystal ball gazing, they had a plan. Conservative, creative and visionary. Or so they thought...

A few days later Charlie was alone in her flat one evening, listening to Mozart, when the phone rang. It was Daniel.

"Hi. How are things in the frozen wastes of Yorkshire?"

"We are all good thank you and the weather is getting more spring-like every day. We might be in for an early one. How are things going in Washington?"

"OK. Endless meetings with boring people who don't like committing themselves to a decision, in case it reflects on their political ambitions. The next job is a bit politically sensitive so I am trying to make sure my contract will not upset anybody at this end."

"Are they paying you this time?"

"Good God no! They don't even know what I am doing, which is why the negotiations are so difficult!"

"Rather you than me. The business plan has been passed by the bank for the purchase of the estate next door and we have put in our offer to William. We are waiting for the owners to come back to him, but I am pretty confident that they will accept it because they know we will look after the place. They have owned it for so long and that must be important to them, for their father's sake."

"Well fingers crossed then. I am sure you and your father will do a fantastic job looking after the place. I think it is very synergistic with your business and will be a great asset going forwards. When do you think you will hear back from William?"

"I suspect it will take at least a week for the family to make a decision, because they disagree about everything."

"OK. Well let me know when you hear anything. I miss you loads."

"Miss you too. When do you think you will be back?"

"I should be finished here by the end of the week and then I am flying up to Seattle to meet Nzinga to discuss some software I need for my rhino project in Tsavo. So, all being well, I should be back in about three weeks or so."

"Who is Nzinga?"

"She is an exceptionally bright computer genius that helps me with the project. You will meet her when we go out to Tsavo in early April. That's if you still want to come?"

"Of course, I want to go with you. I have been really looking forward to seeing the gorillas and all the big game. I have never been to Africa and I have always wanted to see what it is really like."

"That's great then. I will get Nzinga to organise it all at their end, so we can see as much as possible whilst we are there. Well, I better go my darling. Good luck with the offer and let me know as soon as you hear from William."

"I will. You take care. Love you."

The next few days were tense. Charlie tried to make herself busy with the estate management but everything she touched would change if the tender was successful. She found herself constantly staring out of the office window dreaming of all the plans they had for the growth of the business. Her father wore a long hole in the carpet pacing up and down muttering to himself.

Two long weeks past and there was no news on the tender and then the phone rang. Edward answered the phone after one ring.

"Hello William. Is there any news yet?... Oh, I see. Who is it do we know? I suppose he has a bottomless pit of money? Well, I will discuss it with Charlie and Elizabeth but I don't think we can match that. Is anybody else interested?... Well, I suppose it is a very attractive property for the rich and famous. Thank you, William. I will get back to you tomorrow."

"Well, what's happened?" asked Charlie nervously.

"I am afraid we have been substantially outgunned by at least two other interested parties and the price has got up to fifteen million pounds. It is still open to improved offers but I think realistically, it's gone out of our league. We have a nice little successful business here of our own and we must focus on that."

"I am really, really disappointed Daddy. We worked so hard on the offer and nobody else will run it as well as us; to follow on from what their family has done for hundreds of years."

"I am afraid darling, that when it comes down to family disagreements like this, money talks. What has happened in the past or will happen in the future is irrelevant. It's just how much am I going to get out of the will."

"So, who has bought it then?"

"Obviously William couldn't say exactly but a wealthy East European and a Danish businessman that owns a lot of land in Scotland are fighting it out. It could make twenty million pounds in the end."

"It was a once in a lifetime opportunity to buy land next to our own but I suppose we will just have to get used to foreign neighbours." Charlie was trying to be positive but failed miserably.

"I think I will go for a ride up to the moor on Darley, to clear my head. See you later."

Charlie met Mac as she rode out of the yard with a secret tear in her eye. "It looks like one of the Europeans has won the estate Mac. I am sorry. We did try really hard."

"The sun hasn't set yet," said Mac enigmatically.

"And what does that mean?"

"No idea. I must have read it in a book sometime," said Mac defensively. "Have a good ride."

Charlie hacked off down the lane towards Masham Moor and the peace of the open spaces. The sky was leaden with late winter clouds and there was a blustery wind blowing up the Dale. It was getting under Darley's tail causing him to buck occasionally, as she let him take the bit up the long climb to Jenny Twigg. She felt nearer to Daniel up there because of their first ride together and it helped her put the loss of the new estate into perspective. She decided to ring Daniel when she got back to the Hall.

"Hi darling, how are things going in Seattle with Nzinga?"

"Yes. All gone really well. She has got the new tracking system linked in with the satellite array and she is so happy with it. She is such a positive young lady and never gives up until she gets the results she wants. She is a pleasure to work with. How are things your end? Have you heard about the tender yet?"

"Not good news. We have come up against some very strong bidders, so we have lost it I am afraid. Bit depressing really because as you know it was a fantastic opportunity for us and we tried really hard to make it work."

"That's a shame but there will always be people in the world that have more money than us and if they want the same thing it is only going to end one way. I could arrange to blow them up of course!"

Charlie finally laughed. "You are very good at cheering me up."

"I can do better than that. I am coming home on Thursday if that's OK with your Mum?"

"That would be really good. I can't wait to see you. It seems ages. Mummy will be fine. She loves having visitors to cook for."

"I should be with you late afternoon if the flights work out OK. See you soon. Love you."

When Charlie went into the kitchen for lunch, it was full of smoke and the windows were wide open with the curtains billowing in the wind. The Aga door was open and a pan full of burnt cakes was on the lawn outside.

"What on earth happened. It's not like you to burn anything?"

"I was on the phone to Sally; Mac says some American trust fund has bought the estate. I got so involved in the conversation, that I forgot about the cakes."

At that point Edward came into the kitchen with his mucky boots on. "Have you set the house on fire!"

"No. And take your boots off – I mopped the floor this morning."

"Daddy, Sally says that Mac says, some Americans have bought the estate – not the European lot."

"Rubbish. William would know. He is handling the sale. Where does Mac get all this gossip from?"

At that point the phone rang in the kitchen and Edward picked it up. "Hello William. We were just talking about you. All good! OK I see. When did this happen? Who are they – do you know? Is that it then –a done deal? Well, I suppose at least they will speak English – well sort of. Thank you for letting me know William. Charlie has got a new Ferrari you know. You must come over and have a ride in it. Brilliant, I'll tell Elizabeth, dinner at seven on Saturday and if you come before dark we can go for a spin. Great. Good."

"How does Mac know all this stuff?" asked Charlie totally confused. "He said to me weeks ago that an

American family were buying it. They were something to do with publishing he said. I am feeling a bit like a candle in the wind here!"

"He's always been a good source of local knowledge," said Edward "There's not much going on round here that he does not know about."

"Yes, badgers and poachers are one thing, but international property deals being done on the other side of the planet is stretching his network a bit."

"No doubt we will find out the truth in due course darling. I wouldn't worry about it."

"Mummy, Daniel is coming back to England on Thursday, is it OK if he stays for a few days in the flat?"

"Of course, my dear we would love to see him again. He is a very polite guest and your father and I really like him. I'll leave you to make up the flat." She smiled knowingly at Charlie, who blushed like a teenager.

The phone rang again and Elizabeth picked it up.

"Hello William do you want to talk to Edward again. Oh OK. I see. I don't see why not. It will be interesting to meet him. I had better put my best dress on then. ..... OK see you on Saturday."

"What was that all about?" enquired Edward.

"Evidently the new owner of the estate is flying over on Friday to sign some paperwork and William has suggested that he brings him over for dinner on Saturday so we can get to know him."

"Bloody nerve!" exclaimed Edward. "They steal the estate from under our noses and then we have to be nice to them in our own house!"

"Oh Daddy, don't be such a poor loser. We would probably have overstretched ourselves anyway and that was all my fault. I am as disappointed as you are but we will be neighbours and it will only help in the long term if we can get on. Anyway, it will be interesting to see what they are like."

"Well don't expect me to be nice and all cheerful and interested in their Wall Street lives." Edward stomped off to his study to read the paper.

"What do you think Mummy?"

"Well, I was put on the spot really, but I think you are right. In the long term it will benefit us all, if we can get on. It will be interesting to see how the super-rich do things differently to us. They might bring some new ideas we can learn from."

"It's going to be an exciting week with Daniel coming home and meeting the new people on Saturday. Daniel obviously spends quite a bit of time in America so he might be able to help the conversation along if there is a paternal atmosphere," Charlie smiled. "If you need me to help with anything just let me know Mummy."

* * *

Charlie spent the next couple of days tidying up the flat, her mother planned a suitable banquet for millionaires and Edward found some cheap wine in the cellar he had been given by a company rep a few Christmases ago.

Charlie arose early on Thursday morning after a restless night. It was a lovely spring morning, the Shirotae cherry trees were coming into flower with drifts of pure white Thalia narcissus beneath them and the wrens were busy in the garden, planning their nuptials. The first lambs with their snow-white fleeces had been turned out into the Home Paddock and their mothers were constantly bleating to keep them in check and to provide sustenance at frequent intervals. Charlie walked across the stable yard, said good morning to Sally, who was hanging out her newly washed curtains as part of her spring-cleaning ritual, and went into the kitchen for a cup of tea with her mother.

"Is everything OK Mummy? Do you need a hand with anything?"

"I was just trying to decide what you would like me to make for dinner tonight as it's Daniel's first evening back after all his travels."

"I know he likes steak, so why don't we have some of the fillet off that Angus heifer we had to butcher after she broke her leg last month. It should be really tender now after hanging for a while, suggested Charlie.

"That's a good idea and your father would enjoy that too. I will do some of my special chips, because Daniel really liked them when he was here for Christmas."

"I'll make one of my lemon tarts for afters as it's the only thing I am good at!"

"You know that's rubbish. You are a really good cook. Anyway, if you haven't learnt something off me in all these years, I haven't been a very good mother!"

* * *

Charlie had been messing about in her flat after lunch, trying to fill in time before Daniel arrived. She tried on some new Levi's she had bought on her last trip to Harrogate and couldn't decide if they were too tight. Maybe he would like that she thought? She put on her ivory split cuff blouse for the casual look but every detail was meticulously appraised to ensure he would approve. Such is female cunning. She was just about to change outfits when she heard the gravel on the drive warn of a car's arrival. She ran down the creaky stairs and then walked nonchalantly out onto the drive. Daniel scooped her up in his strong arms, swung her around him three times and kissed her passionately on the lips.

"Hi, I have been dying to do that for weeks. You look amazing – love the blouse. Are you OK?"

"I am now – missed you loads. Did you have a good trip?"

"Really good thanks and very productive in Seattle, but I will tell you all about that later. Let me just pay the taxi driver."

"You better put me down first!"

"Good point."

"You're a lucky man. I wish my wife greeted me like that," bemoaned the taxi driver.

Charlie smiled and took Daniel's hand and they went into the Hall kitchen to see Elizabeth.

"Hello Daniel, it's lovely to see you again. Would you like a cup of Earl Grey?" Daniel gave her a peck on the cheek stimulating a big smile.

"That would be wonderful. I haven't had a decent cup of tea in weeks. Has Charlie been behaving herself?"

"That's debateable. She wasn't on her best form about losing the estate next door. I assume she has told you about it?"

"Yes. It's a shame you didn't get it but there is no point in stretching yourselves too far financially, only to regret it later. Do you know who has bought it?"

"All is to be revealed on Saturday. William is bringing the new owner for dinner on Saturday night so you will get to meet him then. All we know, is that he is involved in publishing in America and has unlimited resources."

"What's his name. Do you know?"

"No, William did not say. I think it's still a bit confidential. You could ask Mac – he seems to know all about everything."

Elizabeth poured the tea into the bone china cups she kept specially for royal visitors and cut a slice of Victoria sponge she had cooked in honour of his visit.

"Your mother is the best cook in the whole world," smiled Daniel on his second slice.

"I am hoping I have inherited some of her culinary genes," laughed Charlie.

"So, have you any idea how much they paid…?"

"Too much!" proffered Edward walking into the kitchen. Daniel stood up and shook his hand. "Now then. Did you have a successful trip in the land of limitless money?"

"Daddy stop being grumpy. It's embarrassing."

"Only joking. I am getting used to the idea of living in the fifty-first state and having a party on the Fourth of July," chuckled Edward.

"Actually, I have found that people are pretty much the same the world over – except the Russians who are universally awful. Most very rich people are pretty much normal folk and good to get on with. They have long ago come to terms with their wealth and know how handle it, and respect other people. It's only the nouveau-riche that can be obnoxious, especially those with big yachts," said Daniel with a knowing look at Charlie. She laughed, completely free of her past, thanks to Daniel's cathartic explosions.

"I have got a nice case of Louis Jadot Bonnes-Mares Grand Cru 2005 which I have been keeping for a special occasion, so I thought we could open a bottle tonight and you can tell me what you think, Daniel."

"That sounds wonderful. I really like a nice Burgundy with steak, which Charlie tells me is from one of your own heifers. I feel spoilt already!"

After they had demolished the Victoria, Elizabeth sent them off to get Daniel settled in before dinner. "You let Daniel have a rest for an hour Charlie – he has had a long day and a lot of travelling."

"Yes Mummy. We are over thirty you know."

They walked across to the stables and Daniel gave Darley a pat on the way past his stable.

"Shall we go for a ride tomorrow?" asked Daniel.

"I thought we might do that on Saturday. I want to take you across the North Yorkshire Moors to Whitby in the Ferrari tomorrow. It's meant to be a lovely day and it would be nice to just spend some time with you away from the estate."

"Sounds good to me. Never been to Whitby. They are meant to do the best fish and chips in the world over there?"

"The Magpie for lunch it is then."

"Never had magpie and chips but I suppose this is Yorkshire!" joked Daniel and Charlie tickled his ribs.

* * *

It was a stunning spring morning in the Dale. The rich blue sky was dotted with fluffy white clouds making their

223

way lazily along the moor tops and the dappled shadows cascaded from the budding trees onto the soft greens of the meadows below. The red Ferrari sat expectantly in the stable yard, pristine and glinting in the sunlight. Charlie was loading an F & M picnic hamper into the boot, when Daniel arrived from having breakfast with Mac.

"I wondered where you had gone. What has Mac got to say for himself then?"

"Not much. He is really looking forward to seeing the new owner tomorrow night. He says she is a really nice lady but filthy rich!"

"I thought it was a man who was coming. How does he know all this stuff?"

"No idea. Are we ready for off?"

"Mummy has made us a picnic which will keep us going."

"Till we get the magpies for lunch! Whose driving?"

"It's my car but I might let you have a drive later!"

Charlie pressed start and the V12 Ferrari engine purred into life. The chickens took cover under the feed shed and the resting rooks scattered from the oak trees down the lane. They headed for Thirsk out of Masham along the Nosterfield Road, past the working stone quarries, and on to Skipton-on-Swale over the old stone bridge crossing the river, still swollen from the heavy rains in Swaledale a few days before. They entered the cobbled market square in Thirsk, with the Ferrari exhaust notes bouncing of the tall brick buildings, past the surgery of Thirsk's favourite vet, Alf Wight, better known as James Herriot, and out on the open road to White Stone Cliff. Charlie opened up the prancing horse to the speed limit and they both smiled at the fortissimo. It climbed up Sutton Bank's one-in four gradient effortlessly to reach the top of the western escarpment of the Hambleton Hills with its magnificent views across the Vale of York. They stopped for a while, to take in the panorama and a flight of three Hawk jets from RAF Leeming flew below them along the ridge, bringing a tear to Charlie's eye in memory of poor Thomas. Daniel held her hand. The long run down to Helmsley was Ferrari heaven, slightly in excess of the local limit. Actually, a lot in excess. They stopped at the Black Swan for a coffee and sat in the morning sunshine watching the gathering tourist throng, searching the boutique shops for that perfect gift, whilst the husbands walked inquisitively around the car.

"Shall we move on before we have to talk about torque?" asked Daniel. "Anyway, it's my turn to drive it properly!"

Charlie kissed him on the cheek.

They left the square with Ferrari's tune exciting the jealous husbands and roared along the sweeping road to Kirby Moorside where they turned off and headed for the North Yorks Moors. The climb up through the Dove valley, magical with hosts of golden daffodils carpeting the riverside meadows, and then out onto the high ridge between Westerdale and Danbydale.

"Can we stop for a few minutes, so I can take some landscape shots of the Dales?" asked Charlie.

Daniel pulled across onto a convenient tightly grazed patch of grass and laid out the picnic rug whilst Charlie set up the camera on the tripod. It was a perfect location, with exceptional vistas in every direction. The cloudy shadows drifted lazily across the green heathered moorland, punctuated with heavily fleeced horned

Curlew

ewes, whose daily lives maintained the wonderful landscape. The curlews were calling overhead and the occasional merlin soared into view hunting its prey. When Charlie was content with her collection, she lay down on the rug next to Daniel and they both scanned the mercurial skies. Daniel took Charlie's hand and kissed it.

"Thank you for transporting me to such beautiful and peaceful places," said Daniel quietly.

"We are lucky to have such spectacular scenery on our doorstep. Yorkshire is God's own county you know!"

"It is amazing but why are some patches of moorland a brighter green than others? It's a bit like a patchwork quilt."

"Most visitors think the moors are naturally the way they are, but actually they take a lot of managing to maintain the diversity of wildlife and the oceans of lovely pink heather we get later in late summer," replied Charlie. "Each year the farmers burn off the old outgrown heather in a controlled sequence so the new young heather can emerge which is the lighter coloured squares. The baby grouse and sheep need this young heather to survive and the fresh new flowers attract the bees which make delicious honey from them. Some people who think they know about conservation are talking about stopping the burning but it would be a disaster for the local wildlife, that depend on the new heather plants."

"Conservation is always more complicated than people think because nature is so integrated and if you change one thing it has cascading effects across the whole biodiversity of an area," observed Daniel, with an infinite knowledge of the complexities.

A passing tractor and trailer loaded with big black bales of haylage broke the spell so they drove off towards Whitby, briefly stopping in Grosmont so Daniel could see the steam trains, which evoked memories of his childhood in Africa. They parked on the seafront in Whitby and walked along the quayside, where Captain Cook had set sail aboard HMS *Endeavour* to Australia and New Zealand in 1768. The tenacious herring gulls were still harassing the fishing boats for breakfast and had now advanced to stealing lunch from inattentive tourists.

"So where do we buy the magpie and chips for lunch?" asked Daniel with a wry smile.

"The restaurant is called The Magpie and they do the best fish and chips in the universe and that's official," confirmed Charlie, with great Yorkshire pride.

They purchased their meals and sat on the port wall, looking out to the maritime horizon with the sailing boats bobbing on the restless waves.

"I have to admit the fish is exceptionally good," conceded Daniel, as he threw a chip to a persistent seagull, which was probably not the most intelligent thing to have done. They were soon inundated with an encircling flock of gulls looking for an easy lunch.

They escaped the avian avalanche and headed down to Robin Hood's Bay, a bit further along the coast. An ancient fishing village with its picturesque houses clinging to the hillside leading down to the harbour, it has a history of sailors and smugglers going back hundreds of years. They wandered around for a while, hand-in-hand, enjoying the simplicity of time to themselves. Charlie stopped at a quaint old shop selling Whitby jet, made into interesting jewellery by the local artisans. Daniel bought her an intricate gold cluster ring encrusted with diamonds and the eponymous black stones which Charlie adored and put on her third finger on her right hand.

"One day…" said Daniel.

"I know, there is no rush. I am not going anywhere," interrupted Charlie softly, whilst giving him a long thank you kiss.

Charlie resumed the driving, her new jet ring glinting on her hand, gripping the sumptuous leather steering wheel. She took the Pickering Road, past the RAF early warning site at Fylingdales, and parked on the right-hand side of the road overlooking Newton Dale. She jumped out and got her camera.

"OK, I give up. Why the rush to take a landscape photo. Is it the light?" enquired Daniel.

"Just wait and listen."

"I can't hear anything?"

"Wait. Look over there."

Pure white clouds of smoke billowed over the trees and a loud whistle echoed up the hillside. A steam train pulling old-fashioned carriages appeared from behind the trees and dragged its load around the grand wooded curve of

Newton Dale. Charlie clicked away and got some fabulous shots, whilst Daniel marvelled at the resurrection of such an emotional engineering creation.

* * *

They arrived back at the Old Hall at about seven and decided to spend the evening on their own in the flat, since having eaten their way around Yorkshire, they were not particularly hungry. Charlie put some music on and opened a bottle of wine she had stolen from her father's cellar. She had no idea what it was but Daniel suggested her father should apply for a mortgage the following day. They collapsed on the sofa together and Charlie lay with her head on Daniel's lap, sipping her wine awkwardly. The Mozart drifted around the loft, the wine bottle emptied and they melted slowly into each other's arms.

"Thank you for such a lovely day. My ring is beautiful and I will treasure it for ever. You are always buying me things."

"I like buying you things. You mean the world to me and I'm not going to stop."

"I love you." Charlie kissed him passionately on the lips and he responded holding her head in his hand. "I need you," she whispered in his ear.

Daniel carefully undid the buttons on Charlie's white cotton blouse and pulled the two sides slightly apart. She smiled approvingly. He ran his finger around the edge of her silk camisole top, lightly touching the soft skin of her breast. She closed her eyes, lay her head back and let the feeling permeate her yearning form. His finger slowly lowered the silk and his stroking induced a small moan from Charlie's slightly parted lips. She raised her breasts to his touch and moved her thighs together to intensify her pleasure.

"Please more," she smiled, turning and sitting astride his lap. Daniel slid the blouse down her slender arms and dropped it casually on the loft floor. She put her arms around his neck and he teased her through the thin silk camisole. She responded to his touch and could feel her breasts firm and her nipples becoming erect. The sensuous spiral was starting and she did not want it to stop. Her tummy was tightening and her body was warming to his caress. She leant back, with her hands on his knees inviting him to explore her more. He kissed her neck sensitively, teasing her earlobes with his tongue and then kissing the extremities of her breasts above the silk. She wanted more and pressed her hips more firmly against his. He knew what she wanted but made her wait, with tantalising near touches on the silk. She let out another moan, more desperate this time. "Please."

He responded by pulling down the silk to below her breasts exposing them to his caresses. She felt vulnerable to him but that made her even more excited as her muscles tightened and she pressed her hips more firmly. She arched her back and felt his lips on her breasts. She leant back with his arms around her waist and her whole body cascaded in pleasure.

Charlie fell into his arms. "You are wonderful to me. I adore what you do to my body."

"A musician is only as good as his violin," smiled Daniel.

"I like the symphonies!" Charlie whispered.

CHAPTER ELEVEN

A Labyrinth of Love

The following morning, they woke up late again, having slept for ten hours, which was unheard of for Charlie, normally being an early riser.

"Crickey. I said we would ride at ten o'clock. You can have the shower first whilst I make some tea and toast."

"I want to stay in bed with you all day," pleaded Daniel. Charlie threw a cushion at him.

It was a perfect day for hacking out and they decided to ride around the estate they didn't buy, before the new owners appeared. The sun was already warm as they trotted along the lane towards the neighbours. The stream that trickled along the ditch at the side of the lane was fuller than normal, as it carried the last of the winter leaves along like small sailing boats. The air was still and the occasional barn owl was sleepily perched on a mossy bough, unconcerned with the equines passing. A weasel scampered across the lane and Darley snorted in disdain of such a small creature.

"How far is it to the Manor house?" asked Daniel.

"About ten miles by road but we can take a short cut over Whitton Moor, a bit further on. There is an old track leaving this lane by an old water mill which is on the boundary of the two estates.

"Who owns the mill?"

"They do unfortunately. I always loved it as a child and used to play there amongst the millstones and wooden gear wheels. It would make a wonderful house next to the leat. It's such an evocative setting of days gone by, with the ghosts of dusty millers grinding the corn."

Old Mill Wheel

They dismounted when they got to the mill to give the horses a breather, whilst Daniel and Charlie explored her distant, happy memories

"It is a wonderfully peaceful setting and you're right it does have enormous scope to make a tranquil house with unlimited character. Do think you would get planning permission for it?"

"There is no point speculating really, because it will never happen now, but anything is possible if you know the right people."

They remounted and cantered up the rough track to the moor top where Charlie saw a rare hen harrier swooping down the dale side.

"You don't see many of those these days. They eat a lot of grouse chicks and some unenlightened keepers tend to shoot them, which is a shame because they are such graceful birds."

They just sat for a while on Darley and Byerley and took in the sweeping moorland landscapes, the endless skies, and hillsides falling down into the green pastures of the dales below. They could just make out the silver reflections of the River Ure winding its way along the Dale floor.

"Why is Wensleydale not called Uredale. All the other dales are named after their rivers, Swaledale, Nidderdale etc?" enquired Daniel.

"Do you want the full history lesson or the short version?"

"Definitely the short version."

"The river was originally called Yore and the dale Yoredale and that evolved into the river Ure today. Wensley was the main market town in the Dale so it became Wensleydale for some reason. They then got the Black Death and everybody moved to Leyburn which is now the main market town in the Dale. Wensley is now just a sleepy little village."

"Glad I didn't go for the long version!"

They made their way further along the moor until they could see down into the Dale properly and there, amongst a stand of mature deciduous trees, stood the magnificent house that the American had just bought.

"That is some house!" said Daniel.

"It is a beautiful setting and the house is architecturally well balanced. I love the mellow colour of the limestone. It makes our place look very rustic."

"I actually prefer your old Hall because it has a character all of its own and is less pretentious. Anyway, this will cost a fortune to keep up. I hope the buyer has deep pockets."

"We will find out tonight who the mystery person is. I just hope we can get on and they don't spoil the place with rock concerts and hippos in the lake."

"I quite like hippos. I'll race you back to the triangulation point. Three two one go!"

The Arabs took off at the speed of light, back across the moor. Daniel and Darley took the early lead throwing up divots from the grassy track. The clear, fresh air reddened their faces and Charlie's competitive streak emerged from the depths. She squeezed Byerley with her legs to find another gear and she swept past Daniel beating him to the point by fifty yards.

Daniel rode up to her and kissed her cheek. "You're a fast lady in more ways than one!"

They hacked back to the Hall at a gentle pace, holding hands when the terrain permitted. When they got back into the stable yard they untacked, washed the horses off with a hosepipe and put them back in their stables with a deep bed of straw.

"Let's go and see how Mummy is getting on in the kitchen and have a cup of tea."

"Sounds a good plan to me."

Delicious cooking aromas emanated out of the kitchen door from Elizabeth's industrial labours over the Aga, which was heaving with pots, pans and wooden spoons of every magnitude.

"That smells good Mummy. Do you need a hand?"

"No thank you. All under control. Where have you two been. You look a bit windswept?"

"We've been for a ride over Witton Moor to look at the house, before the new owners move in. Daniel says he prefers our little shack."

"I didn't exactly call it a shack Charlie. Has she always been this contentious?"

"Oh, you've no idea! Earl Grey and a bacon sandwich?"

"That would be lovely thank you. I think we have worked up quite an appetite riding over the moor this morning."

"Mummy what are we going to wear for dinner tonight with the American coming?"

"I thought we should put on a good show, so she doesn't think we are just yokels. I thought I would wear that blue dress I bought in Edinburgh last year. I haven't had a chance to try it out yet. What do you think?"

"I think you would look super in that. I will wear my long blue trousers so we match, with my favourite silk shirt. That should create the right image without being over-the-top."

"What will your father wear?" asked Daniel. "I don't want to let the side down."

"Oh, smart casual is fine. Daddy will probably wear his old cords and the jacket with the rip in it, the mood he is in."

* * *

At the prescribed hour, William's Land Rover Discovery came up the drive and parked outside the front door. Edward and Elizabeth opened the front door to welcome their guests for the evening and Charlie and Daniel hovered by the crackling fire, in the main hall, keeping in the background. William opened the passenger door and an elegant lady in a blue velvet cape with a voluminous hood stepped out into the evening sunshine.

William introduced Edward and Elizabeth and they formally shook hands.

"You have a lovely place here Edward. I love these old stone houses – they have such history. I am so pleased to meet you and I am really looking forward to all the advice you can give me about the estate I have been lucky enough to buy. It has always been my dream to live in the Dales of Yorkshire."

A good start – Edward was impressed. "Can I take your cape?" he asked.

"That's very kind Edward. Thank you so much." She took off her cape to reveal a long blue velvet evening dress, with a very deep décolletage. Edward was even more impressed.

"Do please come through and meet my family. This is my daughter Charlie and her very good friend Daniel. This is Anne Marie Macmillan."

Daniel smiled and Charlie collapsed on the sofa, not knowing whether to laugh or cry!

Anne Marie sat next to Charlie and kissed her on the cheek. "Hello darling. How are you? Long-time no-see!"

Charlie was too stunned to speak.

"So how do you two know each other?" asked a very confused Edward.

Charlie looked at Daniel knowingly. "Did you have anything to do with this?"

"Who me? You know I don't know anything about sheep or badgers!" replied Daniel protectively.

Elizabeth was trying to come to terms with the interrelationships but gave up. "Would anybody like a drink? Edward, go and get a decent bottle of wine and change that ridiculous jacket."

"Yes dear. Of course, dear. Definitely. William come and help me chose the wine."

"Charlie come and help me with the dinner please."

"Do you think they will understand?" whispered Anne Marie in Daniel's ear.

"It will be fine. Just take it slowly. They are lovely genuine people and it will take a while for them to get their heads around the situation – especially Charlie."

"Charlie looks more lovely than ever. I am very jealous."

"Just behave. You've only been here ten minutes. Anyway, she is mine."

Edward reappeared with William. "This is one of my favourite wines, it's a Louis Jadot and we opened the first bottle last night for Daniel and he thought it was excellent. I do hope you like red wine?"

"I adore Louis Jadot, especially some of the 2005s, it's an excellent vintage," replied Anne Marie knowledgeably.

"That's amazing," exclaimed Edward. "This is a 2005. You certainly know your wines!"

Daniel smiled.

In the kitchen the interrogation was in full swing.

"So, who is she?"

"We met her in New England when I was over there with Daniel. She is a lovely lady but I had no idea she had money. It does not make any sense; she was working as a housekeeper at the house where we stayed. I am really confused Mummy."

"She does seem really nice and she obviously likes you but it is all a bit strange. Do you think Daniel knew about it? Did he not say anything yesterday?"

"He never mentioned anything, even when we rode over to see the place but he must have known. I smell a cunning plan. He is always ten steps ahead of everybody else."

"Well, I suggest you play it really cool and let him do the explaining, when he is ready. If she is the genuine buyer and is going to live next door it's good that you two get on so well."

"That's true. I will take your advice and let it take its course, but I am a bit uncomfortable about what it all means?"

"You better get back and I will bring the starters through," suggested Elizabeth.

Daniel and William were in deep conversation about the price of store cattle and Edward was entertaining Anne Marie with tales of the Dales, which she was really enjoying and laughing at the appropriate points, with her arm draped on his shoulder. Elizabeth came out of the kitchen with a tray of smoked salmon terrines. "Shall we all go through?"

Daniel put his arm around Charlie's waist and Edward took Anne Marie's arm and led her into the dining room. "You come and sit next to me my dear and tell me all about how exciting it is to live in the USA." He pulled her chair back for her as a gentleman would. Elizabeth looked at Charlie, raised her eyebrows and looked skywards at the ease with which men are manipulated by a beautiful woman. Charlie smiled back and started to enjoy herself.

"So, Anne Marie when are you planning to move in?" asked Charlie.

"I have no idea. William do you know when we will have the keys?"

"Officially about a month, but they have all moved out so practically pretty well straight away I guess."

"That's wonderful because I want to take Charlie around the house, so she can help me with the plans for any renovations it will need and also, how I go about running the estate. I will not be able to do it without Charlie. I hope you will have the time to help me Charlie?"

Charlie smiled at the three mentions in one sentence. "Of course, Annie anything for you."

Elizabeth looked quizzical and was totally mystified with what was going on, but went with the flow.

The wine was working its warming glow and the conversations drifted from the price of breeding ewes with lambs at foot, to the latest in kitchen design.

Elizabeth got up to fetch the main course and Charlie started to get up to help, but Anne Marie beat her to it. "I would love to see your kitchen to get some ideas," said Anne Marie enthusiastically, scooping up the small empty pots. "I loved the smoked salmon; we eat a lot in New England. The lemon dill dressing was fabulous. Do you have a good local supplier in the Dale?" The two women disappeared into the kitchen already comparing culinary ideas. The Anne Marie magic was not confined to elderly men.

The wine consumption was indicative of how successful the evening went with Edward making three more trips to his cellar. Anne Marie moved places several times to ensure she charmed everyone, but concentrated on Elizabeth who was the one she knew she had to win over. They got on like a house on fire with their common passion for cooking. After the pudding they retired to the main hall sofas, but not until Anne Marie had helped Elizabeth load the dishwasher and tidy up. When they came through, Edward and William were in deep conversation on the window seat and Daniel was sitting next to Charlie on the sofa with his arm around her shoulders. Elizabeth and Anne Marie sat on the sofa opposite.

Elizabeth had become quite enthusiastic. "When Anne Marie gets moved in, she is coming over so we can compare menus and maybe do some cooking together for a barbeque in the summer." Anne Marie held her hand. "I am so pleased we can work together, and all become friends. I can't wait to get started on the house."

"William, have you got a key so Daniel and I can go over to the house tomorrow with Annie Marie and do an initial reccy?" asked Charlie.

"Of course, what sort of time suits you all?"

"Shall we say about ten-thirty?" suggested Anne Marie.

"That's fine. I will meet you there and take you all to lunch at the Blue Lion at East Witton. You will love it there Anne Marie. It's a really old traditional Yorkshire pub with super food," offered William.

"That sounds wonderful, William. I can't wait. I won't sleep I am so excited."

"Well, we better get you back to your hotel in Grantley before they lock you out," said William. "Thank you, Elizabeth, that was a delicious meal as usual. I will be in touch shortly."

Anne Marie gave Edward and Elizabeth a big hug, like long-lost friends, kissed Daniel on the cheek and Charlie got a special one on the lips whilst everyone was getting the coats. "See you tomorrow," she whispered in Charlie's ear. "I can't wait."

Charlie smiled but was a bit bewildered by the whirlwind evening that had just changed their lives forever.

Elizabeth and Edward retired to bed, leaving Charlie and Daniel on the sofa in front of the dying embers of the oak log fire. Charlie stood up and threw a couple more logs into the dog grate and a tornado of sparks flew up the chimney.

"So, Mr Knight. What was all that about?" Daniel knew he was in trouble because she had never called him that before, but her attempt at hiding a smile was transparent.

"It's complicated," he muttered defensively.

"And how did Mac know what was going on before even William knew? I had a sneaking feeling that you were behind it somewhere."

"Mac was completely innocent, so please don't tell him off. He didn't really know what was happening. I just needed someone on the ground here who knew what was going on locally, so we did not get outbid. You were all far too involved and emotional to be in on the plan. Anyway, we did not know if it would work and I did not want to raise your hopes, only to get them dashed again."

"So, who has actually come up with the money?"

"Anne Marie has genuinely bought it herself. I just facilitated the deal."

"But I thought she was your assistant – sort of?"

"She is – just a wealthy one. Actually, a mega-wealthy one. She inherited a media empire worth billions and owns property all over the US including the house at Chocorua where we stayed in New England."

"But why did she let you treat her like a servant when I was there. I don't understand?"

"Anne Marie is a very complicated person. She has oceans of money, so she is not driven in that way. She likes to do exciting things that stimulate her senses. She is desperately in love with you for example."

"But she knows I love you and that will never change."

"She knows that and would never do anything about it seriously, but she likes being near you and if you let her, she will become the best friend you could ever wish for. Very rich people have great problems finding true friends. They always have this fear that people are only friends because of the money."

"As long as you are happy with that Daniel. I don't want anything to come between us."

"She knows how I feel about you Charlie and she wouldn't do anything to hurt me either. Just go with the flow and enjoy being loved by two people! Plus, your mother and father of course."

"I am not sure what Mummy will make of it all?"

"I think she has already fallen under the Anne Marie spell. I am sure if you are happy, she will be fine. Anyway, I have got something else to ask you. I have got to make a visit to Kenya in April and I would like you to come with me. I need to visit my base in Tsavo where we are doing the rhino project and then I want to take you up to the Virunga Mountains in the north of Rwanda so you can photograph the mountain gorillas where we are running the conservation project, I told you about in Croatia. Do you think you will be able to come with me?"

"That sounds wonderful. You know I have always wanted to go to Africa. It will be amazing to be with you in such a beautiful place."

"There is one minor tedious drawback. I have a small job to do in Saudi Arabia afterwards, but it will only take a few days and then we could fly down to Mauritius for a holiday for ten days?"

"Oh, that sounds a really terrible price to pay, but I suppose I will cope!" Charlie put her arms around Daniel and gave him one of her special kisses.

* * *

The following morning the skies were heavy with rain clouds and there was an unseasonal wind from the north. Definitely not Ferrari weather, so they borrowed a Range Rover off Tim and set off for Anne Marie's new house. Just as they turned off the main Leyburn Road, the heavens opened and torrential rain lashed the car; the road barely visible through the windscreen.

"I think the Ferrari might have floated in this lot," joked Daniel, struggling to see the way forwards. "I am not sure what Anne Marie will think of her purchase now?"

They pulled up to the Palladian portico adorning the front of the great stone building, where William and Anne Marie were waiting with huge umbrellas to welcome their first guests inside.

"Isn't it an amazing place Charlie? I adore it. It's got so much potential I can't wait to show you around. I have got so many ideas my head is bursting. But first things first. William, the champagne! I give you a toast. 'The Mansion House!' I am sure we are all going to have a fabulous time here. I am going to make it a happy house, where we can have lots of fun and enjoy the wonderful scenery of the Dales."

"That's if it ever stops raining," laughed William

"It's only rain William, you should try sailing around Tiera del Fuego. Now that's proper rain – this is just a light shower."

Anne Marie put her arm around Charlie's waist and took her into the main sitting room. "Just look at that panoramic view out of the windows, and I love the little lake at the bottom of the field."

"The lake is over five acres Annie; hardly small by English standards!" smiled Charlie.

"Never mind we will make it bigger. Where can we hire a caterpillar? And I want trees all down the drive like you have."

"They took 300 years to grow like that!"

"Yes, but you can get huge trees these days to give you an instant avenue. I saw an advert in the *Yorkshire Post* for Wykeham Mature Trees near Scarborough. We must give them a ring later."

"Are you going to get an interior designer to help you with the inside?"

"No. Complete waste of time. You and I can do it. We will make a much better job in half the time."

So, Charlie was seeing the whirlwind that was Anne Marie, which she saw glimpses of in Hvar.

CHAPTER TWELVE

Chyulu Hills – Kenya – West Africa

Charlie and Daniel disembarked from the Gulfstream G600 private jet, that Anne Marie had casually lent them, into the warmth of the Kenyan capital. They were met on the tarmac by Nzinga, who Daniel had met in Seattle on his last trip to the US, and a very pleasant customs man who made a symbolic check of their passports. Nzinga helped them load their luggage into the waiting Range Rover and they left the airport within ten minutes of landing.

"Charlie, can I introduce Nzinga who is not only super intelligent but amazingly beautiful; she runs all our software programs."

"I am blushing but you can't see it!" said Nzinga. "Is he this embarrassing in England?"

"I am afraid so. We will have to compare notes!" laughed Charlie. "Where are we going, Daniel never tells me anything?"

"Join the club! We are heading to our camp in the Chyulu Hills which is about 200 km and between Tsavo East and Tsavo West National Parks. It will take a couple of hours. Daniel tells me you are a world-famous photographer?"

"Now it's my turn to blush. I love landscape photography, so I am hoping to get some atmospheric shots for a client I am working for."

"That's brilliant. I can take you to loads of places with magnificent views. Mount Kilimanjaro is only about sixty km away from the camp."

"Don't take her up any mountains – she might fall off."

"Very funny, I only tripped over my tether cable to the computer."

"Anyway Nzinga, give me an update on how things are going back at the camp," asked Daniel.

"I am really excited about the new satellite link into the GPS trackers, fitted to the test rhinos. We can see where they are to the nearest metre and the secret video links, that we are not allowed to talk about, mean we actually see them wherever they are. Bomani and Thulani are just fascinated, and spend all day watching them on their iPads."

"Who are Bomani and Thulani?" asked Charlie.

"Oh, just a couple of local thugs we found to beat up the poachers!" replied Daniel very seriously.

"Just ignore him. He wouldn't say that in front of them," smiled Nzinga. "You will like them Charlie – very fit!"

"Who else is based at the camp?

"Jahir, our helicopter pilot, who ferries us about the Park and my best friend Eshe, who is so passionate about gorillas I don't think she will ever find a boyfriend. She is such fun to have around and makes me laugh every day, even when things are tough."

"How is the new solar power unit coming along?" asked Daniel.

"Don't ask! Some days I want to climb on the roof and build it myself. They are so lazy. You just can't find decent workmen anymore."

"We have the same problem in Yorkshire!" joked Charlie. "Mummy usually bakes them a cake and that does the trick."

Nzinga pulled off the main A109 road at Kibwezi and headed up into the Chyulu Hills, soon running out of tarmac and onto rough, ochre tracks amid the parched scrub land. Climbing higher and higher to over 4000 feet, she reached a plateau with clear views across the Tanzanian border. The tri-cratered Mount Kilimanjaro came into view, rising 16,000 feet from the savannah of the Maasai homelands which stretched infinitely below.

"That is an unbelievable, breath-taking view. I must take a photograph of that," exclaimed Charlie.

"There is no rush," added Nzinga. "The view from our camp is even better, especially at sunset when the colours are amazing. Don't worry, there is loads to look at and photograph. I hope you have brought plenty of memory sticks!"

The rutted track led up to the highest point of the hills, where the clouds were captured and the growth of a lush tropical montane forest dominated. They drove into the encampment of half a dozen timber-framed huts with immaculately thatched roofs and rustic walls. Climbing out of the car, they were met with a sea of smiling happy faces, surrounding Charlie with a million questions. Nzinga tried to introduce everybody but the chaos of their arrival swamped the words.

"OK everybody, let's get unloaded and then we can all have a cup of coffee and Charlie will tell you her life history!" ordered Daniel.

"I will carry Charlie's bags and look after her," claimed Jahir. "I am Jahir the helicopter pilot and I can take you anywhere you want to go in Africa!"

"I presume you are paying for the fuel," joked Daniel.

"This is Daniel's special hut which we are not allowed to use, even when he is away for years. This is his private place where he thinks a lot."

"How long have you worked for Daniel?"

"About five years. I flew helicopters in the RAF before that. I met him by chance one day in Mosul, in northern Iraq, and he just offered me this job. It was like a dream for me coming home and doing something about conserving the wildlife."

"What was he doing in Iraq?" asked Charlie.

"He said he was on a fishing holiday, which seemed unlikely, but he is such a sincere guy I trusted him and I have never regretted it for a minute."

"How did you end up in the RAF?"

"I was really lucky because I was raised in an orphanage and was always mad on aeroplanes. They had some extra money from somewhere and sent me to RAF Cranwell."

"Was the orphanage run by a Father Peter?"

"How did you know that?"

"Just a lucky guess. Let's go and have some of that coffee.

Nzinga was busy lighting a fire in a rough stone circle on the ground and two very handsome young men were carrying sticks and logs to help her.

"These are my two bodyguards Bomani and Thulani!"

"You wish!" said Bomani. "Hi Charlie, I am Bomani. It is a great pleasure to meet such a beautiful lady and if I can do anything for you, during your stay, you only have to say."

"What a creep!" laughed Nzinga. "Go and get the coffee and don't spill it like you did yesterday."

"Hi I'm Thulani. I have heard so much about you so it's really nice to meet you at last. I understand you are a world-famous photographer. Your website is amazing. I love the skiing ones from Verbier."

"Thank you Thulani, but I think world-famous is a bit of an exaggeration. How did you get involved in this project?"

"Bomani and I were both on a job in Libya for the British army and we met Daniel near Sirte where Colonel Gaddafi was born. It's a never-ending civil war there and the GNA and LNA are destroying the country. There had been a huge explosion at a munitions depot which gave us cover to get some English people out. Not sure who they were but they seemed important. Daniel appeared at the last moment with some civilian guy and threw him in the inflatable we were using to get back to the ship."

"Sounds exciting stuff!" exclaimed Charlie.

"It was if you like being wet, cold and being shot at! Anyway, he offered us this job in the boat and it seemed a bit less dangerous at the time. I am not so sure about that now. The bloody Somalis are worse than Gaddafi."

"Where has Daniel gone by the way?" enquired Charlie.

"Oh! he will be in bed with Eshe talking about gorillas!"

Charlie looked horrified.

"Sorry. Not physically in bed. They spend hours and hours immersed in gorilla lovemaking and all that stuff," said Thulani back-tracking at ninety miles an hour. How do you like your coffee?"

"Black is fine, thank you. Who were all the other people when we arrived?"

"Whenever the Maasai know Daniel is coming they all get very excited and come up to see him. They are great people when you get to know them. I will introduce you to some of them over the next few days. Their knowledge of the terrain is awesome and they are a massive help to us. One of them brought us some bushbuck for dinner tonight so we need to get that cut up. Do you like bushbuck chops?"

"Is that similar to venison?" enquired Charlie smiling.

"Much better. A lot more flavour and more tender. No red wine sauce I'm afraid and no Limoges to serve it on!"

"I am sure it will be delicious. I like trying new things. If I grab my camera Nzinga, can you show me the best place to take some quick photos of the mountain before supper?"

"Of course. Do you want anything in the foreground or just panoramic? When did you get the D5, it looks fantastic on the Canon website? Can I have a play with it later?"

"Of course. Daniel didn't say you were into photography?"

"It would be rude not to living here I suppose. I just love all the technology and with the new satellite systems we have, I get to see things from unusual angles and elevations that you can't from the ground. Over here is a good location: you can get that Prunus tree in the foreground if you want too."

Charlie set up her tripod on the hallowed outcrop of grey volcanic rock and surveyed the landscape sweeping before her, across the endless grasslands to Kilimanjaro.

Her heart lifted and the sounds of Tsavo infiltrated her mind. The crystal-clear air tenderly brushed her face and the smell of the bush tantalised her senses. This was the real Africa and its magic arrested her soul forever.

"Are you OK?" asked Nzinga after a few minutes.

"Yes. Sorry. Not sure what happened then."

"Don't worry. The same thing happened to me the first time I stood there. This is a very special place to be on this earth."

As the sun slowly set in the west, the skies turned from azure to gold and finally crimson; the waves of light changed the landscape into a myriad of palettes. The acacia trees seemed to catch fire. The hillsides and valleys came alive with moving shadows and the mountain erupted in explosive hues.

"Now then. What are you two up to?" asked Daniel surprising them both. "I hope she is not filling you with all that witchcraft stuff. Can I introduce Eshe? Eshe this is Charlie." They shook hands formally, which felt a bit odd. Eshe was amazingly beautiful. She could have easily been a Vogue model with slender hips, high cheek bones and hypnotic eyes.

"I understand you are running the mountain gorilla project for Daniel in Rwanda?"

"Yes, it is my privilege to work with Daniel on this project and I am so grateful to him for employing me on such a wonderful programme."

"How long have you been here in Kenya?"

"About three years. I did a degree in genetics at Oxford and then a PhD on primate conservation in LA."

"So how did you meet Daniel?" asked Charlie.

"I was so lucky. I was on a summer fellowship at LA Zoo's Campo Gorilla Reserve and I was feeding the young western lowland gorilla females and Daniel just happened to be visiting the zoo. We got chatting and he offered me this job. It was amazing. He is such a wonderful person."

"You didn't by any chance go to Father Peter's orphanage, did you?"

"Yes. It's amazing what a small world it is."

"It certainly is," said Charlie looking Daniel straight in the eye.

Charlie took enough shots to fill *National Geographic* for the next millennium and then they wandered back towards the now blazing fire. The laughter drifted back to them from the camp. The flickering light from the flames highlighted the smiling faces and the smell of roasting buck pervaded the smoke-filled, evening air.

Daniel opened a bottle of Waterford reserve and toasted the team and the visit. Bomani carved the well-done buck from the spit and served it with crispy bread rolls he had made specially that morning. Charlie sat on a Klint safari chair, surrounded by an attentive audience of inquisitive youngsters, hanging on her every word, and asking a myriad of questions about Yorkshire, photography and life with Daniel. Eshe was definitely jealous!

"How long can you stay? You must see the new baby gorilla. Have you ever photographed a giraffe? Do you love Daniel? Can you ride? Have you brought any music?"

The laughter continued into the night, the fire reduced to glowing embers and the star-filled sky looked down on their contentment with their lives.

Mount Kilimanjaro from the Chyulu Hills

The next morning Charlie was suddenly awakened by the squealing of bushpigs outside the camp and sat up with a start. Daniel was nowhere to be seen, so she quickly got dressed and stepped into the cool morning air where she met Nzinga making coffee.

"Where did Daniel go?"

"He left early in the car. He always goes to Elizabeth's grave on the first morning before sunrise. It's like a ritual he has to go through to enable him to carry on. It must be very difficult for you with him being so much in love with her?"

"Our relationship has grown very close over the last year but I know the terrible pain he feels about her death and how difficult he finds coming to terms with it. I just want him to be happy again and am content to just have his company."

"I hope you two can get together because he really seems to like you and you seem a very sensitive person, which he needs so desperately."

"How far has he gone?" asked Charlie.

"The grave is on a prominence above a very special place called Mzima Springs that flow out of these hills. Eshe and I keep the grave tidy and always put flowers there when there are some growing locally. Lots of animals and birds come to the Springs for water and Daniel wanted her buried where she could see them every day. I understand when she was buried the Maasai came from all over Tsavo and stood in a huge silent circle around the grave. They each brought a large round, white river stone from the Galana and placed it on the grave to give it eternal protection."

"Eshe seems very fond of Daniel?" enquired Charlie, with a slight hint of jealousy.

"She is funny. She worships the ground he walks on. If he told her to climb up that tree naked and sing Rule Britannia, she would do it instantly! He is a godlike figure to her and she adores him. But I will tell you a secret if you promise not to tell?"

"Of course."

"She is madly in love with Jahir. If you watch her eyes when he is around, she follows him everywhere. If she knows he is coming, she spends hours choosing the right clothes to wear to impress him and that's difficult living up here. But he just ignores her. It's unrequited love I am afraid."

"So, what about you. Do you have a boyfriend?"

"I am a bit ambivalent to men to be honest. Don't get me wrong they are great fun and I love being with them but I like my work and want a career of my own without being tied to one person. There are plenty of children in the world without me adding to the pile!"

"I am sure the right person will sweep you off your feet one day and you will fall in love," suggested Charlie, smiling.

"Maybe. But not yet. There's the Range Rover coming up the hill. Let's go and meet him and cheer him up."

"Hi. What have you two been planning?" asked Daniel.

"Why? Do we look guilty?"

"Yes very."

"Just girl stuff."

"About men I suppose?"

"Could be. Do you fancy a coffee and then you can tell us all what your plans are for today?" invited Nzinga.

"I thought Jahir could fly us over to Kilimanjaro so Charlie can get some aerial shots of the landscape and maybe see some giraffe from above. Then on the way back, we can call in and see Father Peter at Kimana. She would love seeing what he has done for the children of Africa."

"Is there room for Eshe to come too so she can keep Jahir company whilst we are exploring on our own?" Charlie winked secretly at Nzinga who smiled back.

"I suppose so, but I don't think he is interested!" replied Daniel realistically.

They collected up some warmer clothes in case it was cold on the mountain, Charlie got her camera gear and Eshe was as flustered as a church mouse. Jahir fired up the rotors and they flew towards heaven. Jahir skimmed over the savannah and the flaxen grasses trailed in waves behind them, the birds fluttered from the acacias and the elands scattered. Charlie took a thousand pictures, as Africa opened up before her eyes.

"I cannot believe how beautiful this place is. It's just wonderful. Wonderful!"

"It gets to us all like that the first time. And the next and the next. In fact, every time you fly over the plains of Africa, you touch something that's inexplicable." Jahir said wisely.

As they approached the mountain, Jahir flew up to an open ridge and skilfully landed the helicopter on the bare lava rock. The layered views back to the Chyulu Hills were stunning, with the yellow grasses dancing in the translucent heat haze, giving way to thickets of scrub topped with verdant green montane forests along the spine of the hills, half immersed in white cotton-wool clouds scattering the sunlight in a kaleidoscope of colours.

Charlie and Daniel sat huddled under a coat, for it was cold at the high altitude, whilst Jahir and Eshe explored higher up the mountain side. They said nothing. The panorama before them spoke the words.

When the youngsters returned, Eshe gave Charlie a small posy of wild flowers she had gathered as a hidden thank you for arranging the tryst. Jahir climbed into the helicopter and did a pre-flight check. "I think the rains are coming. We had better get off the mountain."

"Can you fly us down to Kilmana, so I can take Charlie to see Father Peter please?" instructed Daniel as he gave Charlie a hand with her equipment back into the helicopter.

They swooped down the mountain side to the grasslands below and flew the short distance to the orphanage where Daniel was brought up. It was much bigger than Charlie had imagined and the modern schoolrooms were testament to substantial investments. They were met at the gates by an old priest with a weathered, kindly face and a hoard of smiling, giggling children of all ages and sizes. They all looked well-fed and smartly dressed. Not the image pervading newspapers in European capitals.

"Good morning my son. It is so good to see you again after all this time. We have missed you." The priest took

Daniel in his arms and held him as a mother with her young child. Daniel was clearly emotional at meeting his saviour once again."

"Hello Jahir, now, who have you flown in from the gods with you today?"

"Hello Father. You know Eshe of course and this is Charlie from England who is a friend of Daniel's."

"It is a great pleasure to welcome you my dear to our humble orphanage. Please come inside and take tea with me. I want to hear everything about you and how life is, in the green and pleasant lands."

They followed Father Peter, in his flowing traditional black cassock, through an archway into a beautifully manicured cloister, with its mown lawns and a bubbling fountain in the centre. At the far end was his large office, the walls lined with old leather-bound books from floor to ceiling. His desk was a chaos of paperwork with an incongruous computer to one side.

His secretary, in colourful traditional dress, came in with the tea; Earl Grey in china cups with saucers.

"So how long have you known Daniel, Charlie?" asked Father Peter.

"About three years, but it seems much longer."

"Presumably in a good way," he laughed.

"He actually saved my life when I was attacked by three robbers in Croatia and we have been friends ever since."

"A knight by name and a knight by nature. He is a good man and you are very lucky to have him as your friend. Please be kind to him and look after him. We are blessed to have him as a benefactor for the orphanage."

"I will. We seem to enjoy the same things and make each other laugh a lot."

When they had finished tea, Father Peter took Charlie on a tour of the classrooms, the children rising with respect in each room. The facilities were as good as any school in England with computers everywhere and even a small science laboratory. Colourful paintings covered the walls and the air was filled with the happy voices of children at peace with their lot.

Daniel stopped to talk to a group of older students and Jahir and Eshe wandered off to some younger children painting in the art room. Charlie and Father Peter crossed the cloister, to see where the children lived and ate their meals.

"You are doing a wonderful job here Father and it is amazing how Daniel and Eshe have progressed in the wider world with your help, which I know goes a lot further than just education."

"We are very lucky and have some super young teachers, a lot of whom were at the orphanage as young children. It becomes a self-fulfilling cycle that we are trying to spread out across Kenya. We have some amazing supporters like Daniel that enable us to do all this financially. Without his support, none of this could happen."

"Tell me Father, what was he like as a child?"

"Daniel came to us as a new-born baby. His mother was a very wealthy aristocrat from England who fell pregnant to a handsome cavalry officer who knew nothing about the baby. A trusted family servant brought the baby here and we had to find a wet nurse for him. They set up a trust fund for him so he could get a good education and go to university in England if he was intellectually up to it, which he obviously was."

"Is the mother still alive?"

"No. Unfortunately she caught malaria and died about ten years ago. She never got married and there were no other children so she left her estate to her black tenant farmers and very kindly left us some money too."

"Did she ever come to see Daniel as he grew up?"

"She only came once, when he was about five. He was the only white child here, so it was obvious which child was hers. She made no attempt to speak to him but strangely, whilst she was watching him play ball with the other children, the ball came across the grass to her feet. She handed him the ball and he gave her a big hug. She did not respond in any way but there was a tear in her eye as she left. I never saw her again."

"How did he get on with all the other children?"

"He was always very popular with the other children. He was brilliant at all the sports and was always kind and considerate to them. They all respected him and looked up to him. There was even a rumour that he was an alien! Now, I have told you far too much, so please keep it to yourself. We better go and round up the others."

Charlie put her arms around him. "Thank you so much for telling me. He means the world to me and you to him."

As they walked back across the cloister, the heavens opened and the rains started to fall from the black sky in huge droplets. They stood under the entrance arch and were joined by the others.

"Thank you for showing my friends around Father. The place looks as impressive as always and the children look as happy as in my days. I will be in touch." Daniel shook the Father's hand and lingered a second before he let go.

Charlie gave the Father a kiss on his cheek. She was not sure if she should but did it anyway. He smiled and waved them goodbye as they dashed across to the helicopter in the torrential rain.

Jahir got them back safely, if a little bedraggled. The rain was pouring off the un-guttered thatched roofs and running in rivulets across the campsite, disappearing over the edge to the thirsty lands below. Bomani had a fire going under the veranda cover and was busy preparing supper. Charlie disappeared to change into something drier whilst Daniel relied on evaporation from the heat of the fire.

When Charlie returned, Daniel and Thulani were in deep conversation at the end of the veranda obviously discussing something serious. Thulani was showing Daniel something on a map and gesticulating aggressively. Charlie grabbed a drink and wandered over.

"Is everything OK?"

"Thulani thinks he has tracked down the third Somali who killed Elizabeth. We believe he is working near Kismayo in Somalia but it is in a built-up area so our normal tactics will not work. It's on the coast so we can get there by boat at night and surprise them but it will still be quite dangerous unless we can entice him over the border into Kenya. We will have to give it some thought."

"How did you manage to find him?" asked Charlie.

"Thulani says that one of the nurses from the clinic we built in Elizabeth's memory at Mtito Andei had been over to Mombasa to collect some medicines from a wholesaler. She recognised him there, buying some medical supplies. She remembered him from the CCTV we had from the garage where they'd stopped at, after the murder. We have cross-checked it with the wholesaler's security camera and it is definitely the same guy. It's an amazing piece of luck and presumably he was collecting drugs etc for his terrorist group? Supplies are very poor in Somalia and very expensive so that's why he will have come down to Mombasa. We tracked his number plate back to Kismayo with the rhino satellite. Don't mention that to anyone. The US military will get very upset!"

"Could we maybe get him out of the town with an offer of some cheap drugs and then we could ambush him where no one will see?" suggested Charlie.

"You've been reading the wrong books!" laughed Daniel. "Let's have some supper. The rains have given over so we can sit outside and enjoy the celestial show."

CHAPTER THIRTEEN

Landscapes of the Mind – Somalia – West Africa

Daniel did not sleep much during the night and did not talk much either. He was too absorbed with his plans for the Somali killer. They got up early and Bomani had already started cooking breakfast. It was a beautiful sunny day and the trees were alive with birds, chattering away to their colourful colleagues.

"Tea or coffee?" asked Bomani soberly.

"Tea please. The bacon smells good," said Charlie, trying to lighten the mood.

"One of our Maasai trackers dropped it off this morning. He had been following a white rhino and her calf all night near the Springs, so he thought we would like some fresh meat."

"Is Thulani about yet? We need to have a discussion about the Somali," asked Daniel.

"He will be back shortly. Something to do with a woman?"

"I didn't know he had one?" said Daniel.

"Several, I think. That's the problem!"

They were just finishing breakfast when Thulani wandered slowly up the track to the camp.

"Everything OK?" asked Daniel.

"Why is life so complicated?" moaned Thulani.

"Reap and ye will sow!" smiled Daniel.

"What's it got to do with crop farming?"

"Never mind. Get a cup of coffee. We need the help of another part of your anatomy," said Daniel. Charlie choked on her cup of tea.

They sat around the rustic bench, that served as an al fresco table, in the peaceful African morning, planning the murder of the Somali. Charlie thought it a bit surreal, but listened in attentively as they discussed the best way to despatch the soul and dispose of the body. She thought about a more civilised route for all of this, but she knew Daniel needed the catharsis to move on with his life. Anyway, transborder policing with Somalia was poor to non-existent.

"Charlie actually made a really stupid suggestion last night about luring him out of town on a cheap drugs deal and I have been thinking about it all night. I think she might have the grain of an idea. It will enable us to surgically remove him without any collateral damage to innocent natives. They will be desperately short of painkillers, antibiotics and anaesthetics so we could put a package together from our clinic, that looks realistic. We would just need to get a contact number for him, to relay the trap to. Any ideas?"

"Well, we have the numberplate of the van he used, so hopefully, if it was his, we could track it down with the satellite to an exact location in Kismayo," suggested Thulani.

"OK, so ask Nzinga to do that this morning and I will see if I can find out how to get hold of his mobile phone number. Bomani, you get down to the Springs and check on that rhino with the calf."

The two men disappeared to dispatch their tasks leaving Daniel and Charlie alone.

"Can I help in any way?" asked Charlie.

"I want to take you across to see the mountain gorillas when this is over, so can you and Eshe work out a plan and contact our trackers over in Rwanda. They will know the current location of the band and the best way to get to them. Jahir can fly us over to the usual pad near the trackers camp. Eshe can come with us, as she knows all the gorillas by name."

"Can I come with you to Somalia?" asked Charlie.

"No, it's too dangerous and unpredictable up there and I need you to run the conservation programmes if it goes wrong. I have never asked Anne Marie for help but if it all goes awry; she will know people who can help you on the finance side. The young people here are fantastic and can manage the programmes but they don't have the knowledge and contacts to do the high-level stuff and you would be good at that."

"Promise me you will not take any unnecessary risks. I can't lose you again!"

"I will do my best. Right. I better get on the phone to Sebastian and see if he can track down this number."

Charlie went and found Eshe who was very excited about going to see her gorilla band again, as she hadn't been over for a couple of months and there had been a new arrival since. Nzinga and Thulani reappeared after a couple of hours with smiling faces.

"We've got him! We know the exact location, next to a medical clinic on the outskirts of Kismayo. We think he is called Jawara, which ironically means one who loves peace!"

Daniel immediately texted the name to Sebastian in the vain hope that he had used his name on the phone at some time. At that point Bomani returned from his trip to the Springs and reported that the rhino and calf were well.

"I need you two guys to get a couple of AK-47s and some ammunition from that dealer in Athi River. Just say it's for me. He owes me a few favours and he can have them back next week if we don't get shot ourselves!"

"Very funny," said Bomani jokingly. "Can I go back to Libya – it might be safer there!"

"Let's aim to do it on Friday night if he will take the bait?" said Daniel with increasing determination. "I will go down to the clinic this afternoon with Charlie and collect some medical supplies."

* * *

After lunch Daniel and Charlie got into the Range Rover and descended the now muddy red track to Kibwezi and then followed the main road down to Mtito Andei where the pristine white-painted clinic stood, in immaculately lawned grounds. The gateway was adorned with a polished brass plaque on a white marble plinth from the quarry at Kajiado. It simply said 'The Elizabeth Knight Memorial Clinic'.

Daniel and Charlie were met by Karen, a statuesque lady doctor in a crisp white coat. She welcomed Daniel with a big hug and Charlie wondered why there were no ugly ladies in Daniel's life!

"This is a very good friend of mine from England called Charlie."

"It's very nice to meet you, Charlie. Which part of England?"

"North Yorkshire."

"Ah! God's own country. I graduated from Sheffield Hallam University as a doctor and then got my PhD there studying immunology. I love the north of England; one never forgets the green valleys and the purple heather moorland. I have such fond memories of my time there."

"How did you end up in Africa?" asked Charlie.

"It was an amazing coincidence really. Just after I got my PhD, I was out with some friends at a traditional English pub we used as students and I met Daniel sitting on a wall outside, enjoying the evening sunshine after a day's fishing in Ladybower Reservoir. We got chatting and he offered me this job which was a dream opportunity for me, with my work on disease and immunity. It was only later that we realised we went to the same orphanage."

"Life is full of amazing coincidences isn't it, Daniel?" observed Charlie, smiling.

"Don't worry Charlie, I soon rumbled him. He would never go fishing in a reservoir! Come and have a look round our humble clinic."

They wandered around the beautifully kept facilities and small wards where some of the sick children were staying.

"We cannot do complicated medicine here but we have a great relationship with the main hospital in Nairobi and they give us priority access for our children. We do a lot of preventative medicine here and try to educate the younger generation about things like sexually transmitted diseases and managing maternity issues. We only have three doctors and two nurses so we are limited in what we can do, but we hope we are making a difference."

"Karen, can I borrow some medical supplies for a job I am doing on Friday?" requested Daniel.

"Of course. What sort of job and how much do you want?"

"I'd rather not say about the job but a large outer with a few boxes of antibiotics and anaesthetics on the top, so it looks like a lot."

"Sounds intriguing?" said Karen quizzically.

"Let's just say I need to purify the world for now."

"I am all for that. ChaCha will make the box up whilst we have a cup of tea in my office."

"So how did you two meet up?"

"Daniel saved my life when I was on a photographic trip to Hydra and some youths tried to rob me. He just turned up at the right moment."

"I suppose he was on a sea fishing trip!"

"Something like that!" laughed Charlie.

Daniel rapidly changed the subject. "So how is the new mobile x-ray scanning unit working?

"It has revolutionised what we can do here, rather than trail people up to Nairobi unnecessarily. It also means we can treat minor breaks here so patients are in pain for far less time."

"Well, we had better be getting back before the rains start. Thank you for the supplies and I will see they get replaced one way or another."

"It's been very nice to meet you, Charlie. You must bring Daniel over for supper one night and meet my partner, Robert."

Karen waved them off, with the reflection of the car catching in Elizabeth's plaque as they turned on to the road to retribution.

* * *

On the way back up the Chyulu track, the oceans fell down from the sky and progress was tedious, but the trusty Range Rover clawed its way back up the hill to the camp. Just as they arrived Daniel got a phone call.

"Hi Seb. Any luck? That's odd. What language? English! I don't like this. Have you got the number? Great text it to me. And he is openly using his name Jawara? Does he want to get shot? I know, sorry. Thanks, I will get back to you. Give my love to Marika."

"That sounds very positive?" asked Charlie.

"It's almost too easy. Anyway, we're on."

"Is Marika his girlfriend?"

"Good God no. It's his Great Dane!"

Bomani and Thulani were already back, loaded with enough firepower to take on the whole of the Al-Shabaab terrorist group.

"I said two AK-47s."

"I know, but it's ages since we had a good fight!" laughed Thulani.

Bomani started on supper, whilst the others freshened up. Daniel made the phone call, from a new mobile he sourced from his bottomless pit.

"Hi. Is that Jawara? I'm Max. I saw you the other day at the medical wholesalers and the loading guy there gave me your number. I said I was an old friend. I've got some clean medical supplies from a bankrupt clinic in Nairobi, that I can sell you cheap, for cash. Yea, antibiotics etc. It's good stuff. I can text you a list. Yea about half what you pay at the wholesaler. OK ring me back if you are interested but don't leave it too long, I've got other customers."

The wait began.

Just as they were finishing supper and started on a new bottle of Overgaauw Merlot, the mobile rang.

"Yes Ok. No, I can't deliver it to Somalia for that price. How much do you want off the list? All of it. OK. I'll tell you what I will do. I'm coming up to see a friend at Hagadera Refugee camp at Dadaab on Friday night, just on the Kenyan side of the border. I can meet you there if you take the full list and can pay in dollars… OK, it's a deal. I will be there about nine o'clock in the evening. I will be in a blue Subaru truck. Will you be in the same van as at the wholesalers? OK. I will meet you in the car park outside Borehole 5 Primary School on the outskirts of the camp. It should be deserted at that time of night. Ring this number if you can't make it. See you then."

"Do you think he bought into it?" asked Charlie tentatively.

"Seemed to. They are desperate for medical supplies and don't like raiding their own people. The Americans have made it much harder to smuggle supplies over the land border since al-Shabaab bombed Mogadishu. The US carried out two airstrikes targeting the Islamist militants in the vicinity of Qunyo Barrow and Caliyoow Barrow just after Christmas devastating their supply lines."

"Do the terrorists still kill large numbers of elephants and rhino for their tusks and horns?" asked Charlie.

"In the 90s and early 2000s they were killing thousands in Kenya and moving the tusks and horns up through Somalia to the ports. Al-Shabaab acted more as agents and left it to locals to actually collect the ivory and deliver it to them. As supplies started to dry up and the prices to the Chinese rocketed, the Somalis started to come down themselves with better intelligence and heavily armed. Thus, we are where we are. After Friday night, if we are successful, we will have at least completely eliminated one cell and its whole supply chain across to the far east."

"How did you actually track down the other two Somalis back then, without the technology we have now?"

"The locals were amazing. They all loved Elizabeth for the selfless help and limitless dedication she had given them and they tracked the killers route down, by word of mouth, from one village to the next, right across the plains of Africa and into Somalia. To be fair to the American military, when we knew their exact location, I rang a friend in Washington and he contacted the local Commander on the ground. All I wanted was permission to enter their 'war zone' and destroy the bastards myself. Somehow the Commander knew of Elizabeth and offered to do it for me. I gave him the coordinates with a time window and he sent two F16 Viper jets that blew a hole twenty metres deep and eighty metres long where their camp was. He simply sent me a short message back. 'Confirmation mission successful. Vermin exterminated. Glad we could help.' I never knew his name."

"Can we ring the Commander again for Friday night," joked Bomani.

"This one is personal," said Daniel sombrely. "I want to see the whites of his eyes when I pull the trigger." Daniel paused for a moment. "Anyway, onto more pleasant matters. Nzinga, I am going to be busy for the next couple of days sorting all this out. Why don't you and Jahir take the helicopter and show Charlie some of the real Africa?"

Nzinga looked more cheerful. "That's a great idea. We could go down to the Aruba Dam on the Voi River. There will be plenty of elephants there now the rains have come and we might see some lions as well. We could then fly up to the Lugard's Falls on the Galana so Charlie can get landscape shots now there is plenty of water. Does that sound OK Charlie?"

"Sounds amazing. Wherever you think is good for getting some wildlife pictures."

"There will be lots of zebra, gazelles, impala etcetera and hundreds of different birds; but don't ask me to identify them all! The following day we could drive down to Ngulia in Tsavo West to see the black rhinos and we might even be lucky enough to see a leopard. I'll ring a few locals up and see where the latest sightings are."

"Thank you Nzinga," confirmed Daniel. "That's great. If you pick up any sightings elsewhere, it's fine, just to go with the flow. Just make sure Charlie has a good time and sees everything she wants to. Right. It's going to be a busy, few days. Cheers everybody. Here's to successful hunting!"

* * *

The following day, whilst Charlie enjoyed the beauty and sounds of Africa, Daniel, Bomani and Thulani put together the rendezvous plan with the Somali. They tried to think of every eventuality and how they would deal with each scenario. Ambush was the most likely possibility, so they decided to change the meeting point at the last minute to disrupt any chance of it happening. A no-show was of course a possibility, or that the Somali would change the location, but they would abort the mission if that happened. Daniel was very suspicious that the plan was too simple and did not want to risk his colleagues' lives. He organised the pick-up with a friend in Kibwezi and they loaded the drugs and guns in the back. They planned to leave early on Friday morning as it would take about eight hours to get there and they wanted to do some reconnaissance before the Somali arrived, to ensure they were in control of the location.

Charlie and Nzinga flew in with Jahir at supper time after their first trip to Aruba dam. Eshe had roasted a pig and was wearing her best Jahir-enticing dress.

Charlie gave Daniel a quick kiss on the cheek. "We have had an amazing day. The scenery was spectacular and the abundance of wildlife unbelievable. We saw a whole herd of elephants covered in red dust, and I got some wonderful close-ups, thanks to Nzinga. Her understanding of their behaviour patterns was so helpful in letting me get really near. There was a lovely baby elephant with his mother who was so cooperative. I cannot wait to download the cards onto my computer."

"Sounds like you've had a good day," said Daniel. "Eshe has nearly got supper ready so why don't you all freshen-up whilst I find a bottle to drink."

Daniel sat down with Bomani and Thulani and tried to relax but his mind was elsewhere. Charlie and the others came back and they all tucked into the honey-roasted pig. Eshe flashed her eyes at Jahir but he was more interested in the pork.

"So, what else did you see?" asked Daniel.

"Pretty well everything, I think. We saw a pride of lions under some acacia trees looking very satiated. Two giraffes eating the top of another tree and I got a fantastic shot of them. There were huge numbers of Grévy's zebra, Grant's gazelles, impala and every type of bird you can imagine. We didn't see any black rhino but Nzinga says we have a much better chance of seeing them tomorrow. I have some lovely landscape shots of the elephants in the river showing the red soil washing down their leathery skins into the muddy waters."

"Well, I am pleased the rains held off so you could get some good pictures for your files. We will have to go out early one day and get some sunrise pictures when the light is at its best and maybe catch sight of some lions with an early morning kill."

"I see you have got your pick-up ready for the morning. Is everything going to plan so far?" asked Charlie hesitantly.

"So far, so good. I think we have got everything covered that we can think of, but it is always the unexpected that catches you out, as we found last time we went skiing."

"What time are you off in the morning?"

"We needn't leave till about eight, so we will have some breakfast and then set off. Nzinga, have you got tomorrow sorted for Charlie? If you ring Amanze he will know where the rhinos are tomorrow and will probably go with you if he is free."

"All taken care of. He is meeting us at the gates and he thinks he knows where Charlie can get a shot of a leopard that's been loitering around the top of the valley."

"I will bring some long lenses with me in case we cannot get close enough. What time will you get back tomorrow night?" asked Charlie.

"If it all goes OK, I think we will stay in Nairobi and be back for a brunch on Saturday morning. It will break the journey, just in case anyone is trying to follow us or track us. I doubt it but I don't want to risk anyone linking our expedition to this place. Right, we all have a plan. Here's to a successful day's shooting!" Everyone sighed but still drank the Kanonkop Black Label anyway.

* * *

The blood red sun was just starting to descend into the horizon, when the dusty blue pickup turned off the main road into Hagadera Refugee Camp. Daniel and his co-conspirators had covered their faces with scarves, in case of hidden security cameras. They drove around the sprawling United Nations camp, filled with over 100,000 people of every nationality but mainly Somali refugees, sheltering from the interminable conflict over the border. They located Borehole 5 Primary School and could see nothing suspicious, although there were still a lot of people about. Daniel had planned that the real location would be at the Dadaab airstrip, away from the camp, near the main A3 road so they could make a rapid exit if necessary. It was deserted at night and with no security lights or cameras at the remote southern end of the taxi-way. They drove back to a side street, where they could watch for the van arriving at the school without being seen.

"When he arrives at the runway, I will park about 100 metres from his van and flash the headlights. Hopefully he will get out of the van and come towards us. When I am sure he is not heavily armed, I will get out of the car and meet him. I will ensure we have the right man and kill him. I do not intend to move the body – nature can take care of that. I will get back in the car and we simply drive back to Nairobi. If it goes wrong and he, or any hidden terrorists, shoot me first, make sure you kill him before you make an escape. Don't start World War Three – just kill him and leave. Have you checked your AKs?"

"All good," said Bomani calmly. "Don't worry. This is his last sunset."

The minutes ticked by more slowly, as the rendezvous time approached. The pick-up was filled with the silence of professionals preparing for destiny. The streets were quiet as the van pulled into the school and stopped with the engine running and the lights on. A shadowy figure got out of the driver's door and scanned the surrounding area. When Daniel was sure there were no other vehicles accompanying him, he made the call.

"Hi Jawara. Have you arrived at the school? Great. I have moved up to the airstrip on the edge of town. There were too many people around and I thought it would be better for you if we were not seen. Do you know where it is? Great. I will see you there in ten minutes at the southern end of the runway."

The driver climbed back into the van and innocently drove off in the right direction. Daniel let him get well ahead and then followed at a safe distance.

The van pulled onto the airstrip apron and searched the deserted terrain with his headlights. Daniel turned off his lights and entered the airstrip higher up and parked by a building. After a couple of minutes, he turned on his lights and drove down to the van, parking at the prescribed distance. He flashed his headlights. The plan then started to unravel ominously. The van started up again and drove up to the pickup and parked within a few metres. Daniel left his lights on and could see a second terrorist in the van.

"Can you see the other one?" said Daniel urgently.

"I have him covered. If he breathes, he's dead," assured Thulani.

Daniel checked his P30 for the tenth time and opened the car door. Jawara nonchalantly opened his door and stood up. Daniel was sure it was the right target from the video footage. He pulled out his gun and pointed it straight at Jawara's head.

"You are one of the bastards that hacked my wife to death at Nakuru."

Jawara was clearly stunned, his eyes widened and he was shaking with fear as he faced his immediate death.

"No sir. Not me. I wasn't there," he stuttered in a broken voice.

Daniel pulled out a still from the video that clearly showed the guy's face and pushed it in front of the terrified man who was sweating profusely.

"I wasn't there honestly. Please don't shoot me. I am helping the doctor," he pleaded.

Daniel's hand was shaking uncharacteristically. "You lying piece of shit."

Just as Daniel was about to complete the execution, a calm English female voice came from within the van. "He didn't know what had happened until much later. He was only the driver. Please give me a chance to explain, before you seek unwarranted revenge."

For once Daniel did not know what to do. His head was awash with years of planning for this moment of revenge and suddenly the world was not as he had assumed, for all this time. Fact had now been blurred. The female got out of the car. Daniel pointed the P30 at the female.

"Hello Daniel. Please give me a chance."

"Mary! What the bloody hell are you doing mixed up in this?"

Thulani got out of the car and pointed his AK at Jawara, now on his knees in the ochre dust of the taxi-way. "I've got this bastard covered whilst you sort out your social life!"

"I didn't even know you were still in Africa," said Daniel. "How on earth did you get mixed up this whole Somali situation. It's incredibly dangerous up here and you can't trust any of them."

"When Elizabeth and I graduated from medical school, we both came to Kenya and she started her clinic at Mtito Andrei. The situation in Somalia was even more dire so I decided, stupidly, to try and do the same thing in Kismayo. It has been very difficult. The terrorists and their paid lackeys control everything. They murder anyone that gets in their way. We have to keep a very low profile and we cannot raise the funds that Elizabeth did. No wealthy Americans want to pour money into Somalia. When Jawara found out what the other two poachers had done he was horrified. He didn't think about what he was doing driving for them. He just wanted some pocket money to go out with his friends. It was a stupid decision which he will regret for the rest of his life. He came to me for some pills to make him sleep because he was having nightmares about it. We got to know each other and he has been helping me ever since. We are very close and I need him, Daniel. I know you will never forgive him but he is seeking redemption and working very hard to help the poor and dying in the countryside around Kismayo."

Daniel's heart was broken. He had been waiting for ten years to avenge Elizabeth's death and now it was taken from him. He felt failure, indecision and injustice. He walked away into the darkness.

After about five minutes, with Thulani still training his gun on Jawara, Bomani got out of the car and walked slowly over to Daniel who was standing on the airstrip staring into the solitude of infinity. Bomani put his arm around Daniel's shoulders.

"Time to go home boss. Forgive him and walk away. You will never forgive yourself if you pull the trigger. Charlie will never forgive you. Father Peter will never forgive you. And most importantly Elizabeth will never forgive you. She can lie in peace now. Let's go home."

They walked slowly back to the others. Daniel offered his hand to Jawara and he scrambled to his feet. He looked into his terrified bloodshot eyes. "If you ever let Mary down, God help me I will find you wherever you are hiding and pull the trigger."

Mary threw her arms around Daniel, and whispered a 'thank you' in his ear. Thulani loaded the box of medicines into the van and closed the doors.

"If you need any more let Thulani know; he will give you his mobile," said Daniel. "We had better get back before I change my mind. Look after yourself Mary. If you need anything, we will sort it for you."

Daniel and the two boys drove back to Nairobi in silence. There was nothing to say that would fill the desolate space in Daniel's head.

They arrived back at camp the following morning in a torrential downpour typical of the long rains. Everyone was in a sombre mood and the atmosphere devoid of the usual banter. Thulani had phoned ahead and explained what had happened at the airstrip and they all felt a sense of loss in different ways. Charlie put her arm around Daniel and they wandered off on their own to the vantage point overlooking Kilimanjaro, which was shrouded in rain clouds. The rain soaked through their clothes but they did not notice.

"Are you OK?"

"I don't know how to feel; my head says I have done the right thing but my heart feels a deep pain of regret."

"You did the right thing Daniel. He didn't know what had happened. He was just an ignorant accomplice. He shouldn't have been there, but he doesn't deserve to die."

"Mary said Elizabeth would understand but I just feel empty and bereaved," said Daniel sadly.

"Why don't we go for a walk down at the Springs after lunch and you can show me where Elizabeth is buried. I would like that. I know it's a very special place for you; where you feel closest to her. It might help. I am sure she will help you come to terms with what has happened."

"I would like that too," confirmed Daniel.

* * *

After lunch, Daniel and Charlie took the Land Rover down the red-rivered track with the rains still falling in rainbowed torrents from the dark skies. They parked some way from the Springs and Charlie took Daniel's arm as they walked through the sodden grasses and deep mud to the water's head that spilled from the stony bank against the Chyulu Hills. Daniel led Charlie up the path to the prominence where Elizabeth's grave lay covered in the white river stones brought by the Maasai to protect the grave. Daniel bent down to tidy a wayward flower and burst uncontrollably into tears. The years of love and stress etched his face as his tears fell into the dust, as they had at Versailles.

Charlie left him alone for a while and then put her hand gently on his shaking shoulder. He eventually got slowly to his feet and held Charlie close, sobbing on her shoulder. Tears welled up in her eyes too, as his loss overwhelmed them both; her tears trickling down his bare neck. They stood together as the rainbow drifted across the Savanah grasslands towards them from Kilimanjaro and then, as suddenly as they had started, the long rains stopped as they do in Africa. And there before them, drinking from the spring, was the white rhino cow and calf in no fear of the two of them. A small flock of cinnamon bracken warblers alighted on the muddy edge of the spring and drank from the clear waters. A lone white-starred robin sang in the bushes behind them. Daniel lifted up his head and wiped the tears from Charlie's cheeks. "She is the first white calf to be born in Chyulu for several years. She is very precious; we must look after her, you and me."

Charlie took Daniel's arm and they made their way back to the Land Rover.

When they got back to the camp Jahir and Eshe were starting to make supper outside, as the rains had passed for a while. Jahir's hand fleetingly brushed Eshe's back as they

White Rhino

moved around the open grill. Eshe smiled at him. Charlie smiled too and Eshe looked coyly at the ground.

As the sun rose over Tsavo on Sunday morning, Charlie was up early to get some shots from the hallowed rock. As she returned to the camp Eshe and Jahir came out of his tent together hand in hand. When they saw Charlie, Eshe quickly let go and scurried off to her own hut. Jahir nonchalantly strode over to the fire and kicked the embers sending residual sparks into the crisp morning air.

"Morning Jahir. Everything OK?" smiled Charlie.

"Just planning todays flight to Rwanda with Eshe."

"Of course. It's a lovely day for flying high!"

After breakfast they packed the helicopter for the three-day trip. Eshe was staying on for a few extra days to check-up on some more remote gorilla families which had not been seen for a few months. The plan was to fly to Kigali airport and top-up with fuel before heading up into the Virunga mountains where Eshe had arranged for the trackers to be waiting with a pick-up.

Daniel had also been up early and returned the arsenal of guns to the dealer in Athi River. He reappeared in the Range Rover just as they were loading Charlie's final camera equipment into the helicopter. It seemed as if a large weight had been lifted from his shoulders and he was back to his cheerful self.

"Now Bomani, whilst I am away you keep a very close eye on that cow and calf and let the local Maasai leaders know to do likewise. Nzinga, can you and Thulani concentrate on calibrating the satellites to cover that dead area down near the Tanzanian border. And don't drink all the good wine whilst we are away!"

Jahir completed his pre-flight checks with Daniel sat next to him. Charlie and Eshe sat behind. They lifted off into the clear azure blue skies and headed west around the volcanic slopes of Kilimanjaro. And then across the plains towards Lake Natron and on to the rich rain-soaked pastures of the Serengeti. The enormous herds of wildebeest swirled across the grassland beneath the helicopter like a two-dimensional murmuration of starlings in an autumn Yorkshire evening. The Thompson's gazelles leapt and frolicked as if in fun and the Maasai giraffe looked on disdainfully, continuing their lofty lunch. A small herd of bush elephants with two youngsters were drinking at a water hole, enjoying an escape from the heat of the African sun.

When they reached the shores of Lake Victoria, Jahir flew up the lake shoreline until he found a remote beach to land on for lunch. Eshe had brought some sandwiches in an old wicker basket and Daniel rolled out a tweed blanket to sit on. As they ate lunch, a small flock of pink flamingos drifted round the headland with their heads underwater searching for theirs. Daniel sat next to Charlie and put his hand on hers and they smiled to each other as Jahir and Eshe did the same.

In the late afternoon, they arrived at the foot of Mount Bisoke in the Virunga Volcanic region of northern Rwanda. Jahir landed the helicopter in a small clearing of the sylvan landscape and they were welcomed by a chattering group, consisting of the two trackers and their families. They were very excited at seeing Daniel and he was buried in an avalanche of questions and information. He waved his arms to make space but to no avail. His infrequent visits were a reason to celebrate and catch up on all the news from Kenya and beyond. It would be a long evening.

"Jahir, can you and Eshe put our things into the usual tents and I will try and sort out what the plans are for tomorrow." The two tracker's wives latched onto Charlie, enquiring if she was a wealthy benefactor.

"No. no. I am just a friend of Daniel's and he kindly invited me along. I like photographing things and I am hoping to get some of the gorillas."

"So, do you love Daniel?" asked one lady getting straight to the point.

"I think we all love Daniel," Charlie replied cautiously.

"That's a yes then!" the lady laughed. "Come with us; we will show you where we live." Charlie was taken by the hand and lead away for women's talk. She looked back at Daniel, who was still surrounded but managed a perfunctory wave.

The following morning the serious stuff began. One of the trackers had left early, to try to locate the band that Daniel was keen to see and so Eshe could document their progress since her last visit.

"It will be very cold as we get higher up the mountain Charlie and the vegetation is very dense and wet, so wrap up warm. You get a false impression down here in this sheltered spot."

"I've brought my February lambing gear so I will be fine!"

"I know your camera is waterproof but I would keep it in your backpack until we get nearby. The going is pretty tough in places and you don't want to get it covered in mud if you lose your footing."

"Wamwarav, have you heard anything yet about which direction we need to set off?" asked Daniel.

"We have found some nests in the Hagenia forest on the eastern slope, so if we head up in that direction we can home-in as we get more information."

After two hours of heavy slog along narrow rough tracks they stopped for a short break. Wamwarav got on the radio and spoke to his mate who was higher up in the forest.

"Any luck?"

"Not yet. I heard the silverback about twenty minutes ago but they are in very dense forest with gallium vines everywhere, so seeing them is going to be tricky today."

"OK, we will keep following your tracks. When you get near, send us a GPS position and we will work our way to you."

"Are you OK Charlie? It's pretty tough going," asked a concerned Daniel.

"Walk in the park!" smiled Charlie. "You should try rescuing sheep in ten-foot snow drifts!"

After another hour they were no closer. The band had moved further along the slope on some very steep terrain and then it started to rain. A lot.

"I think we better call it a day," said Daniel reluctantly.

"I agree," said Wamwarav. "It's going to be impossible to get near enough for Charlie to take some photos and they will just drift further along that ridge, which I know from past experience is a nightmare, even in good weather. They wearily retraced their steps back down to camp and arrived wet, tired and disconsolate. The wives met them happy and smiling, breaking the mood.

"We've put the generator on, Charlie, so you can have a nice hot shower and then you can help us cook supper. "We are having vegetarian goulash."

Charlie was glad of the shower to warm up but a little surprised at the choice for supper.

"I know we live in the jungle but we are reasonably civilised!" laughed the younger wife.

* * *

Next morning Wamwarav was up very early with his colleague and they set off up the mountain, still shrouded in swirling mist. The forecast was for better weather than the previous day, but this was the rainy season and anything could happen. Daniel spoke to Wamwarav on the radio and they had already seen a young blackback gorilla and could hear others in the distance. Daniel took the coordinates and they set off up a path that Eshe had used on previous visits. After an hour's steady climb, they came to a small clearing and sat on a rotting log to rest and speak to the trackers.

"How are we doing up there?" asked Daniel wishfully.

"We are having breakfast with a silverback and three females; one with a new baby."

"Where are you exactly?"

"About 100 metres higher up than you and across to your left. Keep your voices down because we can hear you from here," came the whispered reply.

"How shall we approach?"

"Come straight up and drop in from above. We are by a big rock on the left as you look down. They are the naturally roaming group and not habituated so move in slowly and tell Charlie to put the camera on silent mode."

"OK, we are on our way. Give us twenty minutes. Her camera doesn't have a flip-up mirror."

"Pinhole?"

"Shut up and watch the band."

They continued the climb as quietly as possible and tracked into the target location, one step at a time. They crawled the last few yards to the rock and there, happily munching away on the Galium vines, were the band of completely wild mountain gorillas in the montane cloud forest without a care in the world. It was one of those magical moments in Charlie's life which she would never forget.

"Can I take some photos?" Charlie whispered to Eshe.

"Yes, of course, but just move very slowly and make as little noise as possible. They know we are here and are not frightened."

Charlie slowly took the camera from her bag and started taking photos of the mother and baby. The silverback male turned his head and looked straight at Charlie and moved his position slightly so he could watch her more clearly but carried on eating.

"He is just checking that you are no threat. He will be fine – just keep going," whispered Eshe.

When Charlie had plenty of shots of the female, she turned her camera on the silverback and got some lovely shots of the sunlight streaming through the vines and casting shadows across his rugged face. He made some low rumbling belches of contentment and seemed to be enjoying all the attention.

Eshe pointed out that two of the youngsters had started grooming each other. "Just video that if you can Charlie. I am doing some work on social bonding in young gorillas and that will be really helpful." Charlie obliged.

After an hour, Daniel suggested they retreat and leave the band in peace. They backed away and the gorillas slowly disappeared from view as the vines enveloped them, and the magic evaporated into life-long memories for Charlie.

* * *

The following morning Jahir started the helicopter surrounded by the families. Charlie received endless cuddles from her new friends, before climbing aboard. Daniel embraced the two trackers with comradeship and received a kiss from each wife. Charlie shook her head imperceptibly and smiled. Jahir waved goodbye to Eshe and she blew him a kiss as he took off.

They arrived back at Chyulu camp, to be welcomed by a torrential downpour, but Nzinga had made a cake and they sat down under cover to relax and relate the news of the last three days.

"All good this end Daniel," said Thulani proudly. "The rhino and calf are still around the Springs and we got the satellite working down on the Tanzanian border so we can monitor stock moving between the two Parks."

"Any news from Mary in Somalia after our sortie the other night?"

"No. All quiet."

Charlie was flicking through her camera shots and shared one of the mother and baby with the team. "We were just so lucky to get such good light and to be so close to completely wild gorillas. It was an amazing experience. Thank you for taking us Daniel. I will never forget the silverback's expression when I started shooting. It said, 'Oh go on then if you must'!"

"Charlie and I need to leave tomorrow from Nairobi. Can one of you run us up there, leaving here about one o'clock?" asked Daniel.

"I'll take you back," offered Nzinga. "Are you going on the same plane that brought you down?"

"Yes, it's picking us up about four o'clock," replied Daniel.

Charlie looked at Daniel quizzically. "I didn't know we were using Annie's jet again?"

"She was just passing and offered to pick us up."

CHAPTER FOURTEEN

The Deserts of Arabia

Nzinga was waved through by security at Nairobi airport and she parked the Range Rover next to the waiting Gulfstream G600 on the tarmac apron. Charlie and Daniel got out of the car and Daniel helped Nzinga unload the bags.

"Hi, how was Africa?" smiled a beaming Anne Marie from the top step of the plane. "Welcome aboard the executive service to Arabia!"

Charlie was taken by surprise to see her and they met half way up the steps with a friendly hug.

"I didn't know you were coming with us. It's a lovely surprise though."

"Can't leave Daniel on his own for too long. He might get into trouble. Has he been behaving himself?"

"Now you two, stop talking about me as though I am not here," Daniel kissed Anne Marie on the cheek.

Daniel and Charlie waved goodbye to Nzinga as she drove off back to her vocation, and Daniel lifted the bags into the hold.

"Make yourselves comfortable, whilst I do the pre-flight checks with Aurora my co-pilot, and when we have taken off, I will come back and catch up on all the news. In the meantime, Lovisa will get you a drink, so just relax and enjoy the flight.

"I didn't know she was able to fly a plane?" Charlie whispered in Daniel's ear.

"Presumably we are about to find out. I would put your seatbelt on!"

"Lovisa is incredibly beautiful don't you think?"

"Hadn't noticed!"

"And the rest. You can't miss that cleavage."

Lovisa returned from the galley. "Can I get you something to drink?"

"Yes please. I guess we had better top-up before we get to Riyadh. It's going to be a dry few days," joked Daniel. "Can I have a Tanqueray and Fever Tree please."

"Mediterranean tonic?"

"Yes please."

"And for you Charlie? May I call you Charlie?"

"Of course. I think I will have the same."

"I think she fancies you Charlie," whispered Daniel grinning.

"Be quiet. Don't be ridiculous."

The Gulfstream took off as smooth as silk, and the seduction of the savannah disappeared into the clouds beneath them. Lovisa reappeared carrying a silver salver with the drinks and some nibbles. She offered Daniel his drink and then leant over to Charlie and served hers, with a charming smile.

"I told you that you would get the smile," laughed Daniel.

"I am not sure how she didn't fall out of that blouse," whispered Charlie.

"I would ask for another drink!"

Charlie poked Daniel in the ribs in response.

"What are you two giggling about?" asked Anne Marie, as she appeared from behind the curtain to the flight deck.

"Oh nothing. Just Daniel being jealous of your crew. That was a very smooth take off Annie. How long have you been flying?"

"An old friend taught me about five years ago when she came out of the USAF and was stuck for something to do. She was really kind and patient with me. I passed all the exams first time and find it quite challenging and exciting. Sadly, she was killed giving an acrobatic display in an old biplane, at an air show in Florida. It really hurt me at the time. I loved her a lot."

"I am sorry. I didn't mean to revive old memories."

"It's fine. I've learned to live with it now thank you, but I still think of her when I take off. Now then, tell me all about those lovely gorillas!"

Charlie related the joys of the jungle trip and how much fun she had had meeting all the young people at the camp, including all the intrigue with Eshe and Jahir.

"And did you get plenty of good landscape photographs for your new book?"

"What new book?"

"I want to work with you on a new book about conservation and the projects that Daniel is doing. Obviously, we can't mention him; he is too anti-famous!"

"That's a great idea but who is going to write it?

"Aurora my co-pilot studied creative writing in Adelaide and has written several successful novels. She has agreed to come and stay with us in England whilst we do it."

"Do I get any say in this?" enquired Daniel.

"None!" laughed Anne Marie.

"I think it's a great idea Daniel. It could raise a lot of money for extra trackers in Rwanda," said Charlie.

"I will think about it. As long as I am not in it and have full editorial rights!"

"I am sure we can persuade you!"

"Let's have something to eat." Anne Marie pressed the button and Lovisa swept out from behind the curtain like a soprano about to sing 'Caro nome' from Rigoletto. She handed out the extensive menus and Charlie wondered where the chef was.

They chatted happily away over lunch and Anne Marie knew Daniel well enough to avoid the 'E subject' until they were on their own. Charlie recounted her safari into Tsavo and promised to go through the photographs with Anne Marie, on their return to England, to decide which ones might be suitable for the new book.

"I better get back to Aurora and make sure she is OK. We are on autopilot but this is her first flight since she qualified." Charlie looked at Daniel and smiled nervously.

"Only joking. She can fly better than me!" Anne Marie disappeared behind the curtain.

* * *

The deep red sun was setting in the west as they flew into King Khalid International Airport just north of Riyadh. Anne Marie taxied across to VIP reception and they were met by two large black limousines. A young man dressed in a traditional white thawb and a red and white checked keffiyeh stepped out of the car. Daniel walked down the steps and the two embraced as old friends. Two bodyguards loaded the luggage into the car and Daniel climbed in, next to his old friend. The car drove off. Charlie acknowledged the protocol and dutifully got into the second car.

"Have a good time," shouted Anne Marie from the steps, "See you in Mauritius." Charlie did not know she was coming to Mauritius but she knew to go with the flow.

The two limousines swept through the beautiful architectural wonder that is modern Riyadh, lit up with a thousand reflections. They entered the ornate gates of the stunning Al-Auja Palace, Saudi Arabia's most secure building, and the cars parked outside the Prince's private quarters. They were met at the intricately carved doors by the Prince's wife, dressed in a traditional black abaya.

"Hello Daniel, it's a great pleasure to welcome you to Al-Auja again. It's been too long." Daniel formally shook the Princess's hand.

"Rashieka, this is my partner Charlie from England."

"I have heard a lot about you Charlie, and I love all your landscape photographs. I enjoy photography myself and I will enjoy talking to you about it later. Please come inside; you must be tired after your long flight."

"It is a great honour meeting you and your husband and thank you for letting us stay in your wonderful home," replied a well-briefed Charlie.

As they walked through the multimillion-dollar palace, the Prince pointed out the historic photographs of the early Saudi Arabia and of his illustrious predecessors. Unlike the other palaces Daniel had been to, Al-Auja was built in a more traditional Najdi style evoking an earlier period in the country's development.

The two men disappeared down a long corridor with a blue mosaic floor laid by local artisans, whilst Rashieka took Charlie to the suite where they were to stay. Rich in locally crafted furniture and subtle decoration, the rooms reflected the simpler tastes of the younger Prince's generation.

"Please make yourself at home," smiled Rashieka. "It's so nice to have someone new to talk to that I do not have to be so formal with. Being a princess can be very boring waiting for the men to make all the decisions!"

Charlie laughed. "Daniel can be a bit like that sometimes!"

"I think we will get on like a house on fire," smiled Rashieka, "I can't wait to show you around Riyadh. We are planning to have a quiet informal dinner together this evening with just the four of us. We will have to observe protocol a bit whilst they are serving the food so I have put an abaya on your bed that you can wear; just have your usual evening clothes on underneath. I will come and collect you about eight o'clock."

"Thank you for making me feel so welcome. I was a bit apprehensive in the car driving across the city on my own."

"It will be fun. Just relax and have a nice bath. If you want anything just give me a ring on the phone by the bed. I am 02. I will leave you to guess who is 01!"

Daniel returned, just as Charlie was coming out of the bathroom in her white towelling robe. "How is my beautiful princess?"

"I am fine. Rashieka is lovely and has made me feel really relaxed."

"That's good. They live a very complicated life with all the politics and sibling rivalry that goes on and I think they enjoy spending some time with ordinary mortals like us!"

"What have you two been discussing?" asked Charlie.

"Just some final details about the little job I have to do for them in the next few days. I will tell you about it later. I will grab a quick shower whilst you put your abaya on. I can't wait to see you in it. Very sexy!"

Rashieka came along at exactly eight and took them through a series of immaculate rooms to a small dining room with intricately carved panelling and adorned with historic items of family interest. The Prince was already sitting at the head of the table but got up and shook Charlie's hand. "Please come and sit next to me and tell me all about England, my second home."

Daniel sat next to Rashieka and immediately struck up a conversation about gorilla conservation. Rashieka was polite and seemed genuinely interested in how things were going.

"Daniel tells me you live in Yorkshire and have a big estate there with an extensive grouse moor?" asked the Prince.

"Probably not big in your terms," smiled Charlie from under her head scarf. "But we have a lot of international visitors and it is a very successful business."

"Do you have any brothers and sisters?"

"No. I think they had me and decided it was all they could handle!"

The Prince laughed and was impressed with Charlie's self-deprecating humour.

Whilst they ate the delicious Jalamah lamb dish, the Prince offered to take Charlie out into the desert for two days, later in the week, so she could photograph the dunes and maybe try her hand at falconry which was one of his favourite relaxations.

"What do you think Daniel? Shall we go and show the ladies how my ancestors lived.? We can get some Bedouin tents set up and spend a night under the stars."

"That would be great thank you. Maybe you could teach Charlie how to ride a camel!"

"I like a good challenge," laughed the Prince. "Would you like to come as well Rashieka? You can show Charlie where to get the best shots of the dunes."

"I would really like that. Can I show Charlie around Riyadh tomorrow whilst you and Daniel are working?"

"What she really means Daniel is, can I spend some money please! Yes of course you can. Take Charlie to our new shopping mall on Al Urubah and have a good time. You better take Kadin with you to carry the bags."

On the way back to their room Charlie whispered, "Who is Kadin?"

"You are highly honoured. He is the Prince's personal bodyguard, who he trusts completely and who never leaves his side except when he is in the bedroom with Rashieka. A very dangerous bag-carrier."

The next morning Daniel disappeared early with the Prince, to some secret location, and he left Charlie to empty the family coffers. Rashieka collected Charlie from her room at ten, accompanied by the most enormous muscular man Charlie had ever seen. Kadin was very well spoken, polite and the last person you would pick a fight with, in Arabia or anywhere else.

When they arrived at the Mall they were met by the General Manager and his top team, at the VIP entrance, and there was much ceremony because a member of the Royal family was visiting their Mall. Charlie later found out that the whole place had been swept for explosives before their arrival and there was a whole regiment of plain-clothed security men on every corner. She was finding out what it meant to be 'Royal'.

"Where shall we go first?" asked Rashieka excitedly. "I need a new suit for a trip to the US, a new handbag and a new gold necklace. He likes the long dangly sort. What do you need?" Charlie was caught a bit off guard as she only usually shopped in Harrogate when she really had to, and at the last minute.

"Err. Will I need anything special to wear for going into the desert? I would also like to buy Daniel a watch for his birthday."

Rashieka knew how to spend money. Kadin was soon loaded with an array of brightly coloured carrier bags but she never seemed to pay for anything. She bought Charlie some ridiculously expensive desert attire and a Patek Philippe watch for Daniel which she wouldn't let Charlie pay for. They had a wonderful day floating around on a cloud of sycophancy and Kadin ensured that they were always a safe distance from lesser shoppers. When Kadin was loading the car with all the day's acquisitions, Charlie whispered in his ear. "She never paid for anything!"

"Don't worry, the Prince owns the Mall, he will get a discount!" said Kadin with the hint of a smile.

When they got back to the Palace, Rashieka organised a time for dinner with Charlie and left her to have a nice relaxing bath to recover from the expedition. As she was lying in the cedarwood-scented bath, Charlie missed Daniel's touch for the first time since leaving England. Africa had been intense, emotional and immersing, but now she was relaxed and her thoughts turned to his cathartic experience with the forgiven Somali and his tearful release at Elizabeth's graveside. Would he now want to be with her properly for the first time?

She dried herself on the sumptuous bath sheet and wrapped it around herself, her hair in a smaller towel twisted onto her head. She helped herself to an apple and mango drink from the fridge and sat astride a barstool, and leaning against the backrest, she read up on falconry on her phone. She had just got to peregrines, when she heard Daniel open the door. She snatched the towel from her hair and shook her head vigorously.

"How is my princess tonight; did the shopping trip go well?"

"It was amazing. We had an army of secret security people, Rashieka bought me loads of presents and wouldn't let me pay for anything. I felt like royalty all day and we had a really good, fun time together. How did you get on?"

"All good. We have pretty well got all the details sorted out and the equipment I sent over is all in the right location. All we need now is a bit of luck."

"I know you don't want to tell me too much but I hope it's not too dangerous?"

Daniel kissed her on the neck and grabbed himself a drink. "You worry too much. Hopefully no one will get hurt this time. The Saudis are worried about the devastation in Yemen and the human consequences. The civil war is really a proxy theatre for the religious animosity between Iran and Saudi Arabia. It has become unwinnable on both sides and is just slipping into a dystopian future for all the children there, who are basically starving to death. We are going to try and take out all the Houthi rebels' internet hubs in one go, so they cannot communicate for a month, which will give the Saudis a chance to tip the balance in their favour and bring the catastrophe to an end."

"Piece of cake then!" quipped Charlie.

"It's quite complicated, but the Saudis have a lot of backup hubs, called redundancy, so if we take out the main internet cable in the Red Sea it should wipe out 90% of the Houthi infrastructure based in Sana'a. Saudi satellites will back up their own systems and other countries affected, like Sudan and Ethiopia."

"You are a genius. Now kiss my neck again. It's more fun!"

Daniel swivelled the chair around so Charlie was facing him but still leaning on the back of the chair. He kissed her sensuously on the lips, put his finger in the top of the bath sheet and spun the bar stool around again releasing the top so it fell to the floor. Charlie was now astride the chair and vulnerable to Daniel's caresses. He kissed her neck again and ran his fingers down her back to the seat. She giggled when he touched her bottom but he gently racked his fingernails across it and she reacted excitedly. Charlie rested her head on her arms on the backrest and Daniel slid his hands up the sides of her now taut body, lingering on the sides of her breasts. She moaned a little in encouragement. He stroked her tousled hair and played with her earlobes with his tongue. He knew she liked that. He knelt down behind her and kissed her back whilst sliding his hands around her waist and along her thighs trapped apart by the back of the stool. She wanted to close her thighs to intensify the pleasure put she was trapped.

She wasn't sure who was seducing who, but she didn't care and just wanted him to continue her pleasure. Still kissing her back, his fingers moved up the inside of her thighs again, and carelessly perhaps, touched her where she now desperately wanted his caress. Instead, his fingers found her nipples, erect with passion. He rolled the tips between his fingers, teasing and pressing, until Charlie lifted her head and leant back against him. She had her eyes closed and moaned again. He intensified his kissing, the caressing, the gentle stimulation of the whole of her trembling body until she came in wave after wave of sensual lust. Daniel lifted her from the stool and carried her to the bed. Charlie opened her eyes, kissed him passionately and started to slowly undo his shirt buttons.

"I love you Daniel. Please let me make love to you. Please."

"I love you Charlie and I adore stroking you. Please give me a bit more time. It will happen one day, I promise."

Charlie smiled and kissed him again. "Of course, my darling, I understand. As long as I can lie next to you and be with you."

Secretly she was getting desperate to be with him properly and wondered if she would ever be able to make it happen.

* * *

The next morning, they were up early. Charlie put on her new, ridiculously expensive desert attire, which Daniel thoroughly approved of, and they met the Prince and Rashieka outside by the cooling waters of the magnificent gold-encrusted water feature. Not quite Versailles, but nearly.

They climbed into the middle of five Range Rovers; the others full of the Royal entourage. And one for the falcons. Naturally. They drove west out of Riyadh, in their air-conditioned cocoons, for about an hour and then headed off-road along tracks for another hour before turning into the golden dunes. They traversed a dried-up wadi, and then up a near-vertical dune and the Prince instructed the driver to stop on the crest. Before them the desert rippled away in a glorious sea of waves to infinity; a perfect landscape for any photographer. Rashieka asked if they could take photographs but the Prince said he wanted to establish a camp not far away and then he would let Rashieka and Charlie drive back with Kadin to enjoy to scenery.

When they arrived at the designated spot, they disembarked and were hit with a wall of heat, which Charlie had never experienced before. She was glad of the special clothing Rashieka had bought for her, which was designed to repel the heat to some extent.

The dark Bedouin tents were soon erected by the efficient team from the fourth Range Rover, which was especially converted to carry such large equipment.

"What are the tents made of?" asked Charlie, who was fascinated by the efficiency of erection.

"Traditionally they were made of black goat's hair and woven by the womenfolk," replied Rashieka. "They were very good at providing shade during the intense heat of the day but also insulated the nomads at night. Most people do not understand that it can be very cold in the desert at night."

"I love all the intricately coloured rugs and well-worn cushions they are laying inside. Do you think we could photograph them when they have finished?"

"Yes of course, but we must be careful not to get the Prince in any of the shots. He is very sensitive about that."

"Of course. Daniel is the same but for very different reasons!" and they both laughed together.

"Why don't we let them finish setting up the camp and get Kadin to drive us back to the ridge to get some landscape shots. I will grab my camera. It's a Nikon, so that should set up a good conversation!"

When the ladies got back from their little expedition, Daniel and the Prince were sitting outside the largest tent, on traditional leather-studded stools, in deep conversation.

"How did the photography go then?" asked the Prince.

"It was breath-taking," said Charlie. "The sheer scope of the horizon and the shimmering colour tones are just unbelievable. Rashieka got some amazing shots with her Nikon, so we have been having a long debate about the pros and cons of Nikons versus Canons."

"I prefer a Leica myself but then I am a bit old-fashioned. My father gave me one as a present when I graduated, and I guess I have just got used to it," said the Prince.

"That's a coincidence," replied Charlie, "I started with a Leica which my father gave to me as a present too. It took some lovely pictures of the Dales."

"It's good at sand dunes too," laughed the Prince. "Let's have some lunch and then we can fly some falcons."

The Prince explained that the falcon is a symbol of wealth in Arabia, similar to the Arab horse. It was embedded into the history of the desert, the culture of the Bedouins and the hearts of the new, vastly wealthy elite. Falcons changed hands for enormous sums and were bred for their beauty, speed and effectiveness. They were a status symbol and his fellow princes of the desert countries, vied to own the best of the different bloodlines.

"My falconer has brought the birds in the air-conditioned Range Rover. They do not like the intense heat at this time of year and prefer their nice cool aviaries at the Palace."

"Are they mostly peregrines?" asked Daniel.

"Mostly, but I have some gyrfalcons from Scandinavia which are bigger and excellent at taking the lure. I will show you shortly."

They drove a short way to an elevated sand dune so they could get a good view of the falcons working. The Prince put a traditional mangalah cuff on his left wrist to protect it from the falcon's sharp talons. The falconer passed him a peregrine which sat calmly on his wrist.

Peregrine Falcon

"You will see Charlie that he still has his hood on covering his eyes so he does not take off prematurely. I am holding him to my wrist with this short leather strap fixed to his leg. That is called a flying-jesses and when I release the falcon, I simply let go of the leather strap. To release the falcon, you simply take off the hood like this…"

The peregrine exploded off his wrist at a lightning speed and climbed to a great height. The falconer swung a lure with a dead quail tied to the end and the falcon swooped to take the prey. At the last second, the falconer snatched it away from the bird and the falcon rose high into the sky again, only to descend at an even greater speed. The falconer repeated the snatch and the falcon soared again. Charlie was really enjoying the dexterity of the falcon and the skill of the falconer.

"He is a fantastic falcon. His speed is electric," observed Charlie.

"He is actually a 'she'!" observed the Prince. "Would you like a go now?"

"That would be amazing. Will she do it for me as well?"

"I will get you a male falcon to try; you might get on better because the males are a bit lighter. We call them tiercels and they are even faster and more agile than the females. Just like humans really!" the Prince laughed.

The falconer gave Charlie a full leather gauntlet, rather than the mangalah, to give her arm a bit more protection and then passed her the falcon.

"Don't lose him Charlie. That one cost me $300,000 last week and I have never released him yet!"

"You are joking?" exclaimed Charlie in fear of losing the bird.

"No. Off you go. Take off the hood."

With that, the falcon took flight and disappeared over a sand dune. The Prince looked at Charlie crossly, for what seemed like an hour.

"I am so sorry. What did I do wrong? Where did he go?"

"Iran, I think," said the Prince solemnly.

Charlie looked at Daniel horrified and did not know what to say. Then the Prince and Daniel burst out laughing and the Prince pointed high in the sky. Charlie could see nothing but as soon as the falconer swung the lure, the tiercel descended at over 200 miles an hour and took it, crashing into the sand, ripping at the quail's carcase and sending a plume of feathers into the air.

Rashieka laughed too. "Don't worry Charlie, he did it to Daniel the first time he came out here," she whispered in Charlie's ear. "He must like you. He only plays jokes on people he trusts."

Charlie and Daniel watched with awe as the Prince worked the bigger gyrfalcons and his love for the birds and the sport were very evident. This was his escape from the world and a return to the life of his ancestors.

That evening the four of them sat around a traditional majlis eating from shared dishes of thareed, a chicken dish with stewed vegetables, spices and ragag bread. Followed by luqaimat with dates and sesame. All washed down with gahwa, an Arabic coffee. The evening was much more relaxed than at the Palace. The staff were despatched out of sight and the girls were allowed to wear their western casual clothes. The Prince and Daniel revisited their times together at university and laughed a lot about their unroyal antics. They were obviously in regular communication and Charlie wondered how much help Daniel was getting from the Prince with his various schemes. Maybe the latest project was built on an old friendship, rather than just money. Charlie and Rashieka got on really well and talked about photography, men and harems. The Prince didn't want the latter and Rashieka made sure he didn't get one!"

After dinner the Prince and Rashieka retired, but not before promising Charlie a camel ride in the desert the next day. Charlie was not sure the gait would suit her riding style but accepted politely.

Daniel and Charlie walked over to their tent and lay outside under the stars on one of the colourful mats.

"Did you know the nearest star to Earth is Proxima Centauri?" asked Daniel.

"I thought I was the astrophysicist?" smiled Charlie, referring to their first meeting on the high ridge above Colsterdale.

"Not with your camera you're not." With that, Daniel rolled on top of Charlie and kissed her passionately.

* * *

The camels arrived early, when there was still a chill over the desert. They were dromedary camels with one hump which have been used for thousands of years to transport people and goods over the endless sands of Arabia. The Prince explained to Charlie how these days camels were kept mainly for racing at various events across the Kingdom and also in the other Gulf States, like the UAE.

"The best camels fetch huge sums of money similar to racehorses, because the races have very large prizes, but betting is not allowed under Islamic law. There are also competitions for the most beautiful camels a bit like your horse showing classes in the UK," advised the Prince enthusiastically.

"My mother has Arabian horses and shows them in classes all over Europe. We have a small stud at home in Yorkshire."

"Ah! You must come and see my mares when we get back to Riyadh. I adore my horses, probably even more than the falcons. You must see my new stallion. He is magnificent. Maybe your mother would like to send one of her mares to him next year?"

"That's extremely kind of you but it is long way to drive!" said Charlie jokingly, not expecting the Prince's reply."

"It is no problem. I will send a plane to fetch it."

"That is an amazing offer but…"

"No buts. It is done. I will organise it all. It will be my gift to you, for honouring us with your presence."

"But…"

"I am the Prince. It is done. Now I will show you how to mount a camel."

Charlie did not know what to do but bowed slightly and followed him to the camel. Daniel looked at Rashieka and they both smiled.

Daniel took some photographs of Charlie riding the camels across the dunes with the Prince but was careful not to show his face. She looked slightly uncomfortable, but put on a good show for the Prince. She looked much happier when they returned and was laughing and joking with him. Something had amused them and the relationship would stand Daniel in good stead when the Prince needed urgent help in the future.

When they got back to the Palace, the Prince kept his word and took Charlie to see his stud of Arabian horses. The air-conditioned barn was enormous and everything was absolutely immaculate. Even the drain covers were polished brass! The mares were incredibly beautiful and the Indian groom brought out the prize stallion to show his paces in the sand arena outside. He simply floated on air and had amazing presence.

"Your mother will be pleased with him. Yes?"

"He is the most aristocratic Arab stallion I have ever seen. Thank you so much for your generous gift. Mummy will be so excited when I tell her."

"That is good. We must keep our Mummies happy!" joked the Prince. Charlie wanted to give him a kiss on the cheek but felt it inappropriate. It was. Very.

* * *

The following morning, Daniel left very early for the two-day trip to carry out the decommissioning work on the Falcon underwater cables; the reason he had come to Saudi Arabia to help his friend. The Prince had also been called away to another Palace elsewhere in the Kingdom and Charlie did not see him again on this visit. However, Rashieka had planned a lot more shopping trips with Charlie to a host of other monuments to the mega-rich. It kept them occupied whilst the men were away running the world. Charlie felt like she had gone back to pre-emancipation times but the lure of infinite wealth and Rashieka's endless enthusiasm and extravagance were addictive.

Daniel returned to the Palace late on Friday afternoon after a successful expedition. The cables had been successfully put out of action for several weeks and, of course, every government in the region had denied responsibility for the action, including Saudi Arabia, which was sort of true!

"What time are we flying down to Mauritius tomorrow morning?" asked Charlie with her arms around Daniel's neck.

"The Prince has arranged for Kadin to take us to the airport at ten in the morning."

"I will be a bit sad to cease being 'Royalty' tomorrow!"

"It will last a little bit longer. We are being flown down in his private jet. A brand-new Boeing 747-8i!

CHAPTER FIFTEEN

The Indian Ocean – A Landscape of Love

The enormous Boeing 747 plane touched down at Sir Seewoosagur Ramgoolam International Airport and was met with all the regalia associated with visiting royalty. Little did the airport staff know it was a gorilla lover and a Yorkshire farmer. The taxi was waiting on the tarmac and no passports were required. If you own a 747 you can probably print your own.

"I feel more at home in a taxi after the last few days," smiled Charlie.

"Hotel 20 Degrees Sud please," Daniel instructed the driver.

"Yes, your highness."

"Just call us Mr and Mrs Day. We are on a secret holiday and we don't want anyone to know."

Charlie liked the Mr and Mrs. It reminded her of their Italian affair.

* * *

The hotel was set on a pristine white sand beach. It had a charming thatched roof and no other properties were in sight. It was a perfect secluded spot to spend a few days together and relax in the warm tropical sunshine.

"Hi, you two. We thought you would never get here!" called Anne Marie as she rushed over and hugged Charlie like a long-lost lover. Lovisa and Aurora both put their arms around Daniel and each kissed him on both cheeks.

"Can I help you with your bags sir?" smiled the porter. "Looks like you're in for a good stay!" Daniel saw the funny side and laughed it off. They all arranged to meet by the curvaceous pool for drinks, after Daniel and Charlie had got settled into the colonial suite.

Anne Marie took charge of ordering drinks. "What are we all having?"

"Anything with alcohol in it! It's been a dry, few days," replied Daniel laughing.

"Was the business side of the trip a success?" asked Anne Marie cautiously.

"Much better than expected. I will brief you later. Your planning was exemplary as usual."

"Glad you approve!"

"Tell us all about the shopping Charlie. Was it as excessive as we are all led to believe?" asked Lovisa excitedly.

"Absolutely amazing and so sophisticated. I bought loads of clothes. I will show you all later. You need a big chequebook to really enjoy yourself though!" Charlie could not give away too much to the two girls about what actually happened; she did not have to pay for anything!

Anne Marie proposed a toast. "Well, here's to a week in the sun. We have all had a very busy year. Let's relax and enjoy ourselves in paradise; away from the real world. Cheers!"

They sat by the pool all evening, watching the sun dissolve from yellow to gold to red, as it touched the far horizon and disappeared beneath the gentle waves of the Indian Ocean. The drinks flowed and the meal of octopus curry with green papaya was unforgettably delicious, and very hot. More drinks required.

Lovisa and Aurora decided to go for a swim in the pool with their clothes on. The alcohol assisting their frivolity. Daniel and Anne Marie drifted off to the palm trees on the far side of the pool, so Daniel could tell her in detail how the successful plan in Saudi unfolded. Charlie was left on her own to enjoy the tranquillity of the island and unwind from the beautiful intensity that is Saudi Arabia. She closed her eyes and, listening to the sea lapping the white sands, fell into her dreams.

* * *

The following morning Anne Marie, Lovisa and Aurora set off on a dolphin safari. They had hired a boat from a local fisherman, because they wanted to be on their own and not be part of a tourist group. He gave them a good idea where the bottle-nosed dolphins would be, but Anne Marie had organised her own sonar device to detect the pods, with her usual efficiency.

After about half an hour; "Over there!" screamed Lovisa as two adult dolphins broke the surface of the water in graceful synchrony. Anne Marie cut the engine and glided towards the pod. As they got closer, they could see there were several cows and calves together, enjoying the warm waters. They were communicating with each other, with a series of squeaks and surrounded the boat with curiosity. Lovisa decided she wanted to get into the water with the dolphins and stripped down to her bathing costume, which was underneath her colourful dress. She slid over the side of the boat and let herself slowly down into the water.

Dolphins

"Mind you don't get eaten," laughed Anne Marie, but the dolphins were obviously used to human contact and kept nudging Lovisa, encouraging her to swim with them. She patted one of the calves, that responded with an endearing squeak, and Lovisa instantly became a life-long dolphin lover.

"Come on Aurora, jump in, it's a wonderful feeling." So, Aurora undressed rapidly and slid into the water. She was immediately rewarded with a playful nudge and Anne Marie managed to get some lovely shots of both of them surrounded by the cows and calves.

"Are you coming in too?" Lovisa beckoned Anne Marie.

"No, I am happy up here."

"Come on. It's really fun."

"No."

"Why not?"

"I can't swim!" she lied.

* * *

When they got back to the hotel, Charlie and Daniel were lounging by the pool in the warmth of the sun. Charlie was wearing her new Adriana Degreas blue, halter-neck swimsuit, she had bought in Riyadh, and was lying on her front getting a tan. Daniel, sporting a white linen shirt and blue trunks, was sitting in a chair next to her, trying to find a good local restaurant on his phone.

"Hi, how did the boat trip go? Did you find any dolphins?" enquired Charlie.

"Found any? We swam with dolphins! It was absolutely magical. Anne Marie took loads of pics of us in the water surrounded by them. Show them to Charlie darling," exclaimed Lovisa enthusiastically.

Anne Marie sat next to Charlie on the sunbed and flicked through the photographs on her phone in reverse order. She overshot the start of the run and there were three close-up photos of Charlie. Charlie smiled at Anne Marie but made no comment about them.

"It certainly looks though you had a good time. Show them to Daniel."

"I can't decide which one is prettier. I think I like the grey, intelligent one in the middle." A typical Daniel observation. "I am not sure you are allowed to swim with wild dolphins, but they seem just as enthusiastic as you two, so I suppose it's OK! Anyway, I think I have found a good local restaurant for dinner tonight. Are you all up for dressing up tonight?"

They were all up for outdoing each other, especially Lovisa who had brought her most revealing dress for Aurora's benefit.

"OK. Meet in the bar at seven and I will organise a carriage and four white stallions!"

When Charlie and Daniel came down to the bar, Aurora and Lovisa were already on their second gin and tonic. Lovisa's red satin dress had more slashes than a rockers Levi's and left little to the imagination. Aurora's dress was a little more restrained, but was very short and very tight. Daniel ordered another round, just as Anne Marie made her entrance in a stunning French number.

"You look wonderful Annie. I absolutely love the dress," said Charlie adoringly.

"I didn't know we could call you Annie," said Lovisa.

"*You* can't," came the curt reply.

"Now then ladies, this isn't a competition. In any case I've won because my outfit is the most different!"

They boarded the Mercedes Sprinter mini coach, with plenty of horses but no white stallions, and drove the short distance to the Noble House Restaurant on the shoreline. With towering palm trees, an uninterrupted view of the fishing boats bobbing on the glimmering sea, and a warm on-shore breeze caressing their faces, they arrived at their table in style. The other guests were impressed. Especially the husbands.

Charlie had Daniel on one side and Anne Marie on the other. Aurora sat close to Anne Marie and Lovisa completed the circle. Daniel ordered two bottles of Taittinger Comtes de Champagne Blanc de Blanc Brut. 2005 naturally. By the time the wok-fried lobster with tamarind sauce arrived, the conversation was bubbling, the faces were flushing and Aurora had her hand secretively on Anne Marie's thigh. Charlie was enjoying being next to Daniel and kept giving him little smiles when one of the others became a trifle indiscrete. Lovisa was flirting with Daniel constantly, even though she would rather be in bed with the other two. And the people at the nearby tables were wondering which film set they were all working on.

"Who's for the lamb massaman with coconut and pumpkin?" asked Charlie, trying to restore some order.

Lovisa wanted a vegetarian dish but didn't know why: and when Daniel pointed out that the lobster, which she had just eaten was not vegetarian, she conceded that, like most vegetarians, she didn't understand what it meant for her or the environment. Anyway, she liked lamb so that was fine! Charlie had a little smile.

Daniel ordered more of the champagne.

After desserts, Lovisa suggested that they all went skinny dipping but she only managed to convince Aurora to go with her, and the two of them disappeared along the beach, away from the flaming torches that were lighting the walkways.

"You will have to get your own taxi back," shouted Anne Marie to no avail. "She's a pilot. She will find her way back. Not sure about Lovisa!"

Charlie, Daniel and Anne Marie were happy to be on their own at last and could talk about Saudi Arabia discretely. Charlie told Anne Marie all about the shopping expeditions and what it felt like to be treated as royalty.

"It was fabulous for a few days," said Charlie. "But I think all the security would become a bit oppressive after a while; no matter how much money you had. Also, although the women were treated with enormous respect, they were still very much secondary to the men."

"Daniel wouldn't like that. He prefers dominant women," laughed Anne Marie.

"I think it's time we went home if you two are going to gang up on me again."

When the three of them got back to the hotel, Daniel got a phone call from Sebastian in Cayman, so he went back to the room to take it. Something to do with a problem the Sudanese were having, now the Falcon cable was destroyed.

Charlie and Anne Marie got a drink from the poolside bar and found a quiet corner to continue their chat.

"When you said Aurora was coming back to the UK with you, to work on our book, I thought that you and she were becoming an item. And she was being very affectionate towards you tonight."

"I really like Aurora. She is very clever and I enjoy her company but the problem is, that I am deeply in love with you."

Charlie was a bit taken aback by the openness of the remark, even though she knew the situation from Daniel. "But you know I love Daniel," said Charlie.

"I know but it doesn't stop me loving you. I have tried desperately to redirect my feelings to the other two but every time I see you, my heart misses a beat. Sorry. I know it's complicated but please don't push me away. I promise I will never come between you and Daniel." Tears started to trickle down her soft brown cheeks and landed on her white linen blouse, leaving islands of sadness across her breasts. Charlie took Anne Marie in her arms as she sobbed, engulfed in the possibility of loneliness.

Daniel reappeared, but Charlie caught his eye over Anne Marie's shoulder and waved him away. He could see the intensity of the moment and discreetly backed away.

"You and Daniel are the only real friends I have and trust, in the whole world. I will do anything for you two. I will always be there for you. I just want to be near you Charlie." She looked into Charlie's eyes, through the tears. "Sorry."

"Please don't say sorry. I adore being with you. I want you to be my soulmate for ever." They hugged again and Anne Marie kissed Charlie sensitively on the lips. They walked back to their rooms, hand in hand, and Charlie left Anne Marie at her door with a kiss on the cheek and a generous smile. "Sleep softy Annie. Let's have some fun together tomorrow."

When Charlie got back to her room, Daniel was on the bed working on his laptop. "What was all that about with Annie. She seemed really upset?"

"She really opened up and said she is very much in love with me, but it will never come between you and me. She was really heartbroken to think I might push her away. I tried to console her but I had to make it clear I really loved you. I am not sure how we should handle it. What do you think?"

"I did try and explain to you how she felt," said Daniel.

"I know, but I didn't realise the intensity of her love. It's very real and I think she is a very lonely soul underneath all the outward appearances."

"I am sure you are right. She is an amazing person, but she needs us both in different ways."

"But she likes kissing me – on the lips!"

"I know it's a bit off-piste but I have known Annie for a long time and we have a very close relationship. She looked after me with enormous kindness in Chocorua, when I nearly died, and I feel very close to her. Not how I feel for you of course, but in an affectionate way."

"OK, as long as you are sure you are happy with it, and you must tell me if ever you are uncomfortable with her and me?"

"I will. Don't worry. Come and give me a kiss."

Charlie lay on the bed next to Daniel. "So, what's the problem with Sebastian?"

"Evidently, when I blew up the Falcon cables, I destroyed two others which were meant to be half a mile away!"

"Oops! Is that a major problem?"

"No. It's fine. Sebastian has sorted it out with the Prince. They have diverted the affected traffic through another Saudi hub. It's quite funny really because it has made the Saudi's job a lot easier. The Prince is very pleased with us!"

* * *

The next two days were peaceful and relaxing. Charlie and Daniel went for long walks, either along the beach or through the plantations. The others swam a lot, enjoying the clear blue waters, and sunbathed in the afternoons. Charlie and Anne Marie lay on a Balinese bed, next to each other, and talked a lot about the new estate in Yorkshire.

"I have been thinking," said Anne Marie, "I want you and Daniel to have the old mill between our two properties, as a present from me. I am getting it renovated at the moment and your mother mentioned how much fun you had there, playing as a child. You two will need a proper house, now you are together, and it will give me great pleasure to know you have somewhere of your own, away from the Hall."

"But you can't just give us the mill. It would be worth a lot of money if you sold it."

"Who cares about the money. I love you both!"

"You are too generous Annie, but it is a lovely thought and I will discuss it with Daniel. He might not want to live with me!"

"Oh, he will, I can assure you."

"Whilst we are on our own, can I ask you a very personal question about Daniel and me? I am too embarrassed to ask Mummy and you are the only person I can ask. But you must promise you will never tell Daniel."

"Of course. We are soulmates now," smiled Anne Marie.

"It's when we make love. He is a fantastic lover to me and makes me very special every time…"

"…………but he is having trouble coming into you because of Elizabeth?" consoled Anne Marie.

"But how do you know that?"

"Because it is worrying him to death and he is frightened he will lose you. He asked me not to tell you that he had discussed it with me. He may appear very macho on the outside but he is a very sensitive soul on the inside and just cannot let go of the past."

Charlie hesitantly opened up. "I am not very experienced in bed with men, but I have tried everything I can think of. He is wonderful to me and plays me like a musical instrument. He can make me come now within a few minutes every time but…"

"We just need to push him over the edge," suggested Anne Marie "Look, I have got an idea. It might not work but let's give it a try. My only advice to you now is, whatever he does to you tomorrow, however much you want it, don't let yourself be satisfied until he is."

"Not sure if I can resist him for that long. He is very sensual!"

"I know, but 'Think of England' for a few minutes!" They laughed and hugged each other.

* * *

At breakfast the following morning, Annie Marie suggested that the three of them take the boat out, anchor off-shore, and spend the day swimming in the sea and sunbathing. "I have booked the boat with reception and asked the kitchen to make us a packed lunch basket and put some nice wine in a chiller."

"That sounds a great idea," said Charlie enthusiastically, "But what about Aurora and Lovisa?"

"Oh, they can go shopping in Port Louis for new bikinis and sun glasses. They will have fun doing that and we don't want them messing up our plan."

"What is the plan exactly?"

"Not exactly sure yet! But it will work!"

* * *

Anne Marie took the helm of the luxury Princess S78 motor yacht and cruised out, over the slight swell, to about a mile offshore and dropped anchor for the day. It was a perfect day. Beautifully warm, with not a cloud in the bright blue sky. Daniel opened the first bottle of wine and they relaxed on the generous sun loungers and beds.

Charlie and Anne Marie took off their sarongs and showed off their new bikinis. Charlie's was bright green, with high-cut legs and a halter-neck top. Daniel pretended not to notice, but Charlie watched his eyes following her across the deck.

Daniel was wearing his canvas shorts and an open denim shirt. Charlie approved but pretended not to notice too. She liked his tanned body; it made her thighs tingle.

The sun rose higher in the sky and it got considerably warmer. The two girls took it in turns to dive into the cooling waters from the bow of the cruiser. As the bikinis got wetter Daniel put more ice in his wine.

The alfresco lunch of fresh sea food salad, with water cress and tomato, was light and tasty, perfect for a soporific day on the Indian ocean. The wine flowed and they all lay back and drifted into their own thoughts under the sunshades.

As the afternoon drifted to evening, Charlie and Anne Marie were lying on sunbeds near the Mauritian flag, becalmed at the back of the boat.

"I love your swimsuit Charlie, but did you bring the one I gave you at Chocorua?"

"No. I thought it was a bit minimal to wear in public!"

"Nothing is TOO minimal as far as a man is concerned."

"I have brought my version which you can wear, but it might be a bit smaller than yours!"

"Smaller?!!"

"If we casually go for a swim shortly, that will give you an excuse to change."

"Do you really think this will work?"

"Trust me. We haven't started yet! I will give you a massage when we get back on deck after changing.

After ten minutes or so, Annie Marie asked Charlie if she would like a cooling swim and they dived into the water together. They swam around the boat a few times to make it look genuine and then climbed back on board. Charlie grabbed a towel and dried her legs, ruffled her hair and tossed her head to shake the drops onto Daniel. He pulled her down and gave her a kiss. She responded, teasing him with her tongue.

"I am off to change into something dry. Annie is going to give me a massage when I get back."

"Can I do that?" asked Daniel, potentially spoiling the plan.

"No, it's fine. You relax. Annie has offered."

Charlie and Anne Marie disappeared into one of the cabins and Charlie put on the Chocorua bikini. The tiny white triangles were taut across her breasts and the gold chains held the miniscule silk between her long legs.

"You look very sexy Charlie, Daniel will love it, as he did in the hot tub at Chocorua."

Anne Marie looked into Charlie's eyes, slid her hand behind her neck and kissed her passionately. "Oops, sorry I got carried away for a moment!" She smiled at Charlie and Charlie returned the affection.

"Now don't forget my plan is for you to try and overwhelm his brain with desire for you. Hopefully his raging hormones will overcome the past. I am just going to help light the fire but you are in control."

Anne Marie changed into a sky-blue thin cotton blouse with nothing underneath and her Chocorua shorts which she knew Daniel really liked. The two of them walked out together on deck. Daniel nearly fell off his sunbed. They all laughed at his reaction. It was a great start.

"That brings back a few very nice memories," said Daniel taking Charlie in his arms and kissing her. "You look amazing and know how to make a man very happy!"

"Annie is going to work on my back from my mountain fall for a bit. Is that OK?"

"Of course. I didn't know it was still a problem?"

Daniel lay on his stomach, on his sunbed, with his head on his arms and his eyes shut, pretending not to notice Charlie, lying there in the sensual silk and gold.

Charlie let out a small moan and said "That's wonderful. Can you press a little firmer please Annie?"

Daniel opened one eye and looked across at Anne Marie, who was working her magic down Charlie's leg muscles. It was a pleasant image for him to have pervading his brain. Charlie had her eyes shut and was clearly enjoying what Anne Marie was doing to her.

Daniel was starting to realise what was going on but his enjoyment of Charlie's body being sensuously covered in oil was stirring his inner feelings. Daniel looked at Anne Marie and she smiled as she slid her hands along Charlie's sides, pretending to massage her. Charlie looked incredibly sexy lying there covered in oil and the tiny golden chains glinting in the sunlight. Anne Marie knew how to light the fuse and Charlie was clearly starting to feel very turned on too.

Daniel was getting immersed in the intimacy and forgot about pretending to shut his eyes.

Anne Marie's plan was working and she undid a couple of buttons on her shirt, pretending to be too hot, to up the intensity. Her beautiful dark-skinned body confused Daniel's brain, but he did not want her to stop. With great skill and sensitivity, she used her hands and fingertips to enflame Charlie's every sense.

Daniel's passions were clearly growing by the minute and Anne Marie decided that now was the time to retreat and leave Charlie and Daniel alone.

"Right, you two, I'm off for a swim. I will see you later."

With that, she dived over the silver bow rails and headed for the shore.

Charlie swung her legs off her sunbed and walked slowly across to Daniel.

"I want to massage you my darling," said Charlie in the lowest sexy voice she could find.

Charlie's tanned skin, covered in oil and Annie's caresses, shone in the sunlight. Her breasts glistened and her beautiful long legs touched his side. She ran her hands over the silk of her bikini and unclipped the tiny gold clasps. She stood before him naked, desperate to feel him inside her. His body started to react to her touch, overwhelmed with passion for her. Charlie was desperate to take control, leant over and kissed his chest, biting his nipples and stripping his shorts from his legs. His body arched with frustration and Charlie slid her long silky leg over his hips so she was sitting on his reaction. Her dominant position released his inhibitions.

"Daniel I am desperate to feel you inside me." She felt his growing passion beneath her and slowly, at first, moved against him. She lifted his hands to her swollen breasts and pressed his fingers against her erect nipples. His response was instant.

"I want you my darling Charlie… now."

Charlie lifted her hips and he entered her heavenly body. She moaned with instant pleasure and she held him tight inside so he could not escape. She leant back to intensify his pleasure.

"Don't lean back."

"I want to lean back."

To feel him inside her was so much more than Charlie had ever dreamed of. He caressed her breasts. She was teased to his touch. He started to pulse inside her. She gasped and gripped. He moaned with pleasure. She gripped again and leant back hard. He thrust one final time and their love affair was fulfilled at last. Charlie collapsed into Daniel's waiting arms with tears of joy and surrounded by an eternal Landscape of Love.

The Ending

A year has swept the changing skies
The mill renewed with ancient ties
Peace astride the prime meridian
Completes a moment of quotidian

Tranquillity sings in weeping willows
The trio rest on garden pillows
The leat flows gently to the sea
Homemade cakes and Earl Grey tea

The summer sun warms smiling faces
Not a thought of distant places
A pheasant calls in distant wood
Others needs not understood

And then a ring to break the spell
To free Dimitri's living hell
A Russian voice pleads help anew
Can Daniel please repay his due

The trio glance each other's eyes
And honour pulls the lifelong ties
Why break the soporific life
But pulses race in conflict strife

The Knight is driven by the Queens
Which one is complex so it seems
To rescue souls from distant past
Another venture looms at last.

Charlie and Anne Marie become increasingly involved in
Daniel's dangerous work in the next two books
in the Landscapes of Love trilogy:

Retribution - Landscapes of Love

Inheritance - Landscapes of Love